Praise for

DEL TORO MOON

"...a wildly original, pulse-pounding tale of a boy carrying on his family's legacy of protecting their rural community from bloodthirsty, supernatural skinners. Medieval Spanish myth meets the Hispanic culture of rugged southern Colorado to create a captivating story of modern-day knights."

—Laura Resau, Américas Award-winning author of *What the Moon Saw* and *The Lightning Queen*

"A rip-roaring monster slaying adventure with heart and humor, cleverly situated in the contemporary mountains and canyons of southern Colorado. This fresh and fun exploration of tough familial relationships, modern knights, and talking horses is sure to appeal to fans of *The Ranger's Apprentice* and equine enthusiasts."

—Todd Mitchell, author of *The Last Panther* and *The Traitor King*

DEL TORO MOON

DARBY KARCHUT

OWL HOLLOW PRESS

Owl Hollow Press, LLC, Springville, UT 84663

Del Toro Moon

Library of Congress Cataloging-in-Publication Data
Del Toro Moon / D. Karchut. — First edition.

Summary: A boy and his family—descendants of Spanish knights and aided by talking Andalusian war horses—must save their friends and their town from a growing horde of supernatural creatures.

Cover Design and Illustration © 2018 by Risa Rodil

ISBN 978-1-945654-14-5 (paperback)
ISBN 978-1-945654-15-2 (e-book)
Library of Congress Control Number: 2018944961

From whence came the cowboy, the history is plain,
He rode out of Europe on a frigate from Spain,
From Mexico southward, and northward he spread,
From the Gaucho and the Huaso, the Vaquero was bred,
Your everyday cowboy, and O' what a sight,
More dashing and daring than a Medieval Knight.

Lyrics by Jack Hannah
Taken from the selection:
"From Whence Came the Cowboy"
Recorded by Sons of the San Joaquin

Used with permission

orst thing about riding point on my first hunt? Waiting to find out if I was going to *die* on my first hunt. Of course, when we Del Toros said hunting, we meant *monster* hunting. Or, as my big brother Ben called it, the family rodeo.

Nervous sweat soaked my hands and neck. It didn't help the sun was dialed to extra crispy. The towering sandstone and granite cliffs surrounding us corralled the summer day and turned the three-square-mile valley into a giant oven. The heat of the soil radiated through the soles of my cowboy boots. Easing from foot to foot, I wondered how long it took to be baked alive.

Tucking my mace—a club-like weapon with an iron ball on the business end—under one arm, I wiped my palms on my T-shirt for the third time. Last thing I wanted was to 'slip yer grip,' as the old saying goes.

Even after drying my hand, I left damp spots on the leather-wrapped haft I oiled just yesterday. As I sat on the living room floor cleaning it, I had wondered how many monsters—the ones we called skinners—the mace had sent into oblivion throughout its long lifetime. A lifetime that spanned four centuries of creepy creature busting, first in old Spain and then in the New World.

"Matt." I jumped at my father's voice. "Enough daydreaming. Focus."

"I *am* focused." *Focused on not throwing up*, I thought. Anxiety tied my gut into a half hitch. I wished those skinners would just attack already and get it over with. I peeked up at Dad. A little parental reassurance and all that.

My father was mounted on horseback a few feet away. He rose in the stirrups and scanned the valley. His face, stern and sharp featured, reminded me of a hawk on the hunt; his black goatee matched the stallion under him.

Man, if I could be just *one fourth* the hunter he was, I'd die happy. I wondered what it would take to reach that goal. I tightened my grip on my mace and glanced at Dad's.

About three feet in length, it hung from a leather loop around his wrist and rested against the saddle skirt. Like mine, the head of his weapon was decorated on four sides with our family's sigil: a crescent moon, its tips curved upward like the horns of a bull. Even though the designs were etched deeply into the iron, generations of monster whacking had pitted and scratched those Del Toro moons until they were almost invisible.

But they were still there—hard to see, kind of beat up, but fighting the good fight—just like us.

The black stallion stomped a front hoof the size of a gallon bucket. Dad patted Turk's massive neck. "Easy, *mi amigo*. We will meet those skinners soon enough."

Skinners. My flesh crawled at the thought of getting my first real look at the creatures. Licking my dry lips, I studied the terrain. The valley's floor was trashed with scattered boulders large enough to hide a skinner or two probably salivating for a taste of fresh boy. A chill ran down my spine. *Don't mess up. Just don't mess up.*

Because messing up meant family members—both the two-legged and four-legged ones—might die.

Yeah. No pressure there.

Speaking of the four-legged. I laid a hand on the shoulder of another family member standing next to me. Family member *and* my best friend: the warhorse, El Cid. The warm, silky coat felt soothing under my palm. As did the powerful muscles beneath it.

The stallion lifted his nose, nostrils quivering, and his ears swiveled around. With a soft exhale, he turned his head toward me. The muscles in the thick neck rippled under a coat the color of weathered chrome. He studied me with an ebony eye half covered by a lock of white mane that hung to his nostrils in proper Andalusian style. Then, he opened his mouth and spoke.

"It's normal, Matt," he said, his voice a deep rumble, "to be nervous. We all are—to some degree."

Turk snorted and curled his lip. "Speak for yourself, old goat."

El Cid ignored him. "You'll do fine." He shook his forelock out of his eyes and butted me with the side of his long nose. "You've been well trained, both by me and your *papá*. And, when in doubt, always—"

"—listen to the warhorses," I finished, repeating one of my father's top three rules. The other rules were "do not get killed" and "do not get your brother killed."

"El Cid." Dad caught the stallion's attention. "Anything?"

The gray sniffed the air again. "Nary a scent nor sound, Javier. We can stand down—at least for the time being."

Another huff of derision from Turk. El Cid pinned his ears flat. I tensed. Great. Just what we needed. Another fight.

"Enough. Both of you." Dad sighed and pushed back his cowboy hat, a Stetson as black as Turk's soul. No, really. His golden amber eyes—a Del Toro trait Ben and I shared with him—narrowed in the afternoon's glare. "So, my son. What do you make of those tracks?" He pointed his chin at the ground in front of me.

I bent over and eyed the dog-like paw prints. They circled past a nearby pile of boulders and disappeared. A single animal. Straightening, I checked for other tracks. *Nada.* Just to make sure, my gaze swept over the landscape.

Around me stretched *El Laberinto* Wilderness Area, a twenty-five square mile mesa jutting up from the prairie. The entire mesa was a labyrinth of deep ravines and needle-thin slot canyons—their openings were dark doorways to no place good. Ben once said the surrounding rock walls with the open valley in the center reminded him of a twisted version of the Coliseum, where folks went to die horrible deaths. The locals of the nearby town of Huerfano, Colorado, just called it the Maze.

"Put in some trails," Ben often pointed out, "and Huerfano could be a world-class hiking and mountain biking destination."

"Except for that one little problem," Dad would respond. "People keep disappearing in it. Permanently. Not good for tourism."

A breeze moaned through one of the slot canyons. The sound made me feel tiny and alone and isolated. *If we got killed, no one would know. Except Ben.* Longing for my brother swept over me. Too bad he wasn't due home for another day or so.

"Matt?" Dad's voice called me back. "Before Christmas."

"Um…skinner tracks."

"Are you certain?" Removing his hat, he stuck it on the saddle horn. He wiped his brow and raked his fingers through hair sprinkled with a few silver strands that I swore weren't there last year. "Not a coyote?"

His casual tone didn't fool me. "I don't think so. Too big." I squatted down and splayed my fingers, measuring the skinner's track; it was as large as my hand. "Not unless we've got coyotes the size of Turk." *And just as mean tempered.* I kept *that* thought to myself. "I think it's just one—"

"Quiet." El Cid stiffened and raised his head.

The hairs on the back of my neck snapped to attention. I gulped, fighting back the impulse to crawl to safety behind him. "Skinner?" I whispered. Out of the corner of my eye, I noticed Turk circling his nose in the air, nostrils flared.

"One," the black said. "About twenty-five strides away and sneaking toward us. Using the rocks as cover."

Before my father asked, I did the math in my head. A horse's walking stride was about two yards in length. "Fifty yards."

"*Bueno.*" Dad screwed his hat down on his head, taking care to cock it just right. "An opportunity for some action, then. Mount up."

Sticking my left foot in the stirrup and grasping the horn, I hopped once on my right leg, then hauled myself into the saddle and gathered up the reins attached to El Cid's halter. My hands trembled. I told them to knock it off. *You, too,* I ordered my heart banging away in my chest.

I ran my hand over the mace's ball for luck. My thumb traced each moon, one after the other, as a soft vibration traveled through my skin from the metal. Wrapping my fingers around the iron head, I squeezed it until my knuckles whitened. *Please,* I said to it silently, *don't let me do anything stupid. Like get eaten by that thing.*

With a quiet word to Turk, Dad edged over to me. He gestured at my mace. "Take some warm ups."

Swinging my weapon in a figure-eight loop on either side of El Cid, I rolled through the basic strikes Dad had taught Ben and me. We both started formal training when we were strong enough to hold an iron mace straight out in front of us for a full minute without dropping our arm. It wasn't until two years ago, when I turned ten, that I was able to do that. Barely.

"Better, no?"

I flexed my shoulders. *No, not really.* "Sure."

"Now, what is the most important thing to remember today?" Dad raised an eyebrow.

"Besides listening to El Cid and the not getting killed thing?" I frowned, thinking what topped staying alive. "Um…"

El Cid let out a long-suffering sigh. "Remain mounted at all costs."

"Oh. Yeah. That."

Dad shifted in the saddle. "El Cid? If things get hot—"

"Really, Javier? You're giving *me* instructions?"

"My apologies." In spite of what was coming for us, a corner of Dad's mouth twitched. "What was I thinking?"

"Clearly, you weren't." The stallion flicked an ear. "But, rest assured. I'll keep the boy safe."

"Hey." Pride elbowed aside my fear. "You guys talk like I'm some little kid…" The rest of the words crept away.

The soft crunch of gravel. Something moved behind a nearby jumble of boulders. A faint drone. I cocked my head, listening. The sound grew louder. Like a swarm of flies or mosquitoes, a buzzing that rose and fell but never stopped until a person was ready to scream. Another rattle of stones—probably under a giant paw.

"Oh boy," I whispered. Goosebumps broke out on my arms. Had Dad felt this loose-boweled when he was my age and faced a skinner for the first time? Doubtful.

Nothing fazed Francis Javier Del Toro, old-school monster hunter, life-long Denver Broncos fan, and a true *caballero*: a gentleman of the horse.

"The first time is the worst." His attention focused on the boulder pile, Dad reached over and squeezed my knee.

Fighting the urge to grab his hand and cling to it—sheesh, what a baby move *that* would be—I simply nodded, not trusting my voice. My heart whaled away, trying to crack open my ribs. Hoping to make a run for it while there was still time. I didn't blame it. Through the thick leather of the stirrup, I felt El Cid's pulse against my calf muscle, its rhythm slower than mine.

I wondered if it was too late to beg Dad to call off the hunt until I was older. Like thirty. I imagined how badly Ben would tease me if I chickened out. *Aw, what's wrong, Matty? Scared of the big bad wolf?* I tightened my fingers around the haft and held on to my courage.

A fly buzzed my nose. I swatted at it. A few more joined in. They pinged off my face like tiny black hail. "What's with all the flies?"

Turk's hide shivered. He danced forward a couple of steps. Dad gave a soft hiss. The stallion eased back, tail lashing like a cat's parked under a bird feeder.

El Cid sniffed. "I saw that."

"Just warming up my legs," Turk said.

Liar, I thought.

More flies appeared. They swirled above our heads in a cloud, casting a shadow. Over the buzzing, I caught another crunch behind the boulders, twenty yards and closing. "Dad?"

"I know. Stand ready."

I reminded myself to breath. *Skinners can't be* that *creepy. Ben's been hunting for three years, and he acts like they're just a big joke. How bad can they really be?*

Pretty bad.

With a roar and a shriek, the skinner burst from hiding. Horror froze me in the saddle.

A bloodied, fresh-skinned carcass. That's what it looked like. Except that the carcass was alive somehow, raw hamburger molded into a wolfish creature. It wore a black cloak tied around its neck. No, not a cloak. Flies. Flies trailed the creature and feasted on the wet flesh. Like pilot fish following in a shark's wake.

The skinner charged El Cid and me. Bile burned my throat. Gagging, I tightened my legs around El Cid's barrel and raised my mace. *Kill it*, a voice gibbered in my head. *Kill it now!*

"Hey, chuck roast." Turk reared. His front hooves boxed the air. "Over here."

In between one stride and the next, the skinner shifted direction. The flies banked around and swarmed after it. El Cid groaned in frustration.

"No, Turk." Dad clung to the reins. "Wait for—"

The black launched himself at the creature. My father cursed in Spanish, then leaned forward in the saddle, his weapon at the ready. Head low, the stallion's powerful legs shortened the distance in a weird game of chicken. With a yelp, the skinner slammed on the brakes, its paws skidding on the gravely dirt. Turk sped up. To my surprise, he shot past the monster.

"*Santiago!*" Shouting our family's war cry, Dad swung his mace in a deadly arc. The skinner's skull exploded. Fragments of bone and gobbets of raw meat flew everywhere. Blood sprayed across Turk's chest and right shoulder and flecked the ground around them.

For a moment, the creature staggered about, wagging its neck from side to side. A small knobby chunk of head was still attached to its spine. It staggered after my father and Turk. My stomach roiled.

Even broken, they are still a threat. Dad's voice rose in my memory. Swallowing my lunch back down, I readied my weapon and pressed my heels against El Cid's sides. "*Santiago!*" The battle cry came out in a croak. A tiny voice in my head rolled its eyes.

El Cid ignored my signal to charge. "Wait."

"For what?

"For *this*," El Cid said.

Bang! The skinner vanished. I gasped. It was like the air had clapped its hands, then sucked away the skinner. A cosmic vacuum cleaner. Only the flies remained. They buzzed around, confused by the shutdown of the buffet, then drifted away.

"That is *so* cool," I breathed.

"Stupid meat mutts." Turk swung around in a high-stepping salsa. "They never learn." His hooves stirred up the dust and crusted his blood-soaked coat. Tossing his mane, he trotted back toward El Cid and me.

My father yanked a handkerchief from his back pocket. "What was that, Turk? I thought we agreed to allow Matt the first strike."

The black's nostrils flared. "*I* never agreed to that, Javier."

"We discussed it this morning." Dad's voice rose in frustration. Grasping the mace just under the head, he spat on the iron ball, then wiped it clean with short, savage strokes. "And what have I told you about rearing before a charge? Bravado like that is going to get you killed. Or one of us—"

"Javier." El Cid's ears snapped forward. "Leave off arguing with that mule and be on guard. I thought I heard—"

Four more skinners exploded from behind the boulders.

2

"**D**ad!" The scream ripped my throat. The nearest skinner leaped at Turk, teeth snapping and front paws clawing. It chomped down on Dad's right calf, then braced itself and yanked, trying to drag him out of the saddle and into the waiting pack.

Terror knifed me. *No. Not my dad.* I started to jump off.

"No, Matt," El Cid shouted. "Stay with me." He jerked to one side. Out of habit, I squeezed my legs and held on.

Cursing in a creative blend of English and Spanish, Dad flipped his weapon around and buried its butt end into the skinner's skull. It cracked like a piñata. "Turk!"

The black planted his hind legs and whirled in a circle. Halfway around, the creature sailed off. With another one of those *bang-claps*, it vanished in midair. Screaming with fury, the stallion barreled into the others and sent them flying. He stomped on an unlucky one, his hoof snapping the monster's spine like a stick of wood. It twitched and jerked, clawing at the dirt. A few moments later, it staggered to its feet, then shook its head and bared its teeth in a mocking grin, ready for another round.

Out of nowhere, a skinner lunged for El Cid's throat. Almost running out from under me, the stallion spun away. The skinner tumbled to the ground, then snarled and leaped again.

"Get away from him!" I swung my mace, my muscles spasming from a combination of horror and panic. The weapon whistled through the air. Clean miss.

Lips twitching in amusement, the creature danced around, circling us. The sickening reek of spoiled meat burned my nostrils and coated my tongue. I gagged, then spat.

"El Cid!" Dad sent another monster into oblivion with a wet crunch, then pointed his weapon. "Go. Make for the Gate."

"Hold tight, Matt." The stallion kicked the creature to one side, then catapulted into a gallop. I grabbed the saddle horn with my free hand just in time to keep from being served up as a skinner appetizer.

Hitting full speed in three strides, he pounded across the valley, weaving around boulders and crashing through bushes. The aroma of crushed sage and creosote mingled with the sharp tang of horse sweat. The chuff of his breathing and the creak of leather filled my ears. Ahead of us, the Gate—a narrow corridor in the southern wall—promised safety. The last thing I wanted.

I tugged at the reins. "We've got to go back and help Dad!" It was like trying to stop the Colorado River in its springtime flood. I braced my feet in the stirrups and pulled harder. With a jerk of his head, El Cid yanked the reins from my hand. The leather burned along my palm.

Giving up, I twisted around and forced myself to look. Even before I turned, I knew what I'd see: Turk riderless. My father sprawled on the ground and a skinner crouched over him, its teeth buried in his throat. *Oh, please, not that. Not Dad, too.*

Sick with relief, I almost dropped my mace.

Eyes white-rimmed with battle rage, Turk gained on us with every stride of his powerful legs. Dad rode low in the saddle, mace at the ready and head turned, watching the pursuit. A tiny corner of my mind marveled that he hadn't lost his hat.

Half hidden in Turk's dust, the three remaining skinners raced after us, strings of venom and saliva flying from their open mouths. One creature dragged a hind leg that was mostly a splintered stick. Chunks of meat clung to it. Even as I watched, the leg grew back. The skinner gave a yip of delight and picked up its pace.

With a surge, Turk caught us. I glanced over. My father's jaw was clenched and his lips were pressed in a thin line. "How bad?" I yelled. "Did it—"

"Matt, no matter what," Dad shouted, "you stay on El Cid."

I crouched lower, rocking forward and back in rhythm with his stride. My ankles and knees flexed with each jolt of the stallion's stride, working like shock absorbers. All the while, I forced myself to stay relaxed, my weapon at the ready.

Just the way Dad had taught me and Ben. The way his father had taught him and his brother and sister. And *his* father before that. Generation after generation. All the way back to our legendary ancestor.

Four centuries ago, Santiago Del Toro had stepped off that frigate and waded ashore to this New World, a magic-enhanced mace in one hand and his Andalusian war-brother by his side. Spain in his wake and a vow to keep.

The thunder of hooves bounced off the valley walls. The echoes grew louder. Or was it my pulse thundering in my ears? Ahead of us, at the top of a short incline, the mouth of the Gate loomed. I could feel El Cid's ribs heaving as he pounded up the slope.

Behind us, the skinners yelped, eager to munch on manflesh or horseflesh. Or boyflesh. I thought of what would happen if those monsters caught me. What their teeth would do to me. What it would feel like to be eaten alive.

Stop it. Don't think about it. Just ride. I leaned forward and stretched out along El Cid's neck, practically burying myself in his mane.

"Fear not, Matt," El Cid panted between words. "No demon-spawned skinner has ever outrun an Andalusian."

Man, I sure hoped that wasn't just bragging on his part. I swore I felt the hot breath of the skinners on my neck.

We hit the opening to the corridor at full speed. Forty yards to safety. Blinded by the shadow, I clung to the horn. Cool air chilled the sweat on my face as the towering walls whipped past me. El Cid stumbled. I gasped, certain he was going down. With a wrench, he caught his balance and flung himself back into the race.

The howls of the skinners bounced off the cliff walls. My stomach clenched. Were they gaining on us? I didn't want to check, because what if they were? The far opening seemed like a million miles away and never getting any closer. It felt like we were running in place.

Sunlight blasted my eyes. I blinked. When I could see again, open grasslands stretched before me, green and gold under a blue sky.

"El Cid. Matt." Dad called from behind us. "We are clear."

Panting, I slumped in the saddle. El Cid slowed to a lope, then a trot, then dropped to a walk, blowing hard. Sweat darkened his hide.

"Oh, man." I pressed my palm on his wet neck. "That was...I mean...*whoa*. What a ride."

"My words exactly," he said.

Turk eased down, matching El Cid's gait. He raised his tail. "Eat *this*, zombie dogs." He let one rip. For a long minute, the whole world smelled like alfalfa. Could've been worse.

Feeling braver, I twisted around and rested a hand on El Cid's haunch. The soaring cliffs of the Maze reminded me of an enormous castle wall. It stretched for several miles in either direction. Shapes moved in the Gate's shadow. Skinners. They milled about, pacing back and forth and howling their frustration. Then they left. The darkness swallowed them up. Bummer that it wasn't for real.

"Dad?" Out of habit, my gaze lifted to the tops of the twin buttes—stony towers that stood like sentinels on either side of the Gate. "How do we know the wards are holding?"

"Do you see any of those *monstruos* following us home?"

An odd tone in his voice yanked my head around. I choked back my anxiety and looked at his leg. A dark, wet patch marred the faded denim just below the knee. "Did its venom…?" I hated the way my voice quivered.

"It only got one fang into me. My boot stopped the other one. Good thing I wore my Tony Lamas, no?"

No, it wasn't a good thing. Not one freaking bit. "How sick can you get from one fang? I mean, shouldn't we tie something around it? Stop the venom from spreading?" Could he die from one fang?

He waved away my concern. "The best thing is home and rest and the evening meal, and my youngest son waiting on me hand and foot." He forced a grin, his face pale.

El Cid snorted. "I ought to *geld* you, Turk," he panted as he walked along. "Showing off. *Again*. Disobeying Javier's orders. *Again*. Then, failing to protect your rider."

Turk bared his teeth. "I didn't see *you* fighting—"

"*Dios*," Dad said wearily. "Give it a rest, would you?"

The two-mile ride back home took forever. The whole time, the shadow of the nearby mountains crept across the open prairie, inching closer to us. But not in a creepy way. The Sangre de Cristo Range was an old friend. It protected our ranch from the worst of the winter storms that roared in from the west.

Breathing harder than I liked, El Cid kept at a running walk, dragging his hooves through the grass and churning up dust and bits of dried vegetation. Turk stomped along beside him, lost in a mood as black as his coat. Me? I swore I aged a year and a half. Even with the summer afternoon being just about perfect—the air filled with the scent of sage and horse, the green-yellow grass lit up from the day-weary sun—all I could think about was getting Dad home.

Halfway there, a new worry crawled up into the saddle behind me. What was I supposed to do once I got him home? I didn't know anything about skinner venom. All I did know was that too much was lethal. How much was too much?

I shot a peek at my father. He seemed okay. Except for the way he slumped in the saddle, one hand resting on the horn. Not typical of a man who always rode head up and heels down.

Just my rotten-apple luck that Ben was still gone. For the hundredth time, I wished my brother was back already.

For the millionth time, I wished my mother was still alive.

I sighed in relief when the top of our barn peeked over the low hill we called the Buffalo's Hump. The house's chimney appeared a few minutes later. Under us, the horses lengthened their strides. Turk stepped out in front and took the lead. Guess he was worried about Dad, too.

"I can feel you fretting right through the saddle," El Cid said. "But you needn't. Javier is going to be fine."

"You're just saying that to make me feel better."

"No, I'm saying that because it's true. Have I ever lied to you, Mateo Del Toro?"

"Only about a bazillion times."

"Ah." A long silence. "Well, only when it was for your own good."

We rounded the hill. I relaxed even more at the sight of our home sweet home on the range. The ranch house and barn sat tucked against the south side of the Hump and faced each other across an open yard of dirt and gravel. The wooden sidings of both buildings were weathered to khaki brown.

Reaching the yard, I spotted a canvas duffle bag on the lowest porch step. I stared at it. At first, my head refused to process the meaning of the duffle. "What's that bag doing…Oh."

My heart kicked like a jackrabbit. I looked around, joy and nervousness wrestling for dominance inside of me. *Maybe now,* I thought, *it'll be different between them. Even a little change would be nice—heck, I'm not greedy. I'd take even one less fight a day.* Before I could point out the bag to Dad, a figure appeared in the barn's doorway.

"Whoa," said a familiar voice, "you guys look like something even a skinner wouldn't eat."

Fingers fumbling, I looped my mace onto the saddle horn, then jumped. I hit the ground running, my boots slipping and crunching on the gravel. "Ben!"

"Hey, Matty." My brother sauntered out of the double doors, his grin mirroring mine.

Ignoring the stupid nickname, I threw myself at him and hugged him, then let go and stepped back. "Man, am I glad you're here."

"Sick of doing all the chores—"

"Dad's hurt. Bit by a skinner."

Ben's smile disappeared. "How bad?" He hurried over to Turk's side, acknowledging El Cid on the way with a nod. He glanced at the injured leg, then peered up. "Looks like I came home just in time, Pop." My brother knew our father hated that term. Which was why he used it.

"Oh, we would have managed. *Reuben.*"

Ben stiffened at the use of his full name. Which *he* hated. Dad's payback. A muscle in his jaw twitched.

Really, guys? I wanted to kick them both right in the seats of their Wranglers.

The black stallion's head whipped around, big square teeth snapping all Rottweiler-ish; he just missed my brother's arm. "Drop the wise-guy routine and help your father."

"Nice to see you too, Turk." Ben offered a hand to Dad. "Stomped on any kittens lately?" Helping our father swing his bitten leg over the cantle, a worried expression flitted across my brother's face. My earlier anxiety bounced back into the red zone.

Wincing from the movement, Dad took his time dismounting, easing his weight onto the wounded leg with a sigh. He flexed his knee a few times, nodded, and ran a hand down his goatee. He studied my brother. "You have grown."

"I guess." Ben shrugged. "Listen, let's get you inside."

"A boy leaves. Two months later, a young man returns."

Ben looked away. Even so, I spied a flush of pride on his face.

To me, he looked like a younger, leaner version of our father. Both of them trim and athletic, their movements quick and sure. And both gifted with features that had earned Ben double, if not triple, looks from girls since he was my age. And still earned Dad sidelong glances and over-bright smiles from waitresses and store clerks.

"Did you walk from Huerfano?" Dad asked. "We would have picked you up."

"I wanted to stretch my legs after that bus ride. Speaking of legs..." Ben started to take his arm.

Our father stopped him. "The injury is not that bad."

"Dad..."

"No, come give your old man a hug first." Still taller by a few inches, he took Ben by the shoulders, kissed him soundly on the cheek, then wrapped his arms around him. My brother stiffened for a moment, then relaxed and hugged back. Hard and fierce.

"Hey, *Papá*," Ben whispered over Dad's shoulder.

"It is a gift to have you home, *mijo*."

Love swelled my chest. A big wad of it pushed a lump into my throat. Part of me itched to join them, wiggling in under one of Dad's arms.

I shoved that thought away. *Sheesh*, I told myself. *Get a grip*.

Movement behind me. Popcorn crunch of hooves on gravel. Then, the rest of our little nuthouse on the prairie family joined us. My brother stepped out of Dad's embrace to face El Cid.

"Ah, Ben." The older stallion blew in delight. "As your father said, a gift to have the family back together again."

"Hey, El Cid." Ben bumped his forehead against the gray's, then tugged on the white forelock. "So, what happened in the Maze? Turk pull a rookie move?"

"While I wish I could blame it all on him, I must admit we were outnumbered. A surprise attack by a pack of skinners."

Ben blinked. "Wait. What? Did you say a *pack*? Since when are there enough of those stinkers to form one? Anyway, I thought skinners mostly worked solo." His head swiveled from our father to me and back again. "What's going on?"

Dad's brows knitted. "The coffer must be compromised."

"Meaning what?" I tried to keep my voice from squeaking. Failed.

He paused, then spoke. "Meaning more of them are escaping from their ancient prison."

My heart froze. More skinners? I tried to imagine fighting an even larger pack. All I could see were the gaping jaws of the one that had attacked me and El Cid. Oh boy.

"And *more* means trouble for us," El Cid said. "Those creatures are clever enough to use superior numbers to their advantage. Such as today when they sacrificed that first creature as a decoy."

"As long as the wards hold, we will deal with whatever is inside the Maze. We always have." Dad stared at the distant mesa, one hand resting on the saddle. Then he shook his head and straightened with a grimace. "But, for now..." He pointed his chin toward the barn. "Mateo. Barn duty. Then, after supper, the five of us will talk. See if we can determine what is going on in *El Laberinto*."

I watched Ben help our father limp inside, my whole being lighter at the sight. Okay then. I turned and tagged along behind the horses. Matt Del Toro—equine indentured servant.

"Wanna go first?" I asked El Cid.

He paused at the water barrel just outside the double doors. "Oh, I can wait. Go ahead before Turk becomes impatient." He stuck his lips in the water and began slurping.

And he takes it out on me, I thought. I followed Turk over to his corner—the one near the back door with a window—and unsaddled him. I wiped him clean of blood and skinner leftovers with a damp cloth, then went to work on him with a grooming tool that looked like an oversized scrub brush. Even with the brush, I had to use my fingernails to scrap away some of the dead flies. Yeesh. I scrubbed my hands on my jeans. "Good?"

He shook himself like a dog, then pawed at the straw. The stalks snapped with each blow. "You missed some."

I gritted my teeth. "Where?"

"On my belly."

"Are you sure?" I squatted down for a look. "I thought I got it all—" A hoof swiped past my head and grazed my ear. I flung myself backward in the straw. "Hey!" Rubbing my ear, I glowered up at him. "Watch your big feet."

"Just pointing out the spot." He stared back, eyes black shiny marbles behind a heavy forelock just as dark.

Like heck you were. "I can see just fine." I cleaned him as fast as I could, shoulders hunched, waiting for a blow. None came. Probably because I was ready for it.

All finished, I sighed in relief at having survived another round. Before he complained about the service, I hurried over to the covered storage bins lining one side of the barn and filled two huge scoops with grain. Balancing them carefully, I carried them to his feed tub and poured them in. The oats pattered against the hard rubber. The sound reminded me of those flies pinging against my face. I shuddered. Double yeesh. "Need anything else?"

"No. Go away."

I rolled my eyes. *Why don't* you *go away? Like to Alaska.*

Turk arrived at the ranch three years ago when Ben started hunting. There was something sharp and cold, like a shard of obsidian, about him. And, from day one, the black stallion wanted nothing to do with me or my brother. After getting thrown off or trampled on repeatedly—all by accident, according to the big fat liar—the feeling was mutual.

Jaw clenched, I stomped over to El Cid and unfastened the cinch's buckle, then yanked the strap from around his barrel with a snap.

He flung up his head. "A bit rough there."

"Sorry." Guilt poked me.

"Was Turk giving you a bad time?"

"As usual." Hands busy, I lowered my voice. "Turk the Jerk."

Leaning his head closer to mine, El Cid blew softly. The warm aroma of grass and grain wafted over me. "Best not let *him* hear you say that."

"Not if I want to live another day." I slid the saddle and pad off, careful not to bang him with the stirrups, and carried the tack to the racks next to the feed bins. Ben's saddle sat there, covered in dust. *Can't have that.* After placing my saddle on its holder, I took a moment to swipe Ben's clean and smooth out the cinch strap before refolding it neatly.

Grinning, I snagged some fresh rags and a clean grooming brush. As I worked, El Cid stood with head lowered and eyes closed in bliss, one hip cocked in repose. White horsehair drifted around my face. I sneezed, blowing bits out of my nose, then spat to one side.

In spite of the barn's peace, the image of the skinner chomping down on my father's leg looped through my head like a horror movie trailer on repeat. I chewed on the inside of my cheek, almost afraid to ask.

"Are you *sure* Dad's going to be okay?"

"I am." El Cid shifted position and cocked his other hip.

"How do you know?"

"Because Javier would've already felt the effect of the venom if he had received a full dose. Or even half a dose. I doubt the skinner injected him with more than a drop or two. So, not to worry. He's a tough *hombre*—he'll be fine."

"Promise?"

"Promise."

Heart lighter, I swept the brush along his spine and over his haunches, my hands on auto-pilot. In spite of the joking earlier, I knew El Cid wouldn't lie to me about important family stuff. If he said Dad was going to okay, then Dad was going to be okay. Simple as that. I moved down to his ribs, whistling softly between my teeth.

After a few minutes, the stallion spoke, eyes still shut. "You missed a bit on my back."

"Here?"

"No, closer to my mane."

"Got it." I gave the spot a couple of swipes.

"And I believe I've a pebble embedded in my right fore shoe. See to it, will you?"

Even though he bossed me around almost as badly as Turk, it was totally different with El Cid. "Anything else, m'lord?"

"Smart mouth."

"Just calling it like I see it. Dad says you take your name too literally sometimes."

One eye opened. "Oh, he did, did he? Hmm. I'll have to work on that." The eye closed. "By the way, I'd like molasses drizzled over my grain this evening."

"Yes, m'lord."

Walking out of the barn ten minutes later, I hurried across the yard. Dad was alive. Ben was home. The skinners were locked tight behind the wards. I practically skipped up the porch steps.

My stomach growled. Patting it, I pondered deep and profound thoughts about meatloaf. The onion-y kind with chunks of bell peppers and topped with a thick slab of tomato paste so hot from the oven it shredded the skin off the roof of my mouth. *Nom, nom.* I slipped inside. The screen door whapped shut behind me.

A combination living room and kitchen welcomed me, illuminated by the sun's lingering rays through the back window. In the living room, a worn sofa and a pair of recliners clustered in front of a stone fireplace. A modest-size television sat next to the hearth. In one corner, a hallway led to our bedrooms. Beyond the living room was a kitchen just the right size for a table and six chairs.

In the other corner sat a large desk, complete with a laptop we all shared, and where Dad homeschooled me and Ben because he couldn't stand the current state of public education. His words, not mine. Behind the desk were floor to ceiling shelves made from leftover wooden planks stacked on cinderblocks. Books of every size neatly lined each shelf according to subject. Topics ranged from metallurgy to edible plants of the Southwest to car repair for dummies. There was even one on how to conduct a Viking burial. My father had read them all. Of course.

But it was the Renaissance Fair-looking object hanging over the fireplace that always caught people's attention: our family's coat of arms. The shield-shaped plaque displayed a silver crescent moon on a sable background. The moon's tips pointed upward like a bull's horn. It took up most of the space above the mantel.

"Dad? Ben?" Hanging my mace on the coat hooks by the front door, I checked my boots for mud or manure. Good enough.

"Here." Dad's voice echoed along the hallway from his bedroom. "Start supper, would you?"

"What do you want?" I yelled.

"Anything but meatloaf," Ben shouted back. "Stuff gags me." A moment later, the shower from our bathroom started up with a *thunk* and a hiss.

"Except you're not cooking," I muttered, "so meatloaf it is." After pulling the Tupperware from the freezer, I placed it in the microwave and punched the thaw button. The machine hummed gleefully over its ability to turn a frozen burger brick into something edible. I added a bowl of green beans to the meal.

Pulling dishes from the cupboard, I grinned to myself because I was setting the table for three instead of two. I started to move aside yesterday's *Denver Post*, then paused. The words

"*El Laberinto*" jumped out at me. Uh-oh. Still holding the stack of plates, I leaned closer.

In the "News from around the Centennial State" section, I read silently: *Possible funding is pending for a joint archeological/paleontological research project for the* El Laberinto *Wilderness Area. The area is located on the eastern slope of the Sangre de Cristo Range in southern Colorado near the town of Huerfano. If approved, the project will be organized and directed by scientists and staff from the Field Museum of Natural History out of Chicago. Dates are still undecided.*

A whisper of bare feet on the wooden floor. Dad appeared, one pant leg rolled up to his knee. A white gauze bandage was wrapped around his calf.

"Did you see this?" I held up the paper.

Pulling a pair of reading glasses from his shirt pocket, he slipped them on and scanned the page. "I did. I spoke to Inez Ortega already." He sighed. "Our good mayor is in favor of the project, in spite of the Maze's reputation. Anything to bring money into the area. However, she said it did not look like the project was going to go through. Lucky for us."

"Lucky for those scientists." Tossing the paper in the trash, I gestured at his leg. "Does it hurt bad?"

"Badly. Does it hurt *badly* is the correct form."

Whatever. "Well? Does it?"

"Nothing that simple aspirin cannot handle. It is more like a bite from a dog than anything else. *Señor* Fortune rode in the saddle with me today."

Thinking back to the conversation with the gray, I nodded. "Because if that skinner *had* tagged you with any venom, it wasn't very much or you would've felt it by now. Yeah, that's what El Cid told me." I finished setting the table, then sank down in one of the chairs.

Dad joined me. Hooking another chair with his foot, he dragged it closer and rested his injured leg on it. He probed the skin above the bandage. "A drop or two just makes a person, or horse, feel sick. Like they have the flu. Horses can handle more because of their larger body mass. It takes a full-on bite with both fangs to kill."

"Does it happen right away?"

"Death? No. The venom spreads slowly. That way, the skinner can drag the victim back to its lair to be eaten later."

My scalp tightened. "Eaten *alive*?"

"Bones and all." Ben appeared, dressed in a worn but clean T-shirt, his wet hair slicked back. "Like a skinner take-out meal. Roman told me that they usually start with your face. Cheeks. Lips. Under the chin. You know, the softest flesh—"

The microwave binged. "Supper's ready," I announced in a loud voice. Anything to shut Ben up.

We gathered around the table. Over our protests, Dad spooned extra helpings of the green stuff onto our plates. And, in spite of his earlier complaint, my brother hunched over his meatloaf, hammering down on it until Dad cleared his throat.

"Sorry." Ben straightened with a rueful grunt. "Guess I was hungrier than I thought."

"I hope you did not eat like that at Kathleen's table." Dad slid another thick slab onto Ben's plate, then mine, before helping himself. "She will think I have not taught my sons manners. Did you thank her and Roman for having you at their ranch again?"

"Yeah, Dad. I always do. Sheesh, I know how to act in public."

"How's Jo? Still ignoring you?" I couldn't resist teasing Ben about his long-standing crush on the Navarre's daughter, who was seventeen and a year older than him. It was one of my favorite brother-chain-yanking. "She still out-hunting and outriding you?" He kicked at me under the table. I pulled my leg to safety with a practiced move and grinned wider.

Pretending to ignore me, Ben finished the second slice of meatloaf and started on the green beans with less enthusiasm. "By the way, Roman said he'd bring us Isabel whenever you want."

Isabel? Chewing, I thought back to the last time we visited the Navarres at their ranch that straddled the state line between Colorado and New Mexico. Sixty or so miles along the crest of the Sangre de Cristos if I were a crow. "Oh, wait," I asked around a mouthful. "Is she that sorrel mare we met in October?"

"That's the one. She's a real fireball." Pride and fondness colored Ben's voice.

"How so?" I wondered if she was going to be like Turk. I hoped not. One in the family was enough.

"She attacked a pack of coyotes that'd been hanging around the Navarre ranch trying to snatch one of the foals." He gave up on the green beans. I didn't blame him. "She hid behind the corner of the barn, watching for them one evening. Then, when the pack showed up, she burst out and stomped two of them into the ground before they knew what hit 'em." He grinned. "That's what they get for trying to pull something around a herd of warhorses."

A question popped in my head. "Dad? Have any of the other hunters ever tried using *normal* horses?" Normal horses— what El Cid referred to as livestock, usually with a sniff of derision.

"You mean for our kind of hunting?" Dad shook his head. "My grandfather tried. And Roman, too, years ago. But it is nearly impossible to train an average horse to stand its ground in the face of a skinner or other kinds of monsters, much less attack or defend us. The Montoyas down in Arizona are trying some crossbreeding, but so far, *nada.*"

"What would happen if we didn't have the Andalusians?" My fork hovered over the last bite of meatloaf. Its moist red topping reminded me of the skinner's peltless body. And there went my appetite. I laid my fork down with a clink and pushed my plate away.

"We would hunt them another way." Dad scooped the leftovers off my plate and added them to his. "Until then, we still have El Cid and Turk. And, soon, we will have Isabel."

"She likes to be called Izzie," Ben said. "We did some training together, just for kicks. And because she kept bugging me for some practice." His face lit up as he talked. "You think Turk is fast? Wait till you see *her* in action. Man, is she going to keep our boys on their toes. Er, hooves."

Dad grunted in surprise. "*You* trained? Without Roman having to break your arm?"

My brother's grin slipped a notch. "Well, sure. Why wouldn't I? Just because—"

"I thought our method was too old-fashioned for you."

Oh, man. My heart sank. *Not this again.*

A muscle in Ben's cheek twitched. He slouched back, one arm hooked over the back of the chair. "Look, I just think there could be a different way to hunt those things. One that's more effective and less dangerous."

"Our way has worked for almost five hundred years. And, in case you have forgotten," Dad pointed his fork at my brother, "we Del Toros have always—"

Ben made a face. "Yeah, Pop. We all know the family's history." His voice deepened, taking on a story-telling cadence that sounded a lot like our father's. "For you, my sons, are the descendants of the knight, Santiago Del Toro. He, along with a band of fellow knights, rid seventeenth-century Spain from a plague of devil-spawned creatures, sealed their evil spirits in iron chests called coffins—"

"*Coffers*," I interjected, "not coffins."

"—coffers," Ben continued without missing a beat, "and then sent the chests across the ocean to the New World to be buried in remote regions."

"That is enough, Reuben," Dad warned.

Ben clearly had a death wish. He kept going. "And with those chests sailed the Knights of the Coffer and their allies, Andalusian warhorses with power of human speech, to stand eternal watch." He waved a hand in the air. "Cue the theme music."

In spite of everything, I laughed. Ben joined me. Until I noticed Dad's expression. Gulping down my amusement, I lowered my gaze and pretended a fascination with my plate.

"Why do you always ridicule our family?" Dad's eyes narrowed. A hawk zeroing in for the kill.

I shifted in my seat and took a swing at peace-keeping. "He wasn't, Dad. Not really. Ben's just kidding around."

"When he mocks our family, he is mocking *me*."

My brother rolled his eyes. "I wasn't making fun of you. I was just—"

"You were. Be a man and admit it."

My pulse sped up. "Dad, I don't think he meant to—"

"You know, you're always saying that." Ben leaned forward and planted his forearms on the table. "About everything I do. *Be a man. Man up.* Then, when I do, you slap me down like some kid." He glowered across the table. A challenge offered.

Dad stared right back. Challenge accepted. "Then act like a man. Old-fashioned or not, you have a responsibility for being part of this family and this family's mission. Without me prodding you every step of the way."

I swore the temperature in the room plummeted twenty degrees. My skin tightened with goose bumps. "Ben. Dad," I tried again. "C'mon. I thought we were going to figure out what's going on in the Maze."

"*Responsibility?*" Ben raised his chin and his voice. "*You're* one to talk."

"What is that supposed to mean?" Dad dropped his fork with a clatter and shoved his plate away.

"I can't freaking believe you took Matt in there today. He's *eleven*. You think—"

"Twelve," I protested.

"—Mom would want him hunting this young?"

I cringed. The Mom card. We rarely played that one. It was too painful. But, once it was on the table, all bets were off.

Dad stiffened. His mouth worked for a moment, then he spoke. "Your mother is not here to make that decision."

"I wish she was." The unspoken *instead of you* stunk up the air between them.

Silence wailed through the house. They glared at each other, re-enacting so many meals and so many fights that I wanted to smash my plate on the floor. Instead, I bolted, banging the table leg and rattling the dishes on my way out.

Bursting out the front door, I stumbled down the steps, then ran across the yard and into the barn. Soft sounds of horse echoed around the dimness. Muted light filtered down from a pair of skylights set high in the ceiling above the loft. My sanctuary since I could toddle.

In his corner by the door, El Cid was a ghost horse. Straw rustled under his hooves as he shifted, head raised and ears pinned on me. He breathed a welcome. "I heard, Matt."

Wrapping my arms around his neck, I laid my forehead against his warm coat. Under the silky hide, the muscles flowed with each movement. He flexed his neck around me and pressed me against his chest with his chin—an equine hug that I was too old for. It felt all kinds of good.

"How come they hate each other so much?"

"They don't." El Cid's voice rumbled through my body. "That's utter nonsense, and you know it."

"It's Ben's fault. As usual." Turk's disembodied voice floated from the other corner. "He's rude to Javier and never listens to orders. Argues about everything. He stinks at—"

El Cid raised his head. "I don't recall asking for your opinion."

"And I don't recall giving a rat's tush."

The stallions squared off, ears flat and nostrils flared. Then the insult slinging began. Dad and Ben. El Cid and Turk. Didn't anyone in my family get along?

I gave up and slipped outside. Just north of the ranch house, disintegrating adobe walls outlined our family's original homestead. Hands stuffed in my pockets, I kicked at the gravel as I wandered over to a crumbling partition and sank down.

When I was little, I used to play in the ruins. I'd pretend I was Gimli on the walls of Helm's Deep, swinging a plastic dustpan for an ax. Killed my first rattlesnake there too, when I was eight, by dropping a chunk of adobe on its head. Good times.

The front screen opened and slapped against the side of the house. Ben stormed out. He stomped down the steps—taking his resentment out on the innocent treads—and across the yard. I sighed.

"Family meeting," he snapped at me over his shoulder. "Now."

"Yes, *sir*." I couldn't resist firing off a salute.

He continued on to the barn. A few moments later, he reappeared, walking beside El Cid, their heads almost touching. They spoke in low tones, Ben complaining and El Cid telling him to stop arguing and listen for a change. Once I caught my name.

Behind them, Turk emerged, a shadow from the shadows. He paused in the doorway of the barn, looked down his long nose at the world, then followed.

My brother and I took seats on the top steps while the horses stood facing us. The warm evening breeze stirred my hair. Folding forward, I rested my chin on my knees. Next to me, Ben blew out a long breath.

"You okay?" I asked.

"Yeah. Same old, same old." He cleared his throat. "Hey."

I rolled my head over, chin still on my knees. "What?"

"Don't let it get to you, Matt. You know how Dad and I are—it wouldn't be a Del Toro family meal if one of us wasn't spitting mad at the other." A corner of his mouth curled.

I couldn't help a faint grin myself. If Ben knew how much he looked like Dad right then, he'd probably kill himself.

The creak of the screen door. Dad stepped out. He had rolled his pant leg down and put his boots on. Just seeing him back to normal eased the tension in my gut. I wondered if there was any supper left.

"Move." He nudged Ben to one side with his foot, then eased down next to him. "About earlier. I should not have said that."

"You mean the part about tying me up and dumping me in the Maze for the skinners?" A glint of amusement danced in Ben's eye. The knot in my stomach loosened even more.

"Oh, I am still considering *that*." Dad fought a grin and lost. He bumped my brother with his shoulder. "We good, *chico*?"

"*Sí, bueno*," Ben drawled, exaggerating his accent.

Dad rose, cuffing him lightly on the back of the head as he walked down the steps. He took a stand, one boot resting on the bottom tread and thumbs hooked on his back pockets. Shifting from hoof to hoof, Turk stared at Dad's injured leg, ears pinned flat.

El Cid noticed Turk's focus, too. "I hope you're racked with guilt. And if this afternoon was any indication of your abilities—*after* three years of hunting, I might add—then trusting you with Javier, or either of the boys, is going to drive me into an early grave."

Turk snorted. "I should be so lucky."

"Please, let us focus on a fight we have a chance of winning," Dad said. "The rising number of skinners means they have found a way out of the coffer. Certainly, nothing new, for we have fought that particular battle—how do you phrase it, El Cid?—for centuries."

El Cid pulled his attention from Turk. "A slow seepage of evil." He eyed Turk, then Ben and me. "Hmm."

My pulse sped up at his expression. Not to mention Dad's comment. "What do you mean, 'for centuries'? Just how often do they get out?"

A shadow crossed Dad's face. "This will be the second occasion in my lifetime they have escaped in such numbers."

Before I asked if two times was a lot, El Cid spoke. "Javier, we're going to need young Isabel sooner than later."

"I just got off the phone with Roman," Dad said. "He and Kathleen will bring Isabel the day after tomorrow. They should be here by noon at the latest. In the meantime, Turk and I will travel to the cave to check the coffer."

El Cid stomped, a clink of steel on gravel. "No, you will not. We will wait and have Roman accompany us. Safety in numbers."

Dad raised an eyebrow. "There is no need for—"

"Got to admit it, Javier. The old goat's right," Turk said. Our father's other eyebrow shot up. "That cave is bad news. I don't want you going in there without backup. Since *we* can't squeeze in there, Roman will have to do."

With a look of frustration, Dad opened his mouth. El Cid shook his head. "Save your protest. You know neither Turk nor I will take you back in there."

Glancing from one stallion to the other, our father sighed, then rubbed the back of his neck. "I see that I am outnumbered."

"And out-weighed," Ben said under his breath.

"Now," El Cid said, "with the addition of Isabel and Matt, we'll be able to field three teams."

In spite of the nerves coiling my insides like a lariat, I puffed with pride. Trying to act casual, I leaned back on one elbow. "Am I going to pair up with Izzie?"

Turk curled his lip. "Right. Like we'd put the two rookies together. Matt'd probably knock her out with his mace. Or she'd dump him right into a skinner's mouth."

"Izzie and I'll partner up, since we have some experience working together. Yeah, I know." Ben snorted at our father's expression. "Don't faint or anything. But, until I can come up with something better, I guess I'm stuck hunting Del Toro style." He stood and gazed northward at the mesa. "Speaking of which—the wards holding okay?"

That doused my brief flare of relief. I rose too and took a stand on the top step. "They held this afternoon, right, Dad?" Even though I knew how powerful the magical wards were—the ones Santiago Del Toro had placed at the Gate all those centuries ago—I wanted to hear my father say it aloud. Again.

"They are holding. And if they fail, *we* will hold. After all, we are the good guys, no?"

"Even if that *good guy* has fallen to one knee?" Affection colored El Cid's voice.

Dad shrugged. "I can swing a mace kneeling."

"He may have to since he's riding Turk," Ben muttered.

I choked on a laugh. Turk flared his nostrils in warning. I knew he'd find a way to accidentally stomp on our feet tomorrow, leaning his weight on his hoof before we could yank our mangled toes free.

Payback around our ranch came in the shape of a horseshoe.

T wo days later, I stood in the middle of the field east of the barn, watching my father and Turk and daydreaming about being an only child. I sighed, then pushed my damp hair off my forehead. The late morning sun was doing its best to bake me into some kind of gingerbread boy. Or maybe it was the waves of hot fury from Ben. He stood next to me, fuming in silence, his mouth flat with resentment. Just to be safe, I inched away.

Being his usual morning-glory self, Ben had snapped at our father during breakfast. Dad had chomped right back. Hard. Skinners had nothing on Dad when it came to chowing down on us for being disrespectful.

"Dude, let it go," I said. "It was like four hours ago. Over nothing. Sheesh."

"Shut up." He swung his mace around like a scythe, decapitating the seed heads from unsuspecting grasses.

No, you *shut up.* Sick of it all, I turned my attention back to the pair.

Hatless, and with his mace dangling from his wrist, Dad stood in the middle of an area the size of a soccer field. At the far end, Turk—sans halter and saddle—pranced in place. Waiting for the signal. Even from a distance, I noticed his hide twitching and his tail lashing and his lips pulled back from his teeth. Psycho horse. Man, was I glad I wasn't facing him.

I fanned my shirt. My body still sweated from our earlier exercise routine. Del Toro boot camp consisted of a long run across the plains for the warhorses and thirty minutes of calisthenics and stretching for us. Ben seethed the entire time.

Then we worked on our balance by running barefooted along the crumbling adobe walls of the old homestead. I was secretly relieved to see Dad do it without a trace of a limp from the skinner bite.

We finished up with mace work, hitting a stack of hay bales as hard as we could. Forehand. Backhand. Jab. Over and over. First with our right hand, then with our left. My teeth clattered from the shock of each strike. Panting in rhythm with the blows, I breathed in enough straw to cover the floor of the barn.

Ben had wielded both his and Dad's weapons, jaws locked and teeth gritted from the strain of the double weight. I wondered who he had been hitting: our enemy or our father. I shook my head and re-focused on the man.

"All right, *mi amigo*," Dad shouted, laughter in his voice. "Before you explode."

With a squeal, Turk launched into a gallop. He thundered toward Dad, grunting with each stride. Clods of prairie grass flew from his hooves, and his tail billowed out behind him like a black cloak.

"Turk Vader." I wondered if Ben would laugh at our old joke.

Nope.

"Hope he misses," Ben snarled. I knew he didn't mean Turk.

"He won't—he's too good. And, anyway, Turk won't let him fail." My brother and me? Turk would dump *us* in an Albuquerque minute.

Dad waited, knees bent, left hand ready to reach, and right hand holding the mace by the middle of its haft. The rumble of hooves grew louder, shaking the ground. My own leg muscles tightened.

"And...now," I whispered.

As the stallion galloped past, Dad grabbed Turk's mane. His fist disappeared in the thick mass. A split second later, his boots left the ground as he flung himself one-handed onto the stallion and into position, all in single smooth move. The mace rested across the stallion's withers. Even bareback, Dad kept his knees and feet in the exact position as if he had been in the saddle. Turk's long mane spilled over his lap like a tablecloth.

Ben grunted. "The guy's a total pain, but dang."

I nodded. We both knew how hard it was to mount a galloping horse. Especially horses as tall as our war-brothers. And while holding an iron mace in one hand. So, yeah. Dang all over that.

Finishing a victory lap, Turk and Dad loped toward us. The black slowed to a jog, then brisk walk. El Cid ambled over and joined us, his muzzle dripping from a water break and Dad's Stetson hooked on his saddle horn.

Dad reached out and plucked his hat free. He put it on, gave it his signature tug, then swung a leg around and dismounted easily. "Who would like to try next?"

"Matty." Ben pushed me toward Turk. "He needs the practice and I don't."

Turk and I eyed each other. "Why can't I try it on El Cid?" I already knew why. It didn't stop me from begging.

"Because Turk is taller." Dad motioned me closer to the black. "And if you can mount *him* at a gallop, you can mount El Cid. Or *any* horse, for that matter."

"And besides," El Cid said, "I'm here this morning in an advisory capacity."

Facing Turk's left side, I placed one hand on his neck and my other hand, holding my mace, on his croup, then bent my left knee and stuck my leg out behind me. With a grunt, Dad lifted me up. I scooted into position behind the black's withers and took a deep breath. "All set."

Taller and thicker than El Cid, Turk stomped along like he was furious at the world. Each stride pounded the earth. As we jogged toward the center of the field, I kept a tight hold of his mane. Just in case.

"Watch your feet," he growled over a shoulder.

"I know how to ride." I fought the temptation to nail him in the ribs with my heels.

He dropped me off, then trotted away to the far end and wheeled around. I let out another steadying breath. *Okay. I've got this*, I lied to myself. I hitched up my jeans, tightened my grip on the mace's haft, and gave the signal.

Turk exploded. He barreled toward me, legs churning and lips peeled back from his teeth. For a split second, I knew what a lamb must feel like when it spied a coyote coming for it. Or a baby seal when it spotted the dorsal fin of a shark in the nearby waves. He lowered his head and lengthened his stride.

"What are you doing?" I hollered. "That's too fast!"

He sped up. The jerk.

Holy mother of pearl! The thunder of my heart matched the black's hoofbeats. With every stride, he grew as big as a Mack truck. I licked my lips and crouched down, my thigh muscles quivering. *Don't miss, don't miss, don't miss...*

I grabbed his mane in a desperate lunge. With a jerk, my feet left the ground. For a moment, I hung one-handed against his side, my arm and shoulder screaming from the strain and the coarse hairs digging into my fingers like wire. I gave a couple of pogo-stick hops, then threw myself face down over his back. The jutting bones of his wither punched me in the gut with every bounce. Gasping for breath, I kicked, then flung my leg around with everything I had.

Too much everything.

His coat was as slick as black ice. I skidded sideways. "Whoa!" I grabbed for his mane.

And missed.

Whump!

I hit the ground so hard I swore my teeth rattled loose from my gums. Vibrating from the impact, I sprawled in the dirt, my lungs convulsing for air. Finally, with a whooping gasp, I sucked in a lungful. Then another. Rubbing my chest, I sat up. A dark shape loomed over me.

"Why don't you save the rest of us the hassle," Turk said, "and go feed yourself to those meat heads right now."

"Yeah, you first." I lurched to my feet. Spying my father walking over, I busied myself dusting off my clothes, not wanting to meet his gaze. Ben and El Cid trailed behind. My brother was laughing silently behind Dad's back.

"Matt?" Dad stopped and pushed his hat back. One black eyebrow rounded upward like the top of a question mark. "Well?"

"It was *his* fault. He's gotten taller or something."

"Oh, sure." Turk flattened his nostrils. "When in doubt, blame the mount."

"Wow. That was embarrassing." Ben sauntered up, still grinning. "Maybe you need a pony."

"Maybe *you* need to shut up."

"Do not use that expression, Mateo." Dad lifted a finger in warning. "It is rude."

I could be a lot ruder, I thought. I swung aboard El Cid and settled myself in the saddle. *Go ahead*, I thought to the gray. *Say something. Then, I'll kick you in the ribs.*

Dad gestured toward the middle of the field. "Ben. Your turn."

"Nah, I'm good. Really. I can do that stuff in my sleep."

"There is always room for improvement, my son."

Ben barked a laugh. "It's mounting a galloping horse, not performing brain surgery. Any idiot with a little coordination and strong arms can do it."

Dad's face stiffened into flat planes and lines. One eyelid twitched.

As usual, Ben missed the signal. "Practicing stuff I can already do? Kind of a waste of time."

"It is mine to waste." Our father's voice was low and even. Another signal.

My clueless brother tried a different tactic. "Have Matt try again. He's the one who stinks at it."

"No way." I gathered up the reins. "He told you to."

"Boys…" Dad began.

"I don't want to work with either of the little rats," Turk snarled. "They can't ride worth spit."

"That's because *you*," El Cid sniffed, "have the coordination of a beer-swilling, overweight Clydesdale."

"My brothers…" Dad tried again.

Turk flared his nostrils and took a stiff-legged step toward El Cid. "Lose the kid and I'll show you—"

"¡Ya basta!"

We all jumped at Dad's roar. Even Turk shied a few paces.

He glared at Ben, eyes blazing gold fire. "*Practice* keeps us *alive* in there." He stabbed a finger northward toward the mesa

with each word. "There will be moments when your horseman-
ship and skill with a mace are the only things standing between
you and death." He stepped closer and crowded my brother.
"Now, get on that warhorse. Because I will not lose you, or any
member of our *familia*, because you thought it was a *waste of
your time!*"

That's when I saw something I'd never seen before.

Fear on my father's face.

Fear that one of us—Ben or I or one of the horses—would
die in the Maze at the teeth of a skinner. Dad had lost his sister
that way when they were teens. It dawned on me that he rode
with that same terror clawing at his shoulders every time we
hunted—saddled with the almost impossible task of keeping all
of us alive. Alone.

Even worse? I knew Ben didn't see it. For a moment, I felt
like the older brother.

The faint rumble of a truck's engine snapped the tension. I
stood in the stirrups and peered toward the Hump. A cloud of
dust drifted up from behind the hill, turning it into a mini volca-
no.

"I bet that's Roman." I craned my neck, trying to catch a
glimpse of whoever was driving along the three-mile dirt road
from Huerfano. *I sure hope so. I could use some backup.*

The thought of the fellow hunter, and my father's oldest
friend, filled me with relief. Roman, and his wife, Kathleen,
were like family. A heck of a lot more family than Dad's brother, Sebastian.

Not that I would know—never met the guy. At least, not
that I remember. Dad only mentioned Sebastian when Ben was
being a royal pain and pushing all of our father's buttons. He
would snarl through clenched teeth how much *my* brother was
like *his* brother.

But Roman and Kathleen? Constant as the Rockies, and fearless referees between Dad and Ben when tempers reached solar flare levels.

"If things ever get too bad between those hot-headed bulls," Roman would remind me at the end of every visit, "you call me, *chico*. Okay? I will drive up with my mace and knock some sense into them."

Without a word, Dad swung up on Turk. They headed across the pasture at a quick trot. My brother let out an unsteady breath, then swiped his mouth along the shoulder of his tee.

"Wow, did you luck out," I said. "He was about to go nuclear on you."

"Whatever. The guy's got issues." He stepped around to El Cid's left side and waved me back. "Move."

"No, I was here first."

"Can't tell you how little I care." He grabbed my arm and pulled. I clung to the horn, kicking.

"Boys. *Boys*." El Cid flung up his head. "I am not a sofa. Ben, either ride behind your brother or walk."

With a smirk of triumph, I slipped my boot free of the stirrup, then leaned forward out of the way. My brother swung up behind the saddle, making sure to jab me in the ribs with the end of his mace. Mumbling under his breath, El Cid broke into an easy lope for home.

The truck's rumble, punctuated by a rattling noise, grew louder. Rounding the south end of the barn, we trotted into the yard just as a trailer rig pulled in. Two figures waved through the dust-covered windshield. I waved back, waiting until Ben slid off El Cid's rump before swinging out of the saddle.

With a crunch of gravel, the rig crept to a gentle stop. Kathleen hopped down from the passenger side and hurried around the front of the truck toward us. Her curling red hair was a fiery halo around her head, and she wore jeans, boots, and a denim shirt as blue as her eyes.

"I don't know who to hug first," she said. "Guess I'll start with my favorite. Get over here, Matt." She opened her arms.

The old feeling welled up—joy mixed with the threadbare wish that my mom was still alive. "Hi, Kathleen." I hugged her back. My ears warmed from embarrassment.

"How's my boy?" Letting go, Kathleen O'Riley Navarre looked me up and down. "Growing like a weed, I see."

"An ugly one at that." A large man joined us, his teeth a flash of white in a tanned face.

"Hi, Roman." I stuck out my hand, hoping the big guy would be satisfied with a shake. Nope.

Built like he could play offensive line for the Denver Broncos, Roman Navarre beamed down at me. His shoulder-length hair, glossy as fine dark chocolate, was pulled back at the nape of his neck with an ornate silver clasp. The sleeves of his turquoise cowboy shirt were rolled up to his elbows, showing off forearms as big as my thighs. He frowned at my attempt at a safe greeting.

"What is this nonsense?" He slapped my hand aside, then wrapped me in a bear hug and lifted me off the ground. My breath whooshed out in a hiss. "How is *mi niñito*? Not so little, eh?"

"Good," I squeaked, wasting the last of my air. He set me down. I stepped back and rubbed my ribs, willing my lungs to re-inflate for the second time that day.

"Kathleen." Removing his hat, Dad lifted her hand to his lips, then leaned over and kissed her cheek. "Thank you, again, for allowing Ben to stay with you each spring. You do not know what it means to me."

"Oh, I think I do, Jav." Her eyes danced. "Otherwise, you two would kill each other."

"My money would be on Ben, now that he has gotten some growth under him." Roman shook Dad's hand, then clapped him on the shoulder. He nodded at my brother, who was inching toward the trailer. "If I had known we were coming up this soon, Ben, I would have saved you a bus ride."

"No big deal." He edged over to the rig.

Roman beamed at the stallions waiting nearby. "My old friends. How are you?"

El Cid blew out a long breath. "Well, Roman, you know I'm not one to complain, but—"

"Except you do," Turk said. "All the time."

El Cid ignored him. "But between the surprise attack, Javier getting injured, Turk being Turk, Isabel's arrival, and fretting over everyone's safety, my mind is awhirl."

Turk started to say something, then shook his head. "Nah. Too easy."

Boom! The strike of a hoof on the wooden floor echoed from inside the trailer. "In case you've all forgotten," called a voice an octave higher than El Cid's. "There's a warhorse still in here. Bored out of her skull." Another bang. The trailer swayed. We gathered around.

"Working on it, Izzie." My brother was already reaching for the latch on the door. "I'll have you right out."

"Thanks, Ben. Glad *someone* with opposable thumbs remembers I'm trapped in here."

Unlatching the metal door, he swung it wide with a clang. "Careful. That first step is kind of high."

"Got it."

I moved closer. One slender, sorrel leg appeared. A long Viking-blonde tail. Then another leg as she nimbly stepped backward.

Once clear of the trailer, she shook herself all over, then flung her head up, flipping her mane to one side. Her coat glowed like fire.

"What's all this?" She looked around, eyes bright. "The paparazzi?

"I zzie." Kathleen gestured at my father and me. "I believe you know Javier Del Toro and his youngest son, Matt."

"Sure, we met last autumn. How's it going?"

"*Muy bien, gracias,*" Dad said. "And welcome." He turned toward the stallions. Before he could make introductions, El Cid stepped forward.

"Welcome, indeed, to your new home." He arched his neck. So did Turk, who shouldered past me. If they had been teenage boys, they would have been puffing out their chests and flexing their arms. "I'm—"

"El Cid," the mare said with a suspicious twitch of her ears.

"Well, yes. If you would care to—"

"The pompous, wise elder," she continued. "Deservedly named after one of the most famous noblemen and knights in Spanish history. Still quite the warrior, but in the twilight of his fighting years. He is fiercely protective of the Del Toro family."

"Why, I beg your pardon," El Cid sputtered. "I am *not* pompous."

"And the infamous Turk." Izzie pointed her slender nose at the black. "Or as the boys call him, Turk the Jerk." Ben and I cringed when Turk glared at us. She chuffed in amusement, then continued. "A savage fighter and a loner, with an ardent loyalty given only to the patriarch of the Del Toro family. Easy to admire, difficult to like."

One of those long, awkward silences. Then Dad barked a laugh. The Navarres joined him, Kathleen looking a little sheepish. A faint blush darkened her freckles.

"Now, girlfriend," she said, "that conversation was supposed to stay between us. Sorry about that, guys," she said to El Cid and Turk.

Izzie flexed her neck a few times and pawed the ground. "Any place I can stretch my legs? That was a long haul in a slow trailer."

"Field on the other side of the barn." Ben jabbed a thumb over his shoulder. "If you want, I'll show you around, then we can—"

To my surprise, Dad stopped him. "Ben, let your brother play the host."

My mouth fell open. "*Me?*"

Ben frowned. "Why?" Alarm colored his face. "You said that Izzie and I were to team up."

"You are." Dad exchanged looks with Roman and Kathleen, who both nodded in understanding. "But it would be good to give Matt and Isabel a chance to get to know one another, too." Dad shooed me away. When the stallions started to join us, he called them back. "El Cid. Turk. A word in private, *por favor?*"

Wondering what Dad wanted to talk with them about— although I could probably guess—I led the way to the barn, Izzie by my shoulder. Even at a slow stroll, her movements were cat-like and quick compared to the stallions. I tried to think of something clever or cool to say, to show her that I was more than just the younger son, but nope. Just a big ol' bucket of *nada*.

I pointed my mace at El Cid's and Turk's corners. "Pick any other spot you want and I'll bring you fresh straw. Water barrel's outside the doors—we keep 'em open most of the time, unless it gets really cold, but that's just during winter. Oh, and whenever you want groomed, just let Ben or me know."

"Feed? Or do I graze?"

"Both. Or either. Whatever you want. For feed, we've got mixed grains, plain oats, and alfalfa. Molasses, too, if you want us to add it to your grain. El Cid likes that sometimes. And if you ever want a snack, there's apples, pears, carrots—"

"May I see the wine list?"

I stuttered to a halt. "The…the *what*?" I knew Turk shared a beer with Dad once in a while, but wine?

"You sound like a waiter."

"Oh." Heat crept up my cheeks. *I am such a dweeb.*

"Seriously, dude, I'm here to help with skinner search and destroy, and to keep you guys safe. I'm not some pretty in pink princess. Got it?"

"Got it." My heart sank right down to my boots. Great. Just what we needed. Another Turk. I wondered why Ben had been so jazzed to have her join the team.

"But I appreciate you trying to make me feel at home. I really do." She butted me lightly with her nose. "Ben was right—you're okay, kid."

My heart rose, both at her words and Ben's. So. Maybe not like Turk. "Want to check out the field now?"

"Lead on, Matty."

I groaned. Should have guessed. *Thanks, Ben.* "Can't we just pretend you don't know about that nickname?"

"What nickname?"

I grinned. "Okay, then."

We headed back out. In the corner of the yard, Dad still spoke in a low tone to the stallions. Roman and Kathleen were following Ben up the porch steps.

Skirting the south side of the barn, we wandered across the field, my boots swishing through the prairie grass, our shadows dark blobs under us. The ever-present breeze stirred the mare's mane and cooled my face.

She halted and looked around. "Nice place. A lot nicer than how Ben described it."

"Yeah, I can imagine what he told you."

"More open terrain than the Navarre ranch." She scanned the area, her ears and nose working like crazy. "But then their place is closer to the mountains. More foothills, too."

"Are you going to miss it?" I asked. "Being with the Navarres and all those other horses?"

"Joking, right?"

"Um…"

"Trust me, I'm not. It's a relief to get away from that new crop of foals. I swear, they never stop. When they're not nursing, they're babbling. Or running around, bucking and chasing each other until they drop dead asleep. Usually right where I wanted to take a nap myself. I don't know how Roman and Kathleen put up with the whole mess."

I shrugged, secretly liking all the times we went down to visit the Navarre family. Josefina—Jo to the world—was like my cool big sister. We always ganged up on Ben. They also cared for any Andalusians mares—*our* kind of Andalusians—who were with foal or had a young colt or filly. The mares were currently guarded by Roman's war-brother, the enormous stud Vasco. Both El Cid and Turk had come from *Rancho de Navarre*, although from different sires.

A question popped in my head. "Hey, did you know Turk?"

"The Jerk? Barely. I was still a young filly when Javier sent for him. He's a few years older than me, you know. But no one seemed to like him much back at the ranch."

"Here either. Except for Dad. For some weird reason that Ben and I *still* can't figure out."

"As long as Turk does his job and stays out of my way, that's all I care about." She swished her tail. "I never thought I'd be stationed up here with him. This is as far north as they got, wasn't it?"

I nodded, recalling all the times Dad told me and Ben about the knights and warhorses who had accompanied the coffers from Spain to Mexico, then onward along the *Camino del Cazador*. "Yeah. They hauled the coffers by ox cart from Mexico, then split up and buried the chests all over the Southwest. Santiago Del Toro volunteered to go the farthest north. That's how my family ended up here in Colorado."

"You guys are lucky."

"How so?"

"Having to deal with just skinners. They disappear—*poof*—when you destroy them, right?"

"Well, yeah. Pretty much. But how does that make us lucky?"

"See, back at the Navarre ranch, we've got *duende*."

"Dew-en-day? Kind of like goblins, right?"

"Yup. Nasty little trolls. They hang out in the foothills west of us. And, man, do they smell when whacked. It's like stepping on a giant stinkbug. They explode into this green troll slime—"

"'Who you gonna call.'"

"What?"

"Never mind."

"Anyway, the slime gets all over everything. The rest of us head up-wind whenever Roman and Vasco come back from the hunt until they can hose themselves off. And, on that charming note, I'm going to stretch my legs."

Izzie trotted a few strides, then broke into a lope, knees lifted high and slender legs churning. Picking up speed, she tossed her head and tore around the field, mane and tail golden war banners.

Something Dad once quoted to me whispered in my head: *Thou shall fly without wings, and conquer without any sword, O, Horse!* I could almost see her wearing pieces of armor—the kind knights used to put on their steeds during the Middle Ages, long tassel-y things fluttering from the saddle skirt checkered in red and blue. Although I had a feeling Izzie didn't do tassels.

Bring it on, skinners, I thought. *Or whatever else slithers out of those coffers. We got warhorses on our side.*

Circling back, she slowed to a bouncing jog and rejoined me. "Oh, that's better," she sighed, blowing out a long breath. "Ugh. I can't stand riding in that trailer."

"Better than walking the whole way."

"True that." Izzie raised her head. Her mane rippled in the rising breeze and flowed back over her withers and along her shoulders. "That big mesa." She pointed her nose northward. "Beyond that low ridge—"

"The Hump."

"Right. So, those cliffs beyond—is that the Maze?"

"Yup. About two miles away."

"You know, I wouldn't mind a little incline work—say, up to the top of the Hump and back down? Get a look at the Maze while we're up there?" She shifted sideways. "You up for a ride? I'd be glad to take you."

"Well…" Swinging my mace, I beheaded some tall grasses. Dad never said *not* to ride with her to the top of the Hump. It wasn't like we were going anywhere near the Maze.

"I just want to get a feel for the lay of the land." She glanced around, then lowered her voice, even though we were alone. "Maybe along the way you could give me some tips?"

"Tips?"

"Yeah." She looked at me with an ebony eye. "I don't want to screw up my first real hunt. You know what I mean?"

"I sure do." I laid my hand on her neck. Red velvet, but warm and alive. "*My* first one was Saturday. El Cid and I went in with Dad and Turk."

"Really?" Her eye widened. "Was it everything you thought it'd be?"

"Oh, yeah. And more."

"So, what was the worst part—" She pricked up her ears and looked east. "Someone's coming."

Squinting, I could just make out someone biking along the dirt road toward our ranch. Couldn't tell if it was a guy or not, but it looked too small to be an adult. Whoever it was sure picked one heck of a neon green for their helmet. They slowed, then stopped at the far edge of the field, one foot on the ground, a hand shading their eyes. The stranger must have caught me and Izzie staring, because they wheeled around and headed back to town.

"Guess he decided the private property sign actually *did* apply to him."

Izzie huffed. "Or *she*."

"What?"

"Could've been a girl, you know. Nothing said the person on the bike was a guy."

I blinked. "Good point."

A faint but piercing whistle. We both looked over. From the edge of the pasture, Dad waved us home.

I lifted my hand in acknowledgement. "Guess we'll explore the ridge later."

"That offer of a lift still stands."

A thrill ran through me. "Okay. But don't laugh at my mounting technique." I looped my mace on my left wrist, then grabbed a fistful of mane, bent my knees, and jumped. With an *oof*, I landed on my stomach. I wiggled higher and swung a boot over.

"Well." Izzie turned her head and eyed me. "I've seen worse."

"Sorry." My cheeks burned. I tightened my legs and gathered up two handfuls of mane. "Okay. All set."

Izzie didn't gallop, she *floated*. Each stride was a graceful roll—so different from Turk's teeth-rattling jolt or El Cid's trampoline-like bounce. She sped up, attacking the terrain with gusto, her stride smoothing out even more. Clinging to her mane, I leaned forward, my legs hugging her slender barrel. The wind hummed a rousing tune in my ears—might have been a Disney movie theme song.

"Roman said you were a good rider," she shouted over a shoulder. "Light and balanced."

Praise from Caesar. I grinned all the way home.

7

By the time we reached the yard, the two-legged members of my family were relaxing in the shade of the porch, all of them with beer bottles in hand. Tilting back in his chair, and with his boots propped on the railing, Dad was laughing with Kathleen. Next to her, Roman sputtered in protest. No Ben in sight, though. Maybe he didn't want to hang with the old folks. Still talking, they rose and strolled inside.

"Thanks for the lift." I swung my leg over Izzie's neck and sat sideways for a moment, then slid off.

"Any time. And I still want to have that talk. We newbies gotta stick together."

My heart warmed. "Count on it."

El Cid ambled out of the barn. "Ah, you're back, Isabel—"

"Still going by Izzie."

"Right. Well, I assume you've a number of questions. If you'd like, we can chat after you've had water. Or Matt can fetch you a snack. Perhaps a chilled pear? I find them refreshing on a hot summer day."

"Water's fine for now. But then, yeah, fill me in on everything I need to know."

"Don't talk yourselves *hoarse*," I said. Dang, but I was funny. "Get it? Don't talk yourselves..."

El Cid flattened his ears. "Go away. Before I feed you to Turk."

Still grinning, I headed up the porch steps and stepped inside. The aroma of pork and green chili, which had stewed all morning, enveloped me in a garlic-scented hug. Mouth watering and stomach growling, I hurried to the kitchen and squeezed in between Ben and Kathleen.

Dad stood at the stove, ladling the almost-lethal stew into waiting bowls. A stack of flour tortillas—Kathleen's contribution—steamed in the middle of the table, hot and bready and misshapen into imperfect rounds. Perfect.

"You know, Jav, I tagged along with Roman just for this." Kathleen leaned over and inhaled the rising steam. "Hmmm. Come to mama."

I took a tiny, cautious spoonful. Spicy porky goodness filled my mouth. Maybe Dad scaled back on the peppers this time. I relaxed and took a bigger bite.

Solar flares exploded in my mouth. Eyes watering, I grabbed a tortilla, slathered it with butter, then shoved in about a third. The bread helped ease the assault on my tongue. Kind of. Gasps of pain circled the table.

"Hot?" My father beamed with pride.

"Shouldn't be a goal, Dad," Ben panted, "to hurt people with your cooking."

"Matt?" Roman dabbed his lips with a napkin. Wincing, no doubt, from blisters. "Your father told us that you went on your first hunt Saturday. *Felicitaciones*." He raised his glass. I saw that he, along with Dad and Kathleen, had switched to iced tea after only one beer.

Alcohol makes a young man stupid and an old man slow,
Dad often said. *And stupid and slow will get a hunter skinned.*

I clinked glasses with Roman. "Thanks." I decided it wasn't
worth mentioning that El Cid had bolted to safety with me. "I
didn't get any skinners, though. But I will. Next time." Nobody's getting hurt again. Not if I could help it.

"Javier?" Kathleen fanned her mouth as she spoke. "Are
you sure you don't want me to check your leg? I brought my
medical bag along."

"No, *gracias*. It is healing fine. However, would you examine El Cid?"

I wondered why Dad asked the red-headed veterinarian to
look at the stallion. Was something wrong with him? A tiny
flame of worry flared up in my already super-heated gut. I started to ask when Roman spoke.

"So, Javier. How many skinners again? That attacked you?"

"Four."

"Five." Everyone looked at me. "There was the one who attacked first, remember? Then, the four others showed up after
that."

"Ah, he is right. There *were* five," Dad said. "That first one
was a distraction. To give the others a better chance. El Cid and
I both thought it might be so."

"Even though those creatures are basically hamburger on
four paws, you've got to admire their cunning," Kathleen said.

"Have you checked on the coffer?" Roman scraped his
bowl with gusto.

"We *were* going to," Ben spoke around a mouthful, "but El
Cid went into mama bear mode. And Turk agreed with him.
They said they wouldn't take us to the cave unless Roman came
along as backup. Or signed a permission slip or something."

"Good." Kathleen laid her spoon down. "They're doing
their jobs, then."

"Too bad Vasco did not come with us." Roman passed his empty bowl to me and nodded toward the stove. "*Por favor?*"

"Why didn't he?" I knew the enormous dappled-gray stallion loved a fight—good, bad, or ugly. After refilling the bowl, I handed it back.

"I asked him, but Vasco will not step one hoof off the ranch right now." Roman dug fearlessly into his second helping, the big show off. "Not with the mares being distracted with their new foals. I told him that Jo is more than capable of running things, but you know Vasco. He is overly protective of the *bebés.*"

Kathleen gulped the rest of her iced tea and pushed up from the table. Dad rose when she did. She waved him back down, then patted his shoulder. "Delicious meal, Javier. Always grateful to have survived it. Well, I'm off to go check on my old friend."

After she left, Dad and Roman began reminiscing about a hunt they had completely and totally screwed up when they were young and stupid. I leaned closer to Ben. "Hey. What's going on with El Cid?"

Ben shrugged. "He's getting old, I guess."

My heart stumbled, as if it had tripped over something in the dark. "May I be excused?" At Dad's distracted nod, I carried my bowl to the sink, then slipped out the front door.

I started for the barn, but changed my mind and headed to the adobe ruins. The thought of El Cid getting older was like a pimple on my chin. Knowing there was nothing I could do about it, I still picked at the notion, making it worse, drawing blood.

Why did it bother me so much? I sank down in the shade of the broken walls, the thick mud bricks cool against my back. It wasn't like he was dying or anything, I pointed out to myself. Heck, he wasn't even close. Leaning my head back, I stared into the everlasting blue of sky.

Ever since I was a little kid, I played a game inside my head that no one else knew about. It was kind of sick, but I couldn't stop doing it. Maybe it was my way of dealing with losing Mom. I'd think about someone in my family dying. Then I'd try to imagine what my life would be like without them.

I closed my eyes and tried to picture a world that didn't have a gray stallion in one corner of it. I couldn't. All my life, I had dreamed of hunting with the warhorse. Me and El Cid. Team Del Toro. We were going to bust up so many skinners there wouldn't be any left. And Dad and Ben would have to find new hobbies. And the Maze would be open to people who wouldn't have to worry about anything more dangerous than sunburn.

"Matt?"

I startled. Kathleen walked past on her way to their truck. A bulging medical pack swung from one shoulder. She opened the cab, placed the bag on the seat, then wandered over to me.

"What's wrong, buddy?"

"Nothing." How could I explain that I was trying on some grief? Just to see if I could stand up under its weight?

"Liar. You're worrying about El Cid, aren't you?" She sank down next to me. "Scoot over. This Irish gal needs all the shade she can get." Shoulder to shoulder, we sat there, watching a maverick cloud ambling eastward on its way to Kansas.

"Is there something *wrong* with him?" I recalled how hard he was breathing when we escaped the skinners. I picked up a pebble and squeezed it, just to have something to hang on to. Just in case.

"Not one bit. In fact, he's in excellent condition considering he's close to nineteen. Not really old—this line of Andalusians is extremely long-lived compared to most breeds—but he's getting up there. I'm leaving a vitamin supplement you can mix with his grain once a day. It'll help him get a little kick back in his kick. I've discussed this with him and he approved. Other than that, I can see him going pretty strong for another ten years, barring any accidents."

"*Ten years?*" That was practically like a second lifetime for me. My whole body lightened. I swore I floated up, the seat of my jeans leaving the dirt. "Really?"

"Have I ever been anything but totally honest with you, kiddo?"

A wave of relief rolled over me. I grinned. "So that means I really *am* your favorite."

She laughed. "Got me there."

Twack. The front screen opened and shut. Dad and Roman, with Ben trailing, marched down the steps and across the yard. In their boots and cowboy hats, they looked like old-time Western sheriffs, eager to hunt down some *desperados.* They only lacked tin stars on their shirts and six shooters at their hips. Except guns didn't work on skinners. All three of them were packing maces.

"Where is my Irish rose?" Roman's voice boomed around the yard.

"Why, 'twould be *wild* Irish rose to ye, boyo." Kathleen patted my knee, then stood and dusted off her jeans. I joined her. "You three gents off to work?"

"Three and a half. Matt?" Dad cocked his head toward the house. "Arm yourself, my son."

Anticipation and nervousness washed over me in a flood of hot and cold. Speaking of flooding, before retrieving my mace from the hooks by the front door, I made a detour to the bathroom. Another rule of hunting: pee when you can.

I passed Kathleen coming inside as I was headed out. "Are you staying here?" I already knew her answer, but I asked anyway.

"Yeah. I'd be more a hindrance than anything, especially since we're short on horses." She flopped down on the sofa, a thick paperback novel in her hand. "Plus, no matter how much I practice, I'll never match your skill with a mace. I don't have the bloodline, and anyway, I started too late in life."

Another question, something I'd always wondered about, showed up. "After you met Roman, and you learned about the whole talking horses and monsters and magical weapons—did that freak you out?"

"No, not really."

I blinked. "It didn't?"

"Actually, I think it surprised Roman *more* that I rolled with it." She laughed at my expression. "Matt, I come from Irish stock, remember? And we O'Rileys have always believed that our ancestors had their own fair share of monsters to battle. All with the help of some legendary weapons and a wee bit o' Celtic magic. Believing in Roman's rather unique background wasn't much of a chasm to leap." She sank further into the cushions and opened her book. "Now, hustle before your father comes looking for you. Oh, and Matt?"

I looked back, one hand on the screen. "Yeah?"

"Tell Javier that I'll re-stock your first aid kit. That said," she shot me a stern look, "you guys be careful. Remember, I'm a vet, not a doctor. I can only do so much patching."

"We will." As I stepped through the door, I heard her whisper words that made no sense.

"*Faugh a ballagh.*"

I jogged to the barn, boots crunching on the gravel. Halfway across the yard, I caught Izzie's voice rising in protest. *Uh-oh. What's wrong now?* I stepped inside the coolness and looked around.

Turk and El Cid waited in the center of the large space while Roman and Dad groomed them with quick, efficient strokes. Off to one side, Izzie fumed while Ben's expression matched hers.

"But that's why I'm here, Javier." She stamped a hoof in frustration. "To hunt and to watch out for Ben. Not to stand around the barn making small talk with the mice while you guys are at the party."

"We don't have mice," El Cid murmured, eyes half closed in bliss as my father brushed his coat. "Turk catches them, then eats 'em."

Dad raised his free hand, forestalling Izzie's next words. "I understand. You are eager to help, and I appreciate your enthusiasm. But this is just to check on the coffer, not a real hunt. You will not miss any excitement. And, forgive me, but I want you and Ben to have a few more training sessions first."

"We *did* do some training together, remember?" my brother reminded him. "When I was at the Navarres? Ask Roman."

"No, no." The large hunter ran a brush down Turk's shoulder. "I think I will skip the family drama this time."

Smart man.

"And, anyway, if this is only a reconnaissance mission," Ben continued, "then it's a good way for Izzie and me to clock some more hours together, even if it's just riding. You're always saying that there's no substitute for time in the saddle." He motioned me over and slung an arm around my neck. "And Matt could ride double with me to the Maze."

Desperate to avoid getting stuck on Turk, and equally anxious not to add more weight to El Cid, I nodded in agreement. "Please, Dad?" I put on my baby-of-the-family face. It worked about sixty-five percent of the time. Good odds.

Dad paused. He rested an arm on El Cid's back and looked at Roman.

The other man shrugged, then bent over and began cleaning Turk's hoof. "Your kids, your call."

"El Cid?"

"Oh, let her come, Javier. Experience is the best teacher and all that."

Dad pinned the three of us with his gaze. "If I give you— *any* of you—an order, and you disobey..." He drew his thumb, curved like a scimitar, across his throat and hissed. *"Comprende?"*

"Sí, Papá," Ben and I answered in unison.

His eyes flicked over to the mare. "Isabel?"

"Sí, Papá."

He fought back a smile. "Another smart mouth." He went back to sweeping the brush along El Cid's spine from withers to tail. "Saddle up. Matt, give Roman a hand."

"Thanks," Ben muttered. "I owe you."

"Big time." I walked over to the saddle rack to fetch Turk's. We could have ridden bareback and often did, but never, ever on a hunt. El Cid wouldn't let us—*any* of us, not even Dad. One of *his* rules.

I don't care how skilled a rider you are, El Cid always said. *It's easier for a human to stay in a saddle. That's why stirrups were such an important development. First used in China, the use of the stirrup spread throughout Eurasia by the great horsemen of the central Asian steppes—*

That's about the time Ben or I would interrupt before Professor Trivia launched into another history lesson.

As Ben readied Izzie, I picked up Turk's saddle and pad with both arms and hauled it over to Roman. He usually rode Turk when he visited and needed a mount. The big black could more easily handle the larger man's weight. Also Roman was probably the only other person in the world that Turk could stand. Grudgingly.

"*Gracias.*" Roman took the saddle by the horn with one hand, then laid the thick pad on Turk's back and slid it backward an inch. "Do you know why I did that?"

"So that all the hairs lay flat and don't pull when the saddle shifts."

"That is right." He lifted the saddle onto the broad back and fastened the cinch, easing the buckle tighter hole by hole. "There. Everything feels good, my friend? Cinch not too tight?"

"It'll do."

Roman shook his head, then laid a massive hand on my shoulder. I forced myself to stand up straight under the weight. "Remember, *chico*, the comfort and well-being of our war-brothers and sisters come first. The fact that we ride upon them does not mean they are beneath us. No, they eat before us, they rest before us. Everything for them first. Next, your father and brother, and the innocents of this world. Lastly, yourself."

I nodded. "The way of the Knight of the Coffer," I repeated the familiar words.

Roman gazed down at me, a smile playing around the corners of his mouth. "The way of a true man," he said softly.

S addled up, we gathered in the yard. I waited in the shade of
the barn, twirling my mace by its leather strap, nervous as a
kid on the sidelines waiting to be picked for the team. Roman's words circled around in my skull. *A true man.* What did
that mean? Did a guy have to be a certain age? Tougher than
other guys? Did it happen all at once? Or would I just wake up
one day and—*bam*—there I was?

I shook myself. *Get your head in the game.* I watched as
Dad swung up on El Cid. It was weird seeing him mounted on
the gray. I reminded myself that they had hunted together longer
than I'd been alive.

"Matt." Ben leaned down from Izzie and bipped me on the
back of the head. "Move it."

Trying to be graceful, I clambered up and settled on the sorrel's haunch behind the cantle. Naturally, I managed to kick her.
"Sorry, Izzie."

"No worries. Nice to have you along."

"Thanks." I re-looped the mace's strap around my right wrist. In spite of the day's heat, a chill rattle-snaked up my spine. I couldn't believe I was going back in the Maze. Swallowing through a mouth that was high plains dry, I wished I had time to run back inside for a water bottle.

"So. Javier. You have a particular goal for today?" Roman leaned forward, crossed forearms resting on Turk's heavy neck. His mace hung from the saddle horn. Longer and heavier than mine, the weapon looked like something from a medieval torture chamber. Short, stubby knobs stuck out from the massive ball. I couldn't see them, but I knew the ball was marked with the Navarre sigil: linked chains crisscrossing each other to form an eight-point starburst.

"Today…" Stroking his goatee, Dad studied me and Ben mounted on Izzie. "Today will be an in-and-out mission only. To see if more skinners are escaping from the coffer. Hopefully, we will not meet too many of them along the way."

"And if more of those meat-creeps *are* getting out?" Ben asked. "Then what? Not to make you mad again, but our *old way*," he made quotes in the air with his fingers, "doesn't seem to be working too good."

Dad's jaw clenched. A twitch of his fingers on the reins. Then, El Cid wheeled around with an angry slash of his tail and bore him away. Roman eyed my brother, his expression frosty.

Ben noticed it too. "What? I was just saying—"

"You know, *muchacho*, you might try giving your old man a break once in a while." Without another word, he and Turk trotted after Dad.

My brother sat motionless for a long moment. "One word," he said over his shoulder, "and you're walking."

Traveling in single file, we rounded the Hump in silence and followed the dirt road east toward Huerfano, the afternoon sun at our backs. Izzie swung her head from side to side, eyes wide and ears in constant motion. Dust rose in a cloud from the horses' hooves and floated around us, fine as cinnamon. I ground my teeth on the grit.

After about a mile and a half, the horses turned their noses northward and we headed toward the Maze. Picking up the pace, they trotted along a sandy trail sidewinding through the brush. With each stride, the cliff walls grew higher—all Black Gates of Mordor-ish. And, with each stride, dread welled up in me to match.

"Ben?" I prodded him in the back. "How *are* we going to seal up the coffer? If it is leaking more?"

"Got me. Last year, I suggested pouring a couple of tons of wet concrete over the thing."

"Would that work?"

"Even if it did, which Dad doubts, we can't get a mixer truck close enough to the cave. Heck, we couldn't even get an ATV back in there."

Neither of us said the other reason we didn't use all-terrain vehicles. An ATV wouldn't stand its ground and fight hoof and tooth for its rider. Or in Dad's case, when he was about Ben's age, sacrifice her life.

We reached the Gate too soon for my taste. El Cid and Izzie sported dark patches of sweat on their necks and bellies, while Turk's coat gleamed like ice-covered asphalt. We halted just outside of the dark opening. A breeze kicked up and ruffled my hair.

A shadow drifted overhead, then another. I looked westward. "Uh-oh." Clouds, thick and gray as El Cid, were snagged on the jagged tops of the range. Even as I watched, they crept in slow motion down the mountain's sides.

"*Dios.*" Dad sighed. Eyes narrowed, he studied the growing storm. "Bad time for rain."

"Why?" Izzie asked.

"With rain comes lightning," he said. "And we are all carry-ing *these*." He held up his iron mace.

"Oh." Flattening her ears, she lowered her head and peered westward, too.

"We must hurry." Roman clucked at Turk.

Side by side, we rode at an extended trot through the Gate's shadow. My skin broke out in goosebumps—I pretended it was because of the cooler air. The only sound was the echoing clink of steel horseshoe on gravel and the sigh of the wind through the narrow passage. I reached out a hand and ran my fingertips along the sandstone wall for luck. My brother did the same thing.

I rode with back tensed and shoulders hunched until we reached the end of the corridor and paused in its shade. So far, so good. I peered around Ben.

I hadn't gotten a good look on Saturday. Too busy trying to stay alive. Now, I studied the area more closely. Below the horses' hooves, the terrain sloped down a short incline before hitting the valley's floor. The faint remains of a dirt road, over-grown and barely useable, wound through massive boulders scattered about. Small, scrubby bushes and clumps of prairie grass poked out between the rocks.

"What's that?" I pointed. About a hundred yards off to one side, a pile of collapsed timbers and what looked like a sheet of tin roofing sat abandoned. "Did someone *live* in here?" My voice cracked with surprise.

"A group of paleontologists did for a few months in the mid-1940s." Dad gazed at the ruined cabin. "As you know, this region of Colorado is rich in dinosaur fossils. But it ended badly one night and the authorities shut down the dig."

"Ended badly like *skinner* badly?" I tried to imagine living in that cabin, oblivious to what was coming for me out of the darkness. Worse, no weapon to defend myself. The skin between my shoulders prickled.

"I heard they ate most of the scientists," Ben said. "The one or two that made it out alive claimed a pack of rabid wolves attacked the camp. Hasn't been any digs in here since."

I thought back to that newspaper article. *Sure hope it stays that way.* Because I knew Dad would do whatever it took to keep people safe from those monsters. Would I?

While Dad and Roman spoke in low tones, I looked around, then nudged Ben again. "Do you know where the coffer is hidden?"

"Yeah, Dad showed me last year. It's in a cave at the end of a slot canyon over in the northeast corner. The entrance is hidden behind a huge chunk of sandstone. And—just so you know—it's a tight fit back in there."

"How tight?" My heart flipped over with a *ka-thud.* Small places and I had a hate/hate relationship.

"Too narrow for the horses. And, it gets worse."

"H-how much worse?"

"You have to crawl through a hole to get into the cave that holds the coffer."

Dismay sucked the moisture from my mouth. I started to ask him just how small a hole, then noticed my father studying me with an odd expression. Glancing down, I made sure I was holding my weapon correctly, and everything that should be zipped was zipped. Check and check. Then what?

"No offense to you, Isabel, but I would rather my sons split up."

"No offense taken," she said brightly, then added under her breath, "this time."

"Come ride with me, Matt." Roman motioned me over. "That way, we can portion out the rookie quotient."

Ouch. "I should've just *walked* here." I slid off Izzie's rump, one hand on her tail for balance, and stomped over to the black stallion.

Turk glared at me. "Watch your clumsy feet this time."

"I know how to mount." Thrusting my left boot in the stirrup, I grabbed Roman's proffered hand and was hauled aboard.

"Could have fooled me." Turk sniffed.

Biting my tongue, I scooted into place behind the saddle. I gripped my mace in one hand and clung to the cantle with the other. "Okay. I'm ready."

"We will ride hard for the cave. Although I do not like the idea of charging blindly into the Maze, speed is our best weapon for now." Dad screwed his hat lower. "Once there, hold up, and we will decide our next move. Isabel? Stay close to El Cid, but allow Ben room to swing."

"Speaking of swinging. Matt?" Roman turned his head enough for me to catch his grin. "I bruise easily."

In spite of the dread crawling along my skin like maggots, I laughed weakly. "I won't hit you, I promise."

"You better not," Turk grumbled. "Watch you don't hit *me*, either."

Don't tempt me, I thought.

"El Cid?" Dad gestured with his mace. "When you are ready, *mi amigo*."

The stallion tossed his head, mane rising and falling like a white-foamed wave. Then, with a snort, he leaped into a gallop. The rest of us followed, thundering down the slope on his heels. We hit the valley floor and spread out.

Turk zig-zagged around boulders and plunged in and out of shallow ravines. The deeper ones he jumped, almost leaving me behind. My teeth snapped together each time we landed. I wrapped one of the leather saddle ties around my fist, hunkered down, and hung on.

Bouncing along, I swiveled my head until I was dizzy, trying to watch all four directions at the same time. Even with the
black's speed, I felt like a gladiator who had lost the fight and
was now waiting for the thumbs down from the emperor.

"Ow!" A fly pinged off my face. Then another. Two more
buzzed my left ear. One landed in the corner of my eye. I
blinked it away. "Roman," I shouted over the wind.

"I know—hold on." He shifted in the saddle. "Turk!"

The black skidded to a halt. I pitched into Roman and
banged my nose on his back. El Cid and Izzie followed suit,
their back legs plowing furrows in the sand. Dust boiled up.

"Guess the 'charge blindly into the Maze' part is over," Ben
said.

I looked around, wishing I could see *through* all the boulders. I imagined hundreds of skinners crouched behind each one,
hungry for payback and a meal, with me as the appetizer. My
gut did a slow barrel roll; I swallowed the panic down and
squeezed my fingers around the mace's haft, leaving sweaty im-
prints in the leather grip.

The horses' breathing sounded loud and raspy in the Maze's
dead air. But not as loud as my pulse thundering in my ears.
Next to me, the sorrel snorted and tossed her head

"Izzie," Ben whispered. "Chill."

Another fly landed on the corner of my mouth. I sputtered
and swatted it away. I wished the skinners would hurry up and
attack. Just to get it over with.

"C'mon already," Ben muttered, scanning the area. Guess
he felt the same way. He held his mace in a white knuckled grip.

A buzzing sound. Then, flies appeared out of nowhere. The
black pests swarmed back and forth over our heads, the noise
more annoying than a hair dryer left on high. Hunching my
shoulders, I tried to drown out the hum. I swore I caught movement behind every rock and bush.

Under us, Turk pawed the ground, tail whipping my legs. "Roman." He pointed his ears at a nearby jumble of boulders.

"I see it. Heads up, everyone."

Something moved in the shadows. The skin on my back crawled up my neck and buried itself in my hair. I raised my mace.

Then, I laughed.

A lone skinner—only a shade bigger than a beagle—crept into the sunlight. It just stood there, naked and shivering, its black eyes blank. I almost folded to the ground in relief. "That's *it*? One little runt?"

I did the math. One runty skinner versus six of us. Okay, five and a half. But, still. Easy as falling out of bed. "Hey, can I take the first crack at…" Turk tensed—never a good sign. I peeked over at Dad and El Cid. "What's wrong?"

Eyes wide, the gray flung up his head. *"Ambush!"*

S kinners exploded out of the rocks like ants boiling from a boot-ravaged hill, spitting mad and looking for a fight. The foremost ones knocked the little decoy into the air; those in the next rank trampled it into the dirt. Braying and howling, they raced toward us in a pack, banging into each other. I sat frozen, heart jammed against the roof of my mouth.

"Too many." Dad rose in the stirrups and gestured toward the Gate. "Go, go. ¡Ándale!"

Turk reached over and nipped Izzie's hindquarters. "Get Ben out of here."

"Hey. Watch it." She stumbled, trying to kick Turk and run at the same time. A skinner leaped for Ben's leg. He yanked it out of reach and swung his mace. Bloody chunks blew every-where. Izzie squelched through a pile of remains and took off, Turk on her heels and El Cid beside him.

The warhorses plowed through the encircling skinners, bones snapping like kindling beneath their hooves. I shifted my grip to Roman's belt and tried not to think what would happen if I fell off. Unable to resist, I looked back.

Heads low, the pack ran flat out. Even so, they were losing the race. I wanted to cheer. *No demon-spawned skinner*, El Cid's words whispered in my memory, *has ever outrun an Andalusian.* Dang right.

Out of the corner of my vision, I caught movement above my head. With a gasp, I looked up. Several dark shapes dropped from the top of a school bus-sized boulder. Something thick and wet and sticky slammed into me; the impact tore my fingers loose of Roman's belt. Weightless, I flew through the air, screaming as I punched and kicked.

Whump!

I slammed into the dirt and skidded a few feet, leaving behind a layer of skin. Burning pain shot through my elbows and lower back. Rolling over, I pushed up to one arm. I shook my vision clear of stars and ordered my lungs to get to work. Next to me, a skinner rose to its feet, lips pulled away from its fangs. It slinked toward me.

Then, a steel-shod hoof stomped down. With a wet splat, the creature burst apart like a smashed pumpkin. Globs of fresh skinner blew everywhere.

"Duck," Roman shouted from Turk's back.

With a curse, I threw myself flat. A hoof slashed past my face, ruffling my hair. Another skinner stumbled over me, its claws raking my back through my shirt. Then it pushed off and leaped for Turk's throat. Breathless, I crawled to the safety of a nearby boulder.

More skinners surrounded us. Standing between me and the pack, Turk crushed the closest beast, then pivoted to meet the next ones. Mangled creatures crawled around, shrieking as they reformed. Roman's mace was a blur.

My mace. Where was my mace? I looked around. Panic tore at me. I spotted it a few feet away. Chest heaving, I lunged to my feet. I grabbed a handful of sand along with the haft, then planted my backside against the boulder. My knees shook. I locked them tight and sucked in an uneven breath, then immediately spat out a couple of flies. One skinner snuck around Turk and slouched toward me, showing off its fangs. The memory of Dad with a skinner hanging from his leg whisked through my brain.

"Come any closer," I raised my weapon in a two-handed grip, "and I'll knock 'em down your throat."

The skinner crouched, preparing to leap. Its muscles rippled under naked flesh. My own skin crawled.

I took a step forward. "Eat iron!" Then I swung my mace like a Louisville slugger.

Totally missed the skinner.

Nailed the boulder.

Whang! Sparks shot into the air. Shock waves zinged up my arms and into my shoulders. Cursing, I swung again. The skinner ducked. Strike two.

Taunting me, the monster danced from side to side, grinning like we shared a secret. Venom dripped from its canines. The stench of rotten meat coated my tongue. I pressed my lips together, wishing I could squeeze my nostrils just as tight. Gritting my teeth, I tightened my grip and lifted my weapon.

"*¡España!*"

The Navarre battle cry. The skinner's head exploded under Roman's mace in a spray of gore. Warm droplets splattered on my face. A pause. Then, with a bang, the rest of it vanished, too. The surviving skinners backed away, growling and snarling. Turk raised a front hoof in warning. Panting, I spat, then wiped my mouth on my shoulder.

"Matt." Roman held out his free hand. Wet leftovers dripped from the head of his mace. "Hurry."

I sprinted toward him. Right on cue, my toe caught a rock. With a cry, I tripped and skidded on my free hand and knees, taking more skin off my palm. To my astonishment, I managed to hang on to my mace. Reeling to my feet, I flung myself toward Turk; he seemed a million miles away.

The pack crept closer. Heart hammering against my ribs, I stretched for Roman's hand. Our fingers almost touched. *I'm not going to make it. There's too many of them.*

A rolling thunder filled my ears. The rumble grew and grew, getting closer with every second. I could almost feel its power vibrating through the soles of my boots.

"Santiago!"

Like a winter blizzard roaring in over the mountains, El Cid plowed into the pack. Izzie was right behind him. Skinners flew into the air just in time to meet Dad's mace. His weapon rose and fell—hammer strikes of reckoning. Every stroke a kill.

"Whoa," I whispered.

An iron hand grabbed my arm. "Do you need an invitation?" With a grunt, Roman jerked me off the ground and hauled me onto the stallion's broad haunch. "Go, Turk!"

"No, I'm not leaving Javier—"

"As if I would let anything happen to him," El Cid shouted, grinding another skinner into the ground. "Get the boy to safety."

With a snarl that matched the skinners', the black kicked his way clear of the pack and took off. I threw a desperate glance over my shoulder. To my relief, my family pounded after us. Beyond Dad and Ben, skinners wiggled feebly on the ground like smashed beetles. Even so, they tried to drag themselves along with legs dangling or heads half formed. I grimaced. Yeesh. Zombie dogs, all right.

We sped for the Gate. Izzie and El Cid caught up with us, both breathing hard.

Not Turk, though. Even carrying two riders, he sailed over rocks and bushes and ravines without breaking stride. Each thrust of his powerful legs kicked the earth beneath us and sent it spinning.

A fierce, dark thrill welled up. As if the stallion's strength and speed became mine. As if his lungs and heart were mine. Did my father feel this way when he rode the black? Leaning to one side, I squinted into the wind.

The Gate. My heart rose at the sight.

A low word from Roman. Turk slowed. Powering up the slope, Izzie took the lead and shot through first. Ben rode stretched out low over her neck, a jockey in a race. Turk and El Cid chased her heels. The cool air was a punch to my chest. The warhorses' hoof beats echoed off the stone walls, as if an entire cavalry ran with us.

Suddenly, a blast of light and warmth and the open range. The horses slowed, then wheeled around and stopped, blowing hard and snorting. I squinted at the Gate.

The foremost skinner slid to a halt just inside the opening. From the shadow, it glared at us, teeth bared. The rest of the pack milled behind it, shapes in the darkness.

I leaned around Roman for a better look, wincing as the movement pulled at the scratches. "What happens if they try to leave the Maze?"

Dad and Roman exchanged glances. Then, with a faint smile, my father hooked his mace on the horn, then swung out of the saddle and dropped to the ground.

"Really, Javier," El Cid grumbled. "Is this necessary?"

"Necessary? No. Educational? Yes." Dad strolled forward a few yards and stood there, holding his weaponless hands out.

"Is he *baiting* them?" Ben asked.

Roman nodded. I noticed he kept his weapon at the ready. "It is very hard for a skinner to resist a human on foot. After all, we are their favorite meal."

"But won't the wards stop them?" I glanced up at the tops of the buttes on either side of the Gate. "I mean, would the skinners even *try*?"

"It depends on how hungry they are." He paused, then added. "Or if there is enough of them."

"You mean enough to swamp the wards," Ben said.

"*Sí*. While the queen's wards are *muy* powerful, they cannot hold back an overwhelming force at one time. In a mass assault, some creatures *will* get through. That is why we hunt on a regular basis. To thin the evil we guard."

I thought of the descendants of the Knights of the Coffer living secret lives all over the Southwest: The Navarres in New Mexico. The Montoya's enormous extended family—currently led by four sisters—down in Arizona. The Reyes clan over in Utah. And more hunters spread across Texas, Nevada, and California. For the first time, I wondered just how much evil had been dumped in the New World.

"And you two should know, especially *you*, Ben, that one of the finest and most respected hunters alive is that *hombre loco* right there." Roman pointed his mace at our father.

Chewing on that statement and my lower lip, I eyed Dad. The whole time, the skinner snarled and growled, pacing back and forth—a shark cruising the waves for surfers. Its mad eyes never left my father.

Dad took another step and spread his arms wider.

Guess it must've been pretty hungry. The skinner crouched down, then belly-crawled out of the shadow and into the light. Raw flesh gleamed wetly in the afternoon sun. It crept closer, one paw, then another. Flies swooped and soared overhead with glee.

My heart stumbled. "Dad..."

Kaa-rack!

A lightning bolt shot from the top of one of the buttes. I jumped. So did Ben and Izzie. I blinked and waited for my vision to clear.

A pile of leftover skinner steamed on the ground in front of the Gate. Tendrils of smoke wafted toward us—it smelled like a convenience store hot dog. The remaining creatures melted away and disappeared into the Maze.

Ben and I looked at each other, wide-eyed. "The *wards?*" I asked. "Every time?"

"Faithfully," Dad said, strolling back. Ignoring El Cid's comments about hunters who just can't resist showing off, he remounted, then lifted his hat and saluted the buttes. "*Gracias, mis viejos amigos.*"

My brother chuckled. I gulped. Was he was laughing at our father? I peeked at Dad.

Ben pointed his mace at the mound of smoking monster. His eyes danced. "Talk about getting...*Thor-ed.*"

I groaned, secretly relieved. Dad shook his head, then leaned over and placed a hand on Ben's neck and pulled him closer. He said something in a low voice.

My brother's face flushed with pride. He shrugged. "Just doing what you taught me, Pop," he said, eyes locked on Izzie's ears. The faint smile stayed on his face. It matched the one on Dad's.

Man, I'd go up against a pack of skinners. By myself. In the dark. Without a mace. Every day. Just for *that.*

Overhead, the sky darkened. More clouds shoved into place, lining up for a chance to dump their load on us. A rising breeze sent the grasses bowing and waving.

"Home, gentlemen." Dad tipped his hat at Izzie. "And *señorita.*"

She rolled her eyes.

The horses' hooves swished through the grass as they dragged themselves home. Foam coated their necks and chest. El Cid's coat was speckled with flecks of red, turning him into a roan.

I looked back at the Maze. "Sure was a lot of skinners," I said to Ben. "Wonder how we're going to get to the cave. And how's Dad going to seal it up again?"

"Guess we'll find out sooner than later." He nudged Izzie closer to Turk. "Hey. You okay?"

I peered down. My T-shirt looked like a butcher's apron—it matched Turk's coat. "I'm good, but this shirt's history." Bummer. It was my favorite one, too.

"Scared the cow patty out of me when you fell off. Don't do that again. Okay? I mean it. Or I'll have to kill you."

"Matt?" On the other side, Dad took my shoulder and twisted me to one side. I stifled a hiss. He frowned.

"Think I scraped up my back when I hit the ground. Stings like crazy. Tore up my elbows, too."

Dad nodded. "And you, Turk?"

"Nothing worth mentioning. I've been bit worse by horse flies."

Still gripping my shoulder, Dad spoke to Roman and Turk. "*Muchas gracias.* To you both. For this one."

The hunter waved off Dad's gratitude. "Matt did well, no?"

"Sure he did." Turk snorted. "Except for falling off. And missing all of his swings. And tripping over his own feet—"

"Dad?" I interrupted the black. "How're we going to get to the coffer with all those skinners around?"

"We will figure it out." A line appeared between his brows.

"Whatever the plan, we mustn't rush into anything." El Cid flattened his ears. "The wards *are* holding, after all."

"But for how long?" Izzie jogged a few steps to catch up. "If more of those meatballs find a way to slither out…"

A low rumble overhead. Another one followed. I gulped and stared down at my mace. Slowing, El Cid lifted his head, nostrils working. The breeze lifted his mane.

"How long?" Dad asked.

"Ten minutes if we're lucky. Turk? Isabel? Best speed for home." With that, he broke into a weary gallop.

We lost the race with the storm. Splashing into the yard, I spotted Kathleen leaning over the porch rail, waving her cellphone. Already chilled from my sodden shirt and jeans, I tensed.

"Uh-oh." Izzie blew her dripping forelock from her eyes. "Something's wrong."

"Roman, we've got to roll," Kathleen called. "Jo just texted. The Morrigan is in labor and having complications…" Her voice trailed off. "Looks like you guys saw some action. I'll fetch my bag."

She met us in the barn. "Who's first?"

"I just got some scrapes," I spoke up quickly, "but Turk got bit." I hid a grin at my coup.

"Then, I'll start with him." She waited until Roman and I dismounted, then ran her hand over the black's right side. "Hmm, looks like a puncture, all right." She bent closer, fingers wiping away skinner and mud, and peered more closely in the dim light.

"It's nothing." Turk shifted away. "You said the Morrigan is in danger?"

I blinked in surprise at the note of worry in the stallion's voice. Until I remembered that the black mare, named after the Celtic goddess of war, was his dam.

Kathleen hesitated for a moment. "Not in danger per se, but she's struggling with the delivery. The foal seems determined to make its debut earlier than we'd expected."

"Then get out of here. No, I'm all right." He shook his head and mane, showering us. "A drop or two of skinner venom isn't going to bother me."

"Yes, go, Kathleen. We will be fine." Dad loosed El Cid's cinch as he spoke. "At least you will make better time with an empty trailer."

"What about Matt?" She eyed me. "He's a mess. Maybe I should examine him before I leave. Just in case."

"I'm fine. Really." I held up a battered elbow. "See? Nothing more serious than this." *Get tough or go home,* I reminded myself. *Show them I can take it.* I disregarded the lingering pain—it was becoming numb, anyway.

"Well, if you're sure…"

"We are." Dad nudged her toward the door. "Now, go. The mare needs you more than we do."

"And you know how Vasco gets at times like this. We need to hurry before you have *two* patients to worry about." Roman took her arm. A few minutes later, they drove out of the yard, the empty trailer dancing behind them.

Working in silence, we took care of the warhorses. Dad switched mounts with me. Guess he figured Turk and I had had enough of each other. El Cid dozed while I cleaned him. Good. He needed the rest.

I took a calming breath. There was something about being inside of the barn while it rained. Storms and monsters outside.

My family warm and safe inside. I breathed in the smell of straw and horse and rain-washed prairie, trying to dissolve the leftover jitters.

My head had other ideas. The same two questions kept tumbling around in my skull. How were we going to get to the cave with all those skinners running around? And how were we going to stop more from escaping?

After serving El Cid a late lunch, I steeled myself and walked over to Turk. "I, um, I want to say something."

He raised his head, jaws grinding in a slight side to side motion. A few grains of oats dribbled out of the corner of his mouth. "Well?"

"Thanks."

"For what?"

"For earlier. In the Maze," I said. "Thought those skinners had me."

"I didn't do it for you." He chewed some more then swallowed. "Now go away so I can eat in peace."

Sheesh. Family.

Slogging through the puddles, I missed the warmth of the barn. Every bruise and cut made a point of re-acquainting themselves with my nerves. I plodded up the porch steps. My legs grew heavy with each step, as if my boots were filled with concrete. Then my vision blurred. I leaned against the railing for a moment, panting, as I waited for the odd dizziness to go away. Had I hit my head when I fell?

Feeling only a little better, I sucked in a shaky breath, then opened the screen door. Its squeal announced my arrival.

"Remove your boots," Dad ordered from the kitchen. "Then, come here."

I toed them off, left them by the door next to his and Ben's, and padded into the kitchen. My father stood by the sink, rummaging through the first aid kit. He held up a familiar dark brown bottle, then put on his reading glasses and checked the date.

"*Bueno*," he grunted. "Still effective."

I grimaced. "Oh, man. I hate that stuff. Can't you use medicine from this century?"

"Nothing works like good old-fashioned iodine."

Nothing burns like good old-fashioned iodine. I gritted my teeth through the treatment on each elbow. "You didn't do this to Turk." I flapped my arms to soothe the sting.

"He is larger than me." Dad motioned for me to turn around, then lifted my shirt to my shoulder blades.

Cold air wafted across my bare skin. I shivered, wondering why it felt so chilly in the house. *Must be my wet clothes.* Another wave of dizziness, mingled with nausea, swept over me. A clammy sweat broke out on my face and torso. "Can we do this later? I don't feel so good."

A long silence.

What's taking so long? "Dad, can you hurry up, please?"

"How close did the skinners get to you?"

"You mean, besides the one who slammed me into the ground and rolled around on top of me, trying to chew off my face?" I joked weakly.

Another long silence. I was starting to hate them. Plus, I really wanted to sit down. Then, he touched a spot on my lower back. A white-hot pain flared.

"Ow!" I flinched away. "Warn me next time."

"Matt." He gripped my arm, holding me still. "You have a bite wound."

Panic squeezed its fist around my throat. I opened and closed my mouth. Nothing came out. I licked my lips and tried again. "H-how bad?"

"One puncture mark. Not too deep, but…"

He didn't need to finish the sentence. I knew already. Depth didn't matter. It was how much venom got into my body.

"I gotta sit down." On wobbly legs, I groped for a chair.

My knees folded. He caught me before I hit the linoleum, then swept me up in his arms. Hoisting me higher, he hurried out of the kitchen and across the living room. I swallowed, fighting the queasiness that worsened with every stride.

"Dad?"

"You will be all right, my son."

Ben appeared. "What happened?" Eyes wide, he stepped aside as our father brushed past. "What's wrong with Matt?"

"A skinner got him."

Dad carried me into my bedroom. The small room felt airless and dark. Too dark. Had the storm gotten inside our house somehow? I tried to warn Dad and Ben, but my tongue was a fat, lazy worm.

"Quickly, Ben. I need you to…" The rest of the words faded away.

Pain knifed me again. The agony spread in waves throughout the rest of my body. My jaw tingled, telling me I was seconds away from throwing up.

Then everything was a blur. Vomiting, shaking with fever, my body curled in a ball from cramps. Hands moving me when all I wanted to do was sleep. Ben's voice breaking as he spoke. My father forcing some nasty tasting stuff between my lips. I choked on the water that followed, spilling it down my chin.

Then nothing.

I left for a while. Don't know where I went. Just floated around in the darkness. No feeling. No sight. No sound.

Except…

I thought I caught a low murmur, just on the edge of my hearing. Was it Dad? Or Ben? Whoever they were, they whispered the same words over and over.

Hail Mary, full of grace…

৵৹৵

With a jerk, I was conscious. Where was I? I peeked through a slitted eyelid. Wherever it was, it wasn't as dark. The amber glow of the bedside lamp welcomed me back, as did the familiar weight of my old quilt. For a few moments I lay there, afraid to move in case the pain was waiting in ambush. I never wanted to hurt that badly again. Couldn't imagine—and hoped like heck—I ever would.

That low murmuring from earlier. I peeled the other eye open.

My father was seated on the edge of the mattress, head bowed and elbows propped on his knees. A rosary dangled from his fingers. I squinted past him. Ben lay spread-eagle on the other twin bed, his face slack with sleep.

Dad. I mouthed the word, but nothing came out. I worked my tongue and tried again. "Dad?"

He raised his head. His eyes were red-rimmed with exhaustion, and he had on the same shirt he'd worn on the hunt. Sure smelled like it. Placing the beads on the nightstand, he leaned over me.

"How are you feeling, *mijo*?" he said in a soft voice.

"Like Turk went a couple of rounds on me." I managed a grin. "He didn't, did he?"

"Not this time." A faint smile lit up his face. He cupped my cheek, his fingers calloused but gentle. "Do not frighten your old man like that again. Okay?"

"Not planning on it."

"Thirsty?" At my nod, he picked up a drinking glass from the table and held the straw to my lips. "Slowly. Make sure it stays down."

The water washed away the sour taste of vomit. After a few pulls, I sighed, then glanced at the darkened window. "What time is it?"

"Around four."

"In the *morning*? You've been here all this time?"

"All night." Ben sat up, his hair flattened on one side. "When we weren't running out to the barn to check on the Jerk. Between the two of you, the timing stunk."

"Turk okay?"

"He is fine." Dad rose, straightening his back one vertebra at a time. *Crack, crack, crack.* "Except for lying about how badly he was bitten. If he pulls an act like that again, *I* will kill him."

"You'd have to get in line," Ben yawned, "behind El Cid." He rolled off the bed and staggered to the doorway. "I'll go check on the horses."

"And start some coffee, *por favor*?" Dad called after him. He turned to me. "Are you hungry? Some toast and tea?"

Toast and tea sounded pretty good. "And bacon?"

"Let us see how your stomach handles toast first."

I managed a few sips of tea and half a slice of dry toast. Even that wore me out. I woke up a few hours later. Rubbing my face, I grimaced at the feel of dried sweat and crusty flakes of I didn't want to know what.

Morning sun outlined the lowered blinds. The other bed was empty. Across the hall, I caught the hiss of the shower. *Great. There goes all the hot water.*

I lay there for a while, walking my fingers around the familiar patterns on my quilt. Our great-aunt Dolores had sewn matching ones for me and Ben when we were little. Dad always said she was destined for sainthood because she had given up a comfortable retirement in Arizona to come live with us after

Mom died. She stayed until we were old enough not to burn
down the house whenever Dad and El Cid hunted.

Pushing the covers to one side, I eased off the mattress and
took stock. Sore in places, especially my back, but ignore-able. I
pulled on sweat pants and a clean T-shirt then shuffled out to the
living room, my knees trying to remember how to walk. With
every step, I felt stronger.

Dressed in clean clothes and hair still damp from a shower,
Dad lay stretched out on the sofa, eyes shut and hands clasped
behind his head. "Better?"

"Yeah. Moving around helps."

"If you would," he said, eyes still closed, "show your face
to El Cid. He has been threatening to crash the front door."

I stepped outside. The thick scent of rain-washed sage and
damp earth filled my nose and mouth. Across the yard, Izzie
loafed in the shade of the barn. She tossed her head in greeting
then called over her shoulder.

"Hey, El Cid. Guess who's up and walking around on two
legs? I'll give you a hint—it's not Turk."

El Cid burst out of the barn at a fast trot, nostrils tight with
worry. I thought for a moment he'd come right up the porch
steps. "Matt…"

"I'm okay." I walked down, the wooden treads warm under
my bare feet, and wrapped my arms around his neck. "Really."

"I don't know which of us was more alarmed, me or your
father. Please don't get bit again."

"Already promised Dad." Looking past him, I noticed Turk
limping out of the barn, his movements slow and stiff. Standing
broadside to the sun, he lowered his head and closed his eyes.

Something tugged at my heart. "You too."

"Me too *what*?" El Cid asked.

"Promise me that you won't ever get bit either."

"Silly boy." He chuffed, then curved his neck and pressed me to his chest.

11

"**A**re you sure you shouldn't be resting?" Reaching around, El Cid nosed me as I groomed him. "That's all I've been doing. For three whole days." I swept the brush along his ribs. "I'm sick of hanging around the house. Besides, Dad said going with you guys this afternoon would be good for me. Fresh air and sunshine and all that." I worked for a few moments, then asked. "So. *You* feeling okay?"

"I assume you're still worried about what Kathleen said. Well, you needn't be. I know how to pace myself." He sniffed. "I'm not elderly."

"I know."

"I'm in my prime, thank you very much."

Grinning, I finished up, then tossed the brush across the barn. It landed in the wooden storage bin with a satisfying thud. I flung up my arms. "Score."

"What's taking you two so long?" Izzie called from outside. "I could've run to the state line and back."

With El Cid on my heels, I hurried out of the barn and into the afternoon sun, joining Turk and Izzie. A few puffy clouds— sky sheep—meandered eastward, their shadows rolling on the ground. Man, but it was good to be outside.

And alive. Alive was just fine with me.

My father appeared. He strolled down the porch steps and walked over, all city-spiffy in clean jeans, polished boots, and a sports coat over a white shirt. No hat, though.

"Isn't it kind of early for a town council meeting?" I asked. Facing El Cid's side, I grabbed some mane, twisted my fingers in the wiry hairs, then bent my left knee and stuck my foot out. One-handed, Dad grasped my lower leg and lifted me up. Once mounted, I shifted into the natural dip behind El Cid's withers.

"The council will meet later this evening. However, I wish to speak to Inez Ortega beforehand. In private."

El Cid sighed. "Don't tell me she's back at it again."

"She is." Dad's sigh matched the stallion's. He ran a hand along the massive neck. "Our mayor is still seeking a way to bring that project here, even though the other council members are more wary. But she might be able to convince them. Argue that the dig will help repair the Maze's reputation, especially if it is successful."

Izzie cocked her head. "Successful like they find a truck-load of fossils?"

"Successful like no one gets eaten." Turk snapped his teeth, then chuffed. "Nothing like leftover body parts to put a damper on tourism."

"Too bad we can't tell them the truth," I said.

"About the skinners?" The black snorted. "No offense, Jav, but your youngest is an idiot."

"Turk..." Dad began

"But why can't we?" Izzie interrupted. "Tell the mayor and council, I mean. Some of the older folks around the Navarre

ranch know about us hunters and what we do. They're cool
about it. Kathleen told me once that an elderly lady stopped her
in town and blessed her. Said she slept soundly knowing we
were around. 'You are our shield against the dark things of the
night.'" Izzie clopped her lips. "Has a nice ring to it, don't you
think?"

"Sadly, it's a different era," El Cid said. "Back then, belief
in things skewed toward the mythical end of the spectrum was
acceptable. Somewhat. But with each new generation, humans
find it harder to believe."

I frowned. "Believe in monsters, you mean?"

"And in heroes." Dad glanced at his watch. "I must go. El
Cid? South today?"

Yeah, go south, I thought. *South is good. Away from the
Maze.* My head knew the wards kept us safe. The rest of me always looked over one shoulder.

El Cid took his time answering. He lifted his nose and
swung his head in a circle, pretending to read the wind. Turk
flattened his ears. It irritated the fire out of him that Dad left it
up to El Cid to dictate the horses' daily workout.

Hiding my grin, I ducked my head, then leaned forward and
smoothed a hank of mane. Out of the corner of my eye, I noticed
Dad fighting back a smile too. I remember when Ben once asked
our father why he didn't just *tell* the stallions how far and in
which direction to take on their daily run.

"You give *us* orders all the time," my brother had added,
pushing it as usual.

I had cringed at Ben's tone and hoped Dad would let it pass.
To my relief, he had only shrugged.

"Our war-brothers know what is expected of them on the
hunt, especially El Cid. I trust him to keep himself and Turk at
an optimum level of strength and endurance without instructions
from me. And besides…"

We waited. Nothing. "Besides *what*, Dad?" I prompted.

He hesitated, then spoke. "This relationship we have with the warhorses—it is one based on respect and equality and a warrior's bond forged in battle, no?" At our twin head bobbles, he continued. "I cannot *order* them to do anything, except under a rare situation, for we are fellow hunters. In the same way, I must not appear to favor one over the other. *¿Comprende?*"

"I don't get it...Oh." I nodded. "So, that's why you let El Cid be in charge of their workouts."

"A small gesture for my old partner. To make up for Turk being, well, *Turk*."

"Thought you didn't do faves, Pop," Ben said.

"Between the warhorses? No. Between my sons?" He waggled a hand back and forth.

Even my brother had laughed.

Dad slapped my knee, pulling me from the memory. "Not too much today, Matt. Rest when you return. If Ben is still napping, get him up and tell him I want the older straw bales rotated to the front of the stack before they rot." He climbed into the truck and drove off. We waited until the dust, apparently bored of hanging around the ranch, drifted away.

"Well? Which way?" Izzie asked, moving up beside us. She pranced in place, hide twitching and tail slashing. "Like they say in the movies, I feel the need for speed."

"See the trail running south?" El Cid pointed his nose. "Follow it. About two miles, you'll come across an unpaved road that runs west from Huerfano to the foothills. Quite popular—"

"Do you *ever* shut up?" Turk wheeled around and broke into an extended trot, gravel pinging under his steel shoes. A few strides, then he hit the accelerator and lit out, his tail a black banner.

"—with ATV enthusiasts and dirt bikers—"

"Sorry, El Cid," Izzie said, "but I've got to agree with the Jerk this time. Enough talking. Let's kick up some dust."

The sorrel beside us, we tore across the prairie, my body moving in rhythm with El Cid's stride. Tears leaked from my eyes; I hunched lower, left hand buried in the gray's mane. In my other hand, I carried my mace balanced across the stallion's withers. To my right, the mountain range was a grandstand. I pretended the whoosh of the wind in my ears was a crowd cheering me on.

"Hold on, Matt." El Cid warned over his shoulder.

Just in time, I tightened my legs around his barrel. A split second later, El Cid leaped into the air with a grunt—an Andalusian Pegasus. His powerful hindquarters hurled us across a narrow arroyo. I glanced down at the dark wound in the earth. Then prairie grass again. Landing, I barely kept my seat, skidding forward until he evened out. Then it was off to the races again, Izzie in the lead by a half-length. Letting her surge ahead, El Cid shifted down into cruising speed. Good. He didn't need to be pushing it.

The horses were streaked with white lather by the time I sighted Turk. El Cid's sweat soaked the seat of my jeans. We slowed to a trot, then eased into a walk, the gray's hooves stirring the dust. His ribs rose and fell beneath my calves.

"What took you so long?" Turk's neck and chest gleamed like polished black marble. "Thought you could out-run the old goat, sweetheart."

"Oh, go kiss a rattlesnake," Izzie fired back, sides heaving.

"Don't encourage him," I said. "He'd probably kill the poor thing."

A high-pitched whine caught my attention. For a split second, I thought it was flies. *Those* kind of flies. El Cid swung around, ears pricked toward the east. My hand shielding my eyes, I squinted.

A cloud of reddish-pink dust, lit by the lowering sun, billowed behind several dark shapes moving toward us. The whine of dirt bike engines deepened into a rumble.

Turk and Izzie joined us. "Is this going to be a problem?" she asked.

"Nah. They're cool. Just some guys from town." I watched as a pair of riders careened over ruts and through potholes, their bikes' front fenders flapping like waving hands with each bounce. They coasted to a stop a few yards away. One of them lifted a couple of fingers off the handles in greeting.

"Hey, Ethan."

"Nice ponies, Matt," he said with a grin. His helmet partially obscured a mass of freckles threatening to take over his features. "When're you going to ditch them and come ride with us? I've got an extra bike."

"No way. I've got more horse power than your two tricycles put together." I grinned back. But inside, a tiny flame of envy flared up. I wondered what it'd be like to live in town. Maybe have a bike, too. To hang out with friends my age—and species—without dodging awkward questions about my family.

Family.

I slipped my fingers beneath El Cid's mane and pressed my palm against the blend of warmth and strength. To remind myself who family was. And always would be.

"Wanna race?" The other rider twisted the throttle; the engine wailed in protest and the stink of gasoline poisoned the afternoon. Then, with his free hand, he thumbed the air horn duct-taped to the handle bars. The blare about took the top of my head off. I winced.

Not the warhorses, though. They were equine statues crafted from marble and onyx and red granite. Not an ear twitched. Not an eye blinked. Heck, even their manes and tails froze in place. Pride swelled my chest.

"Knock it off, Chris," I said. "Can't you see that you're freaking them out?"

"Whatever." He let off on the throttle and horn. "So. Do you want to?"

"Race?" Man, did I. Wanted to in the worst way. A chance to show off the speed and agility of an Andalusian.

"How about along the trail to those trees and back?" Chris pointed toward a clump of piñons a hundred yards along the dirt path.

"Nah, I'll pass. Too rocky for them."

El Cid flicked his ears back—two fingers pointing accusingly at me. I ignored them, as well as Izzie's angry snort. Sorry, not sorry.

"Yeah, you're probably right. And anyway," Ethan craned his neck, "the trail's kind of narrow."

"Not if you're in the lead," Turk said loudly.

Shut up, I mouthed at him.

Ethan looked around in confusion. "Did you just say—"

"Oh, man, what time is it?" I pretended to look at a watch I wasn't wearing. "I was supposed to be home an hour ago. You know. Chores and stuff. Well, gotta go. See you guys later."

I squeezed my legs, hoping El Cid would get the message. To my relief, he stepped out, then broke into a trot. I heard the other horses fall in behind us. After a few minutes, Izzie and Turk shouldered past and loped on ahead of us.

As El Cid jogged home, head bobbing in time with his gait, I chewed on a realization. Something that I'd always known, but never really thought about. One that didn't taste so good.

None of my friends—like a *real* friend, someone outside of my family—had two feet. Did that make me weird? I didn't used to feel that way, but now I wondered.

Was I a freak?

12

"**D**ang it." Hissing, I reached down and massaged my bare foot, the one that just discovered the kitchen table's leg. Nothing like a stubbed toe to wake a guy up. I limped over to the cabinet and grabbed a box of Cheerios, taking some of Ben's favorite cuss words out for a spin—under my breath, of course, in case Dad was around.

Except that the smell of brewed coffee and the open kitchen window told me my father had already left for his morning run to town and back. Ben, as usual, was still asleep. He hated mornings and mornings hated him right back. With extreme prejudice.

Yawning wide enough to pop my ears, I hitched up my pajama pants and swung by the sink for a clean bowl. Idly, I glanced up.

An enormous ghost floated outside the window.

"Holy beans!" My heart slammed into my throat and lifted my feet clear off the linoleum. The box tumbled from my hand as I fumbled for a weapon that wasn't there. Little round Os spilled across the floor.

"Good morning, Matt." El Cid peered in at me, nose pressed against the screen. The tiny wires formed a diamond pattern on the soft skin between his nostrils. "Did I startle you?"

"Whatever…gave you…that idea?" I gasped, rubbing my chest.

"My apologies."

"What are you doing sneaking around on that side of the house?" Pulse still thundering, I scooped up the cereal with my hands and tossed it in the bowl. Close enough to the three second rule. "Besides giving me a freaking heart attack." Glaring, I snagged the milk carton from the refrigerator and flopped down at the table and blew my hair from my eyes.

"Simply taking a turn about the place." He eyed my cereal. "Might I have—?"

"No." I hunched over my bowl. "Go scare the pjs off someone else."

"Ungrateful child." With a sniff, he wandered off.

"Yeah, yeah." I finished my bowl, then munched my way through a second one, wiping out the last of the milk.

The front screen creaked open. Dressed in shorts and running shoes, Dad walked in, panting and wiping his face. Sweat soaked his T-shirt.

"*Buenos días, mijo.*" Passing by, he ruffled my hair.

"Hey, Dad." I wrinkled my nose and waved a hand in front of my face. "Ewww—gross."

"What are you saying?" He paused. "That I smell badly?"

"Like road kill on July asphalt."

"Disrespecting your *papá*?" Before I could duck, he wrapped an arm around my head. "Not a prudent idea this early in the morning."

"No, wait." My spoon clattered to the table. I grabbed his forearm with both hands. It was like pulling on a steel bar. "I didn't mean—"

Too late. With his free hand, he turned my head and snuggled my face into his armpit. "Smell *this*."

I thrashed from side to side, breathless with laughter. "Get off of me." I finally struggled free and pushed him away. "Some people would call that mistreatment of a minor, you know."

"Or a minor mistreatment."

"Funny." I picked up my spoon. "Who went with you this time?"

"Turk." He snagged a paper towel. Leaning against the sink, he blotted his face. "He complained the entire time about the pace."

After what happened in the Maze, El Cid had practically ordered Dad to stop his morning workouts, or at least take one of the horses along. Turk agreed with El Cid. Yeah, I almost fainted. Seated on the porch, Ben and I had sat back and watched our father, fists on hips, argue with them.

Dad had pointed out that he was just as safe jogging along the road as he was in his own house. It wasn't like he was going to go running around *inside* the Maze wearing a "free sample" sign.

"More importantly, I refuse to live a life of fear. My father would not. Nor will I let my sons. No, we live our lives facing into the wind."

"Then either myself or Turk will accompany you." El Cid shook his head when Izzie started to protest.

"I do not need a four-legged Secret Service agent following me each morning." Dad's hand sliced through the air. "End of discussion."

The gray stomped a hoof. "No, Javier, this is *not* end of discussion. Because this isn't just about you. It's about Ben and

Matt. What would they do if something were to happen to you?"
The unspoken *they have lost one parent already* hovered in the
air.

Dad had folded like a cheap card table at a bake sale in a
high wind.

It had been an accident. Mom had been driving home after
running some errands in the larger town of Walsenburg about an
hour east. Nice summer day. Not much traffic on the state high-
way. Just another vehicle in the wrong lane at the wrong time.
Dad always joked that Mom would've been spitting mad at the
universe if either of us boys had been in the car, too. He made
himself talk about her to us, even though it tore chunks out of
him. Sometimes, I wished he wouldn't try. It just made it worse.
Worse for Ben, who remembered her better. Worse for me listening to the false cheerfulness in Dad's voice.

Shoving those thoughts away, I finished my cereal. Dad
propped his foot on a chair and examined the bite mark on his
calf. "How is it?" For once, it was nice for *me* to be doing the
asking instead of the other way around, thank you very much.

"In another week, it will be nothing but a scar."

Battle scar. Just like mine. I took a deep breath. "When are
we going to go check on the coffer?" Half of me wanted to. The
other half wanted to slap myself upside the head for suggesting
it.

"You sound like Isabel. She asks me that same question
every time she sees me. So eager." He shook his head. "But,
very soon, for it looks like the mayor may get the council to al-
locate funds toward the dig. Time is working against us."

At that moment, Ben staggered into the kitchen, eyes narrowed into slits. One cheek was creased from the pillow, and his
hair looked like it was trying for a Mohawk but didn't quite
make it. With a groan, he sank down at the table and stared at
my empty cereal bowl.

"We're out of milk." Rising, I grabbed my dish and placed it in the sink. "Sorry."

Ben made a face, then lisped something. It sounded like "ewe zugh."

"Want me to go get some more? El Cid and I'll make a run to the 7-Eleven." The convenience store on the outskirts of Huerfano got a lot of our business. El Cid and I sometimes went there for a soda, which I had to split with him. The guy had a thing for Mountain Dew.

"Like he'd take you," Ben rasped. "He's in full-out smother mother mode."

"It is just his nature. You know how he feels about you boys." Dad nodded toward the hallway. "Matt, my wallet is in my jeans. Take a five." As I left the kitchen, he cuffed me lightly on the head. "I want *all* the change back this time."

After dressing in jeans and a hand-me-down shirt of Ben's, I snagged my mace from the hook beside the door and slipped outside, pausing to block the screen door with a heel before it slapped shut. On the south side of the barn, Turk dozed, his ebony coat a solar panel. One back leg was bent in a hip-cocked posture.

"My straw needs changed," he said, eyes still closed.

Whatever. "Where's El Cid?"

"In the pasture. Seeing a man about a horse."

I rolled my eyes. That joke was barely funny the first seven times he said it.

Movement from beyond the barn. The crunch of hoof on gravel. El Cid appeared. He strolled over, his ears half question marks. "Did I hear my name?"

"We're out of milk. I told Ben I'd go get some."

"No, Matt. It's too dangerous. Plus, you still need to rest."

"I'm *good*. Really. I've been good for almost a week now. And Dad said it was okay for us to go."

The gray flattened his ears, nostrils flaring in frustration. "I might as well be livestock for all that anyone listens to me." He stomped over to the porch in an equine huff.

"Hooves okay?"

"Javier cleaned them earlier."

"Just checking." I figured as much, but I wanted to show El Cid that I knew my job.

He sidled sideways up to the porch. "Well, don't just stand there. Mount up."

Using the middle step as a mounting block, I threw a leg over, then clambered up and settled into position. I threaded my right hand through the mace's leather loop. "Okay. All set."

Izzie ambled around the corner of the barn. A forgotten stalk of grass hung from the corner of her mouth like a cigarette. "Where are you guys going?" The stalk jiggled up and down as she spoke.

"Into town for milk." I leaned over and plucked out the grass.

"Can I come?"

"Sure."

"No, you may not," El Cid said. "Bad enough I have to guard this one. I don't need another novice in my care."

She raised her head, ears pinned tight. "Just because you're a stallion doesn't make you the boss of me. I'll ask Javier—"

At that moment, angry voices exploded from inside the house. I swore the screen door bulged outward from the force. Burying my fingers in El Cid's mane, I stiffened, debating if I should go back inside or take off. Maybe keep going past Huerfano until we reached, oh say, Missouri.

"You never listen to me." My brother's voice rose. It was followed by a thump and a crash. Ben slamming his chair into the table. "Why are you afraid to try something different?

Scared to find out you're not the great hunter everyone says you are?"

Dios. Sometimes, I wished I was an only child.

Before I caught Dad's counterattack, El Cid fled with me. He broke into a lope after two strides, and, as the old saying goes, we lit out for the territories, rounding the Hump at a gallop. He didn't slow until we reached the dirt road to town. Fine with me.

With my mace resting across my lap, we jogged along in silence. The only sound was the dull thump of hoof on dirt and the *brr-cheep* of grasshoppers. The tall prairie grass waved a good morning at us from either side of the road. Under me, I could feel every roll of the gray's muscles, his movements as natural to me as breathing. Just being horseback helped loosen the tightness in my chest.

"I hate it when they fight."

"I know, Matt."

I studied my fingers wound in his mane. When had the hairs gotten so white? "I hate *them* when they do."

"No, you don't. You simply dislike the fact that they forget how much it bothers you when they quarrel. As if you matter less to them than the opportunity to hurt each other." He arched his neck, then spoke again. "Rest assured—you do not."

"I don't what?"

"Matter less. In fact, you could not matter more. Not to your father, who would sell his soul—and count it cheap—to save you from harm. Not to your brother, who loves you more than he knows right now." He swung his head around and looked up at me with an ebony eye. "And, certainly, not to me."

I swallowed twice before the tightness in my throat would go away. Embarrassed, I changed the subject and checked behind us. "I guess Izzie decided not to come after all. Dad probably told her—"

"Matt." The stallion slowed to a walk. "We have company."

Panic walloped me in the gut. *How'd they get past the wards?* I whipped around, my fist spasming around the mace's haft.

"A little jumpy, are we?" El Cid asked.

"Nope. Not one bit." I huffed out a long breath. "What is it with people ignoring our private road sign?"

Wearing a lime green helmet that matched her T-shirt, a girl about my age pedaled toward us on a mountain bike. Something about her bike—as well as her helmet color—seemed familiar. Was she the stranger from the other day?

El Cid halted. She slowed, too, then stopped and hopped off. Below the hem of her cargo shorts, both her knees sported impressive scabs.

"I didn't want to spook your horse." She walked toward us, the bike clicking cheerfully beside her.

"It's cool."

She gazed at me. Her eyes were dark brown, almost black, and tipped up at the corners. Face scrunched in curiosity, she studied us. "How can you control your horse without a bridle or saddle?"

"Voice commands."

"Voice commands?"

"Yeah. Like a circus horse." El Cid swelled in indignation. I choked back a laugh.

Holding the handlebars with one hand, she leaned sideways, getting a better look at El Cid. "She's gorgeous. Is she an An-da...something?"

"Andalusian." I blinked, impressed she knew her breeds. "And, she's a he," I added before the stallion ballooned up any more. "This is El Cid."

"Oh, cool name. And my bad. Sorry, boy." She started to pat him, then paused. "Can I...?"

"Sure. He's like a big ol' dog—loves being the center of attention." Man, was I going to pay for these remarks later, but I couldn't resist.

"Andalusians originated in Spain, right?" She ran her palm along his shoulder muscle.

"Yeah. Spanish knights used them as warhorses during the Middle Ages." *And for other kinds of battles.* I smiled to myself.

She combed her fingers through his mane, then sighed. "I always wanted a horse. I'm Perry, by the way."

"Matt." For a moment, I wondered if I had brushed my hair—or teeth—before leaving the house. Probably not. Great. "Do you live around here?" I knew all the local kids. I would've remembered her.

"Just moved back with my mom. Well, back for *her*, not me. She grew up here."

"*Here*? In Huerfano?" I didn't know of anyone who returned after leaving.

"We're just here for the summer. Mom's the assistant director of the dig."

My heart slammed to a halt. For a moment, I couldn't speak. "W-what dig?"

"The one in the Maze. Kind of sudden, so maybe that's why you haven't heard about it. Everyone's scrambling." Perry gestured behind her. In the distance, a dark green station wagon idled by the side of the road. Even as I watched, the vehicle turned around, bumped over the ruts, then drove slowly back toward Huerfano. "Mom's scouting out the best place for the bulldozer to punch a new road to the site."

"N-new road?"

Perry nodded. "To haul all the camping gear and equipment into the Maze. And to pick up supplies throughout the summer."

Questions piled up in my head—I plucked out the nearest one. "What are you talking about?" *Oh, man, don't let it be what I think it is.*

She stopped playing with El Cid's mane and pulled off her helmet. Her hair, black and cut short enough to frame her face, was spiky with sweat. "The paleontology dig? The Field Museum's site? Bunch of scientists crawling all over *El Laberinto* playing Jurassic Park?" She made a face. "And Perry sitting around camp, screaming bored out of her mind."

El Cid snorted and flung up his head, startling her. As the stallion began backing up, I wrapped a hank of mane around my hand. "Um, I just remembered something. I gotta go. See ya."

"Oh. Right." Perry stepped back. "Well, nice to meet you, Matt." She put on her helmet and fastened the strap. "Maybe I'll see you around this summer."

I sure hope not. With a weak smile, I nodded. El Cid spun around so fast, I almost fell off. Only my grip on his mane kept me from doing a rear-planter in front of Perry. We bolted for home.

13

"Slow down. Both of you." Standing on the porch, my father tugged on one boot, then the other. "Start at the beginning."

In a jumble, El Cid and I filled him in. Dad's face tightened with every word. Nearby, Turk and Izzie listened in, ears swiveling and tails lashing their hindquarters. As I finished, Ben appeared with the truck keys in his hand. He handed them to our father without a word. Just as silently, Dad took them.

Between rounds, I guessed.

"Everyone stay here. I will return shortly." Dad reached inside the door and snagged his hat from the hook, then pulled it low over his eyes. "Perhaps I can catch up with Perry's mother and get more details. What is her name?"

"I didn't ask." I slipped off El Cid. "Can I come, too?" I shot a glance at Ben. He leaned a shoulder against the porch post, his face sullen. I knew then that I'd be riding shotgun in the cab.

"Well, *I'm* certainly coming with you, Javier," El Cid said. "It's easy enough to follow you along the road."

"I better come as well," Turk said. "Check out what's going on."

Ben sneered. "Yeah, like *that's* not going to look weird or anything. A guy driving a truck with a pair of horses trotting behind."

"Make that a *trio*." Izzie shook her forelock out of her eyes. "I'm sick of being left out of everything around here."

Dad blew out a long breath. "Change of plan. Matt, you and I will saddle up and ride out with El Cid and Turk. Izzie, you may come along as well."

I caught my brother's attention. "Ben?"

"Pass."

"Oh, c'mon, Ben." The sorrel stretched out her neck and nosed my brother. "Don't be a poopster—join the parade."

"Nah, I'm good."

"You and Javier can be mad at each other some other time." She caught the hem of his T- shirt between her teeth and tugged.

To my surprise, Ben barked a short laugh. "All right. I'm coming already." He pulled free. "Sheesh, hold your horses."

The entire family groaned.

Ten minutes later, we were jogging east, riding side by side in a mismatched cavalry line. For a while, the only sound was the jingle of the buckles on the horses' halters and the clop of hoof on earth.

"There." I pointed along the road. A white SUV rumbled toward us, a plume of dust billowing behind it.

"Perry's mother?" Dad asked.

"No, she drove a station wagon."

We stopped and waited on the shoulder. My eyes kept drifting northward toward the towering cliffs. The Gate was a black mouth open in a silent scream. Did something move in its shadow? The hairs on my arms lifted. *Stop freaking yourself out*, I ordered.

"I don't understand." El Cid locked his ears on the approaching car. "Did the driver not see the *Private Road, Dead End, No Turnarounds Allowed* sign?"

"Maybe they can't read," Izzie said.

"Maybe they don't care," Turk growled.

The SUV reminded me of the vehicles they used on safaris in Africa. Big and boxy, with large, plastic crates and bulging duffle bags strapped to the luggage rack. It slowed. The dust caught up with it, then wafted toward us. I narrowed my eyes as the fine grit settled on my face. Izzie sneezed.

The driver lifted his hand in greeting as the vehicle rolled to a stop next to us. It had out-of-state plates, but I couldn't tell which one. Wasn't Colorado or New Mexico. Holding onto the saddle horn, I leaned to one side. The words *The Field Museum of Natural History: Chicago* and an image of a Greek-like temple, decorated the vehicle's door.

Motor idling, the man powered down his window and stuck his head out. His scalp gleamed through white hair cut short enough to make a Marine proud. "Hello there. Oh, I mean, *buenas tardes*," he added, getting both the pronunciation and time of day wrong. Ben and I winced.

"Good morning." Dad nodded once. "Can I help you?"

"I hope so. I'm looking for the old cut-off that used to connect this road with the *El Laberinto* Wilderness Area trailhead. I think I've come too far west. Or perhaps it's so overgrown, I've missed it."

"You have. Forgive me, but this is private property, so you will need to go back to Huerfano and—"

"Actually, it isn't. Private, I mean." The man's smile was polite, but just barely. "I've checked and double-checked with both the county and the state. While this section of road is privately owned by a Francis J. Del Toro, all this land," he gestured from the Hump to the Maze, "is public domain. Which means it belongs to the good folks of Colorado." Sunlight bounced off the man's horn-rimmed glasses, the lenses thicker than the bottom of a drinking glass. His gaze took in my father's faded shirt and dusty boots. "Speaking of Mr. Del Toro, I was told his ranch is at the end of this road. I need to speak with him as soon as possible. Do you work for him by any chance?"

Dad narrowed his eyes. Ben coughed, then bent over, pretending to adjust his stirrup while I bit my lip, fighting my own grin. Turk snorted in anger and stomped. Eyeing the black stallion, the man shrank back in his seat.

"*I* am Francis Javier Del Toro."

"My apologies. I thought…well, it doesn't matter." The man turned off the engine, then eased out of the truck, careful to keep the open door between his lanky frame and Turk. He adjusted his glasses and peered up at my father. "Dr. Philip Allbury. The Field Museum. Chicago." He paused, then added. "That's in Illinois."

A muscle twitched in Dad's cheek. "What do you wish to speak with me about so urgently?"

I noticed Allbury didn't offer to shake Dad's hand. "Actually, more of a courtesy call before the bulldozer arrives. It's scheduled to be here by the first of next week. That gives us just three days to decide."

"To decide what?"

"Why, where to put in the access road to the site. The mayor suggested that we might be able to use the old abandoned one. Just have the bulldozer clean it up." He nodded back down the road toward Huerfano. "That would make the shortest route to our camp, as well as easy access to town for supplies. And, hopefully, not bother you too much." His eyes flicked over Ben and me. "Are these your sons?"

"They are."

"Well, you and your family are welcome to stop by and see what we've unearthed. I know how children love dinosaurs." Allbury beamed at Ben and me. We looked at each other in disbelief.

Dad pushed his hat back on his head. A crease appeared between his brows. "Then it is true? There will be a dig in the Maze?"

"All summer. I'm planning on being up and running within the next week or so. That's when the last of my crew gets here. Hopefully. Organizing paleontologists and other specialists scattered around the world is like herding cats—"

"Dr. Allbury," Dad interrupted him. "I do not know how much you have heard about the Maze, but I must warn you. It is a dangerous place. A number of deaths have occurred there over the years." He stopped at the low hum of an engine.

Shading my eyes with my hand, I stood in the stirrups. A station wagon, the green one that belonged to Perry's mom, drove toward us. A tiny part of my brain wondered if Perry was with her. Then I wondered why I even cared.

The second car slowed and parked behind Allbury's. A woman, wearing jeans and a white shirt with the sleeves rolled up, stepped out. Her blonde hair was pulled back at the nape of her neck. Shaking her head in disbelief, she stared at my father. A growing smile curled the corners of her mouth.

Perry clambered out from the passenger side. Her gaze darted from my brother and father to the horses then to me. Making a face, she pointed at the woman. *My mom,* she mouthed.

"Well, well." The woman strolled nearer. Her blue eyes crinkled at the corners. "If it isn't Javier Del Toro. Bet you don't remember me."

"*Dios mío*," Dad breathed. To my amazement, he swung out of the saddle. "Liz Vandermer?" Removing his hat, he clasped her hand. "You have not changed a bit."

"Flatterer." She laughed. "It's been a long time."

"Since senior year in high school."

"Right before, actually. That's when my family moved to San Diego."

"That's in California," Ben said in a low voice. I choked back a laugh.

"And these two have got to be yours. Talk about peas in a pod." She looked at Ben, then me. "You must be Matt. Perry said she ran into a boy riding a gray horse. Considering a horse was involved, I'm stunned she remembered your name."

"Yeah. I mean, yes, ma'am." I pretended not to notice Perry cringing in mortification.

Dad pointed his chin toward my brother. "And Ben is my oldest."

The woman waved Perry over. "Perry is my one and only pride and joy." She started to sweep the girl's bangs from her eyes.

"You're killing me here, Mom." She dodged away with a practiced move. Her mom just laughed.

El Cid shifted. At that moment, Roman's words returned. *Our war-brothers come first. The fact that we ride upon them does not mean they are beneath us.*

"And this is El Cid," I blurted out. "The sorrel is Izzie. And Turk's the black one." As soon as I said those words, my whole head burst into flames. Who, in the normal world, introduced their horses to strangers? A dweeb, that's who. But, dweeb or not, I wasn't going to sit there and pretend half my family didn't exist.

For a split second, I saw just how wide a gulf there was between my family and others. Not good or bad. Just different.

Like a totally-different-solar-system different. I felt better when Perry threw a thumbs-up behind her mother, who gave me a warm nod. I ignored Ben's snort.

"You two know each other?" Allbury edged closer to the other scientist. His eyes widened behind the lenses. "Oh, that's right. You grew up here, didn't you, Liz."

She pointed toward the Maze. "I used to hunt for fossils at the foot of those cliffs when I was Perry's age. Whenever I could dodge Javier and his family. They'd chase me off, telling me it was too dangerous and that something bad would happen to me if I didn't stay away. '*El Laberinto* is no place for a little girl,' his father used to say. 'Go home where it is safe.'" She smiled at Dad. "Even back then, you guys were a tad overly vigilant about the place."

"We were trying to keep you safe."

"I know. But there's no need to worry about me now. I'm back with a crew and the support of the Field Museum. Not to mention some extra funding from Huerfano's council, thanks to your mayor."

"Liz, you and the other scientists must not go in there. People have disappeared or died in there in record numbers."

"See, Philip? What did I tell you?" She sighed. "Really, Javier. We're not kids anymore. Enough with the whole 'there's a bogeyman in the Maze' thing already."

Out of the corner of my eye, I spotted Perry edging over to me. Remembering what Dad did earlier, I swung out of the saddle. For a split second, I wished I wore a cowboy hat, just so I could take it off.

"What are they talking about?" Standing on tiptoe, she craned her neck, looking northward. "About the Maze being dangerous?"

Before I could answer, Dad spoke again. "I will not allow any road to be built across my land."

"Oh, Javier—" Dr. Vandermer began.

"Excuse me." Allbury held up a finger. "Not to belabor the point, but the new road will run across *public* land. So you see, my good man, you really have no say in this matter."

14

"**M**att." A hand nudged my shoulder. I jerked awake. For a moment, I stared up at my father, my throat slick with sweat. Man, was I glad to see his face. Because I'd been locked in one twisted nightmare.

I dreamt I was blundering around the Maze, struggling to see through a thick fog. The moisture on my lips tasted liked salt water. I tried to catch up with El Cid, who was always a few strides ahead, appearing, then disappearing, his gray coat blending with the mist. I was afraid to call his name in case the skinners heard me. I tried to reach him, but my legs felt like weights were tied to my ankles. All the while, I knew there was something I had to do. Before it was too late. Something for El Cid...

"I-I can't find him," I gasped.

"Who?"

"El Cid."

His face softened. "Only a dream."

I nodded. Even as I thought about it, the memory grew thinner and thinner, like fog when the sun came out. Fine with me. "Is it time?"

"*Sí*. Get a move on." He left, boots beating a rhythm on the hallway's wood floor.

I yawned and stretched, thinking about last night. I swore I had just crashed into bed after staying up late with my father and brother planning how to safeguard the scientists. It had felt all kinds of good to be part of the discussion, even though I didn't contribute much.

"The best way to learn about the family business is to be involved in the family business," Dad had said last night. "Especially at the strategic level."

We all threw out ideas. But, in the end, we came back to doing what we do best: ride hard, swing hard, and wipe out as many of those stinkers as we could before Vandermer, Allbury, and the rest arrived and set up camp. Reduce the skinner population so they'd be less of a threat.

"Isn't it called a 'war of attrition' or something like that?" Ben had said. He laughed when Dad's jaw dropped. "See, Pop. I listen to your history lessons. Sometimes," he added.

"What about the coffer?" I had leaned back on the sofa, my feet propped up on the coffee table and a bowl of buttery popcorn on my lap. "Won't do any good if the skinners are escaping as fast as we kill them."

Ben reached over and snatched the bowl from me. "Gimme that."

"Hey!" I grabbed at it.

He slapped my hands away and held it higher. "Too slow and too low."

Dad cleared his throat in a meaningful rumble until we stopped. "That is why our first task is to reach the coffer and seal it. This is also a good time for you two *hombres* to learn another use of your maces." He eyed me. "And, Matt, about the cave."

"Ben already told me. Pretty tight back in there, I know." I hoped I sounded braver than I felt.

After one more spine-popping stretch, I threw back the covers and rolled out of bed and into my clothes, then joined Dad in the kitchen. Outside the window, the sky was the flat gray before dawn. On the counter, the coffee machine mumbled complaints to itself as it labored away.

Over the crunch of cereal and toast, I heard my brother stumbling across the living room. He appeared and sank down at the table. Without a word, Dad poured him a cup of coffee— light on the sugar, heavy on the milk—and set it in front of him. While Ben attempted to kick-start his brain, I finished my breakfast, one eye on our father.

He stood at the sink, chasing down one aspirin after another between gulps of water. At four tablets, I started to worry.

"Bad headache?"

"Not as yet." Before I could ask further, he headed for the front door. "Five minutes, gentlemen, then we ride."

By the time the sun hoisted itself up and over the eastern horizon, the six of us were waiting just outside the Gate. My gaze drifted skyward. The tops of the buttes glowed red and gold in the beams of the rising sun, all beacons of Gondor-ish.

"We will try the same tactic as the other day." Dad circled his right arm a few times, then flipped his mace end over end and caught it by the haft. "Hopefully, this time, it will work."

Something niggled at me—something about the coffer. I shrugged the thought away. *Dad knows what he's doing.*

We started through the Gate's shadow. I looked up. The walls rose and rose and seemed to pinch together at the top. Shivers climbed up my spine—wish I could've said it was from

the cool air. The creak of leather and the thump of hooves echoed and rebounded inside the corridor.

"Dude," Izzie muttered to Turk. "Can't you tiptoe? You
sound like an elephant."

"Iz, hush," Ben murmured. He laid a hand on the mare's
neck. "Not now."

Way too soon for my taste, we emerged into the growing
light. The valley opened up below us, washed by a pinkish glow.
Pretty, if a guy wasn't worried about being eaten by a monster.

"Ben, take the lead," Dad ordered. "Head for the cave. Do
you remember in which canyon it is hidden?"

"Yeah." Ben secured his mace's leather strap around his
wrist, Izzie prancing beneath him.

"El Cid, you and Matt next. Stay close to Ben. Turk and I
will take up the rear."

"Dad?" The nagging worry from earlier returned with a
question I couldn't ignore. "If more skinners are getting out of
the coffer, won't we be charging into an even bigger bunch of
them?"

"Wow." Ben frowned and peered northward across the valley. "That's an encouraging image."

Dad tugged his hat on tighter. "All the more reason to ride
fast, no?"

"Stealth and speed," El Cid said to Turk and Izzie.

Izzie flicked her tail. "Got it."

"Turk?"

"I know my job."

El Cid flattened his ears. "See that you execute it, then."

"Isabel?" My father touched the brim of his hat in a salute.
"You have the lead. Good hunting."

She gathered her hind legs beneath her, then leaped down
the incline. Ben leaned back, his feet braced in the stirrups. El
Cid and I followed.

Hitting the valley floor, I hunched down further and tried to make myself as small of a target as I could. My pulse pounded in rhythm with the stallion's hoof beats. Even with El Cid's speed, I tensed each time we thundered past a boulder or large bush. They weren't going to ambush me again, I swore to myself.

Riding low in the saddle as well, my brother angled toward the northeast corner of the valley. Izzie's mane and tail were gold banners in the wind. I glanced behind—Dad rode several lengths back. Rear guard.

The valley's northern wall loomed up. Blowing hard, El Cid slowed to a trot. Massive slabs of stones lay where they had peeled away and fallen from the cliff face. I trailed Ben around the debris. He and Izzie halted by an enormous block of yellowish sandstone the size of an eighteen-wheeler. It leaned against the cliff at a forty-five-degree angle. I could just make out a dark opening—a little higher and wider than a man and roughly triangular in shape—behind the stone. More rubble was piled in front of the entrance. A chilling breeze wafted from the opening. It also smelled like rotting meat—or something worse.

Turk trotted up, Dad scanning the area. "So far, so good."

"So, this is it?" I asked. "The cave?"

He swung down from the saddle. "Behind this block of sandstone, yes. We are fortunate it hides the entrance." He patted my knee. "Are you going to be okay?"

"I'm cool." He lifted an eyebrow. I shrugged, then slipped to the ground. "Too bad that chunk of rock didn't block up the cave permanently."

Ben joined me and eyed the cliff. "Still think we should try dynamiting this whole area."

"We have talked about this before," Dad said with a trace of exasperation. "Your grandfather, and great-grandfather, and great-great-grandfather, tried every way they could think of to block this accursed hole. Including dynamite. Nothing works for long."

"Why?" I leaned against El Cid's warm shoulder.

Dad toed the pile of rubble. "My guess is that the evil trapped within eventually leaches through."

"Just as it ultimately leaches out of the coffers," El Cid added.

Toxic ghoul waste, I thought. "What about the wards? Roman said they don't always work."

"This is true, but unless they are overwhelmed by sheer numbers, the wards will hold the longest. They are even more potent than our maces or the coffers. We can thank the memory of Her Highness for that."

Her Highness being Joan, Queen of the Crown of Spain during the early sixteen hundreds. She had blessed everything—the maces, coffers, and especially the wards—before Santiago and his band of brothers had boarded the ship for the New World. I marveled that a royal blessing could still be so powerful after four centuries.

"Ben. Matt. Once we reach the hole, I will crawl through first, then you two follow." As he spoke, he hooked his Stetson on Turk's saddle horn, then pulled out a small headlamp, the kind backpackers used, from his shirt pocket. He fastened it around his head.

"What about the horses?" I dragged myself over. "Are they going to be okay?"

El Cid shot me the ol' stink eye. "I'll pretend I didn't hear that. And, Javier? If I give a warning neigh…"

"I know. But no heroics, my friend. We can defend ourselves in the cave if the pack shows up. You three flee to safety."

"Oh, sure," Izzie said under her breath. "We'll just do that very thing."

"Good luck." The gray bumped Dad's shoulder with his nose. "Boys, listen to your father. Do exactly what he tells you."

"Yeah, Ben," Turk said. "Surprise us."

Turning sideways, Dad squeezed behind the block and disappeared. My brother pulled me in front of him and gave me a push toward the gap.

"Girls first."

"Funny." In spite of the dread tightening its fist around my throat, I made a face over my shoulder then slipped inside the crevice.

Trailing the fingers of my left hand along the sandpaper surface, I hurried after Dad, leaning slightly to one side. Light filtered from overhead, where the uneven edge of the block met the cliff. With each step, I swore the walls were closing in on me. I wondered what Ben would do if I suddenly spun around and clawed my way through him to escape.

It'd serve him right.

When I was little, Ben thought it'd be funny to stuff me in one of the empty feed bins. Although the bin always seemed plenty big to me when I was scooping grain out of it, it sure didn't feel roomy when he closed the hinged lid and latched it. Squished into a ball, arms pinned against my chest, I had less than an inch between me and all four sides. No matter how I squirmed, I couldn't move. Worse, the lid pressed against my face.

I screamed forever. I had also wet my pants by the time my father rescued me. El Cid came tearing in from the field, barely in time to stop Dad from giving Ben a serious whupping with his belt.

Lost in the memory, I bumped into Dad. I took a step back, rubbing my nose, and peered past him. A stone wall blocked the end of the canyon. "Where's the cave?"

"Look down."

At knee height, a black hole gaped at me. A hungry maw eager for boy. I gulped.

Dad adjusted the headlamp and clicked on the light. He swung his head from side to side, the beam dancing over the stone, then squatted down. I knelt beside him.

"A short crawl through the tunnel, then we will be in the cave. Think of nothing but following me."

Not trusting my voice, I nodded and made sure the mace's loop was tight around my wrist.

"Here we go." On his hands and knees, Dad vanished into the darkness.

15

Before I lost my nerve, I scooted along behind him. The sand stuck to my sweaty palms. Reminding myself to breath, I focused on the bouncing light and the soles of Dad's cowboy boots. As I crawled along, my breakfast threatened to join me in the tunnel. Swallowing, I kept moving.

Dad's boots paused, then stood and shifted to one side. I sped up. Banging my head, I scrambled to my feet.

"Okay," I wheezed, "that wasn't so bad."

He squeezed my shoulder. "You did well."

I looked around. About the size of a freight elevator, the cave's roof was only a couple of yards above Dad's head. My boot heels sank into the deep sand covering the bottom. I tried not to think about how much rock rested above us.

Ben appeared. He rose and dusted his hands on his jeans. "Smaller than I remembered. Kind of like your worst nightmare, huh, Matty?"

"*You're* my worst nightmare."

Dad hissed through his teeth. We both knew what that meant—knock it off before I knock your heads together. He turned in a slow circle, then stopped. "There."

The size of one of those plastic milk crates that nobody uses for milk, the iron chest sat on a stone ledge about waist high. Etched with alternating symbols of multi-rayed stars and crosses, it rested on four round balls for feet. Iron rings were welded onto each corner, just below the lid. Ben crossed himself. My fingers did the same.

One corner of the lid curled up, as if someone—something—had pried it open.

Our father sighed. "As I feared."

A dark shape moved in the gap under the lid. Black smoke, shaped like a wolf's snout, poked out. My heart lurched.

"Weapons," Dad ordered.

I raised my mace shoulder-height in a two-handed grip. Next to me, Ben did the same. The smoky muzzle paused, then oozed back inside.

Goose bumps broke out my arms and neck. "Was that a...a *skinner?*"

"Its spirit, yes," Dad said. "Or more accurately, its essence. Be vigilant, but do not fear. If it escapes, we have a margin of safety, for it will not become fully corporeal until completely exposed to sunlight."

He motioned us to one side of the cave. "Sit down and place your backs against the wall. Otherwise, the shockwave will knock you down. Ben?" He pulled off the headlamp and handed it to my brother. "Hold this. Keep it aimed at the coffer."

I hunkered down next to my brother. "What shockwave?"

"From the mace." Dad rolled up one sleeve, then the other. "Now, watch and learn."

Taking a stance in front of the ledge, he dug his feet into the sand, then gripped the mace in both hands. He pointed the weapon at the coffer. A challenge and a warning.

"*Stamus contra malum*," he said in a ringing voice. The words echoed in the tiny space.

The echo continued, morphing into a low hum. My lungs froze. Sweet mother of pearl, was that flies? Were there skinners lurking in the tunnel, waiting to chow down? What about the warhorses? "Ben..."

"It's coming from Dad's mace."

The humming grew louder and deeper, like an army roaring in the distance. I thought I caught a whiff of hot metal. The mace began vibrating. Dad shifted his weight, arm muscles corded from the strain. He sucked in a deep breath, then stepped forward and touched the coffer's lid with the iron ball.

"*Stamus contra malum,*" he shouted again.

Kaa-rack! Blue-white light blasted my eyes. A split second later, an invisible fist punched me in the chest. My head slammed against the rock wall; stars popped like fireworks in my vision. The cave spun around, taking me on a tilt-a-wheel ride.

"Matt!"

Ben sounded like he was hollering through a pillow. He yanked on my shirt. Ears ringing, I shook my head, then gripped his arm. He pulled me upright.

Dad lay sprawled on his back, still clutching his weapon and gasping for breath. A wisp of smoke spiraled upward from the mace's head. My gaze flew toward the coffer.

It was bathed in a bluish neon-y glow and sealed up tighter than a cinch on a bronco. There wasn't even a seam between the lid and the chest. As I watched, the glow faded back to a dull gray.

"Matt." Ben held one of Dad's arms.

I grabbed our father's other arm and helped him sit up. "You okay?"

"Not really, no." Opening and closing his jaw, he rubbed his chest, then held out a hand. Ben hauled him to his feet. I hovered nearby, not sure what to do.

Out of the corner of my eye, I spotted something. A flash of red in Ben's headlamp. Almost afraid to look, I slowly turned my head. Alarm tied a bow in my gut. "What the heck is *that?*"

"What?" Ben peered around.

"Up there." I pointed. Another coffer, made from some kind of dull, reddish metal and smaller than the other, sat in an alcove above our heads. It was shoved back, as if whoever put it there was trying to hide it.

My brother aimed the light. "Did you know there's another coffer in here, Pop?"

Dad rolled his head from side to side, wincing. "*El Cofre Rojo.* Also known as the Red Casket."

"What's in it?" *Oh, please, not more monsters.* I remembered what Izzie told me about the goblins—the *duendes*—near the Navarre ranch.

"I do not know."

"Y-you *don't?*" I glanced at Ben. He looked as astonished as I felt.

"It arrived in the middle of the night when I was a boy. I awoke to the sound of voices coming from the front porch. My father and a stranger. Then, I heard my father agree, reluctantly, to keep something in our cave. By the time I had reached the door, the stranger was gone and *El Cofre Rojo* was sitting on the lowest step."

I stared at the chest. "And you never asked him about it? Or who brought it?"

"Oh, about a thousand times. But *Papá* said that it would be better if I stayed ignorant. He passed away before I could learn more." Dad winced and rubbed his forehead.

A million questions swirled around inside my skull. I started to ask the first one, but stopped myself. "You okay?"

"I will be fine." Sighing, he held up his mace and spat on it. A sizzling sound, like oil on a hot griddle. "Still too hot." He waved it back and forth, then staggered a step, then another one. Then, his legs gave out. He crashed to the ground, falling to his knees. The weapon dropped from his hand. Ben caught his shoulder before he planted his face in the sand.

"I am a little dizzy." Breathing deeply, he motioned Ben's hand away. "Thank you, but I will stay down here since I have to crawl back anyway. Matt, take my mace. Go first."

I belly-swam back through the tunnel, dragging a mace from each wrist and trying not to get sand down my pants. Dad trailed behind, taking twice as long.

Clear of the cave, I stood up and shook myself all over, like a dog after a swim. *Never again. I don't care how many skinners slither free of that coffer—I am never, ever, for as long as I live, going in there again.*

We hurried out to the horses. A few yards away, Turk and Izzie stood on guard, tails to us, and ears and noses on full alert. El Cid waited by the opening. He stiffened at the sight of my father.

"Javier?"

"I am fine. Here, Matt. Let me have that." Retrieving his mace, he sank down on a rock, laid it across his knees, and kneaded both temples with his fingertips. "My sons. Always make sure you take aspirin *prior* to sealing the coffer. Trust me on that."

Questions lined up in my mouth. I clamped down on them.

Dad must have read my expression. He smiled faintly. "Go ahead."

Okay. "Will *any* of our maces work?"

"As long as a descendant of a knight holds it, yes."

"So, how does it actually work?" Ben rested his mace across his shoulders, hands hanging over both ends for support. "I heard you say something. Wasn't Spanish."

"*Stamus contra malum*. Latin for 'we stand against evil.' Remember those words. You may need them someday to save your life."

"*Stamus contra malum*," I whispered to myself. Just in case.

Dad pushed to his feet. "Time to leave. I am not up to dealing with skinners right now." He plodded over to Turk and grasped the horn. It took him two tries to get his boot in the stirrup and haul himself into the saddle.

"How many times have you done that?" Ben asked, swinging onto Izzie's back. "Nailed down that coffer?"

"Counting this time?"

"Yeah."

"Twice. The first time, I came to with a bloody nose and your grandfather dragging me out by my heels." Dad grinned weakly. "Hopefully, it is sealed tight. At least, for a while." He signaled Turk, who trotted away.

Maybe it was the blast from Dad's mace that scared them off. Or maybe the skinners somehow knew that the coffer was closed for good, and that no more of their fellow hamburger hounds were coming out to play. Whatever it was, we made it all the way across the valley and through the Gate without any sign of those creepsters.

Still, as El Cid and I galloped along, I checked every shadow. You know. Just in case.

For the next three days, it was nonstop search-and-destroy, though really more the former than the latter. Every time we spotted a skinner, it tucked tail and hauled you-know-what. Drove my father insane because the one time we needed to get up close and personal with those things was the one time they were playing hard to get.

Worse, the bulldozer showed up right on schedule first thing Monday morning. For several days, the T-Rex roar of the diesel engine filled the air as it gouged a road across the prairie. Even though it was more than a mile away, Dad stomped around in a foul mood, snapping at me and Ben. For once, my brother had the sense not to poke the bear. Finally, by Wednesday, the bulldozer finished and crawled back to town.

The next afternoon, as I spread fresh straw around the barn, El Cid stuck his head inside. "Care to accompany me?"

"Where to?" I wiped my face on my shirt.

"To the bright lights of Huerfano. I told Javier that I'm in need of a refreshing beverage after listening to that awful mechanized drone for the last three days."

"Do a little Dew?" I dug in a pocket, pleased to find a couple of dollars. "Sure, we can split one."

"Excellent. Plus, I wish to take a look at the new road."

"Give me a minute." I put away the rake and wheelbarrow, then slapped bits of straw from my hair and clothes. Checked my hands. Good enough. Balancing on an upended bucket, I motioned him over.

"No, Matt. Saddle me, *por favor*."

"Why? We're not hunting."

"But we *are* going into town. And there's no need to stand out more than we do. The locals already have a distorted view of our family. The less we call attention to ourselves, the better."

"Is there something going on?" I hauled his tack over and hoisted it up on his back.

"No more than usual." He shifted from side to side, settling the saddle more comfortably. "You know what I mean."

"Yeah, but it doesn't mean I have to like it. Too bad folks can't handle the truth." I reached under him, caught the cinch, then pulled it around and buckled it. A rare loneliness washed over me. *It'd be nice to have a friend who got me. And didn't think we were oddballs.*

"Talking horses and magical weapons and creatures that go bump in the night are all just too much for the average person to believe in. You know this. And what people don't understand, they fear. And what they fear, they often grow to hate. Isabel, Turk, and I might be captured and taken away to be studied. Javier might be declared an unfit father. You and your brother would be placed in foster care."

"*Dad?*" Disbelief stilled my hands. "*Unfit?* I mean, he's strict about stuff. And he makes us do too many chores, but c'mon."

"Think about it, Matt. What loving father would knowingly expose his child to monsters rampaging nearby? And expect the child to fight said creatures using a medieval weapon while mounted on horseback?"

I laughed. "Since you put it that way, we'll just have to fake normal."

"Well, as normal as any family really is," he said dryly.

We jogged out of the yard, the afternoon sun hot on our backs and our shadows leading the way to town. Reaching the newly bulldozed road, we stopped. My gaze followed the shortcut as it left our road and curved northward toward the Maze.

"Wonder where the paleontologists are going to set up? I mean, they wouldn't camp *inside* the Maze, would they? After what Dad told them?"

"Oh, they'll establish their base in the very worst location, I'm sure. Just as I'm certain they've written off Javier as some sort of isolationist nutcase." He lowered his head and sniffed the raw soil, blowing away bits of dead grass. "The more pressing question is how soon do they arrive?" He sighed.

I did, too. "Still want that soda?"

"More than ever." He broke into a jog.

Reaching the town limits, El Cid slowed to a walk. His shoes rang like gongs on the asphalt. Only one car passed us. The elderly driver lifted a couple of fingers from his truck's steering wheel in greeting as he pulled out of the mini-mart's parking lot.

"Matt?"

A girl's voice. I looked around. Across the street sat a row of small houses, most with dirt yards, and all of them in need of a coat of paint. To my surprise—and uneasiness—Perry stood in the doorway of the nearest one. I swallowed, my mouth suddenly dry and useless. Which was good, because I had no idea what to say.

"Thought I heard a horse." Letting go of the screen, she stepped to the edge of the porch.

Fingers fumbling, I twitched the reins, signaling El Cid to stay put. He ignored me. Instead, he ambled up her driveway. Stupid horse.

"Um, hey, Perry," I said.

Dressed in the same cargo shorts and sporting a black T-shirt that declared not all those who wander are lost, Perry jogged down the steps and slowed as she neared El Cid. Her black hair framed her face in delicate wisps. "Are you riding all the way into town?" She stroked the stallion's neck. "Hi, big guy."

"Just to the 7-Eleven." I poked a thumb over a shoulder.

"Which has got to be the coolest thing ever."

"What do you mean?"

"Other kids ride their bikes to the store. *You* ride a horse. Gotta love the rural life." She looked past me. "So where's Brad?"

"*Brad?*"

"Your brother?"

El Cid laughed, then covered it up with a snort. Perry's eyes widened, then narrowed.

"You mean *Ben?*" I said hastily. "He's at home."

"Oh." Her fingers combed through the gray's mane.

I looked around, trying to fill the silence. "This your house?"

"*This* place? No way." She made a face. "We're just renting it until the site is up and running. I think Mom picked this dump to make the camp look better." She shuffled her feet. "So, um…would you like a soda or something?"

"Sure." The answer tumbled out of my mouth before I could catch it.

"We can sit on the porch if you need to keep an eye on El Cid."

Worked for me. Being inside a girl's house seemed like too much of a commitment. I swung down, trying to be like Dad. One smooth move.

Chewing on her lip, she glanced back at the open screen. "Might as well get this over with."

"What?"

"My mom. And I apologize in advance."

I opened my mouth to ask why, then closed it. Instead, I smoothed my hair, wishing I had changed into a clean shirt before I left home.

"Mom?" Perry raised her voice. "Matt Del Toro's here."

A clanking-thud, like a bag of tools being dropped. A muffled exclamation. Footsteps. Then, Dr. Vandermer appeared, dusting her hands on her jeans.

"Hello, Matt." She tucked a strand of pale hair behind one ear. With a smile, she joined us on the porch. "Nice to see you again. How's your father?"

"Fine, thank you." I couldn't help staring at the mother's blue eyes and blonde hair, then Perry's dark eyes and black strands. *Wait. What…*

Dr. Vandermer noticed my confusion. "It's okay. People always ask, and yes, Perry is my daughter. And, yes, she is adopted, and yes, she is Chinese. And, she's also one amazing individual."

"I'll just step to the end of the porch now," Perry said, "and throw up."

Dr. Vandermer ignored her. "Would you like to come inside, Matt?" She eyed El Cid. "Although I don't know what to do about your horse."

"We'll hang out here," Perry said before I could answer.

"All right, then." She opened the screen and paused. "Per, make sure you finish organizing your stuff for camp before supper. I'm sick of tripping over piles every time I walk into your room."

"Yes, mastah," Perry muttered, slurring her words. "Igor obey, mastah." Squinting one eye, she hunched a shoulder.

I laughed at her imitation. She grinned back.

"Want to try that again?" Dr. Vandermer did that parental eyebrow lift that I knew so well.

"Sorry," Perry said out of the corner of her mouth. It seemed to satisfy her mother. Shaking her head, she disappeared inside. *Whump.* The screen slapped shut. Message delivered.

We took seats on either side of the top tread, the porch's shade a relief from the lowering sun. El Cid nickered, then pointed his nose at the vacant lot next door. I nodded. With that, he wandered away and began grazing on the sparse grass.

"Wait." Perry flapped a hand at the gray. "You just let him walk around loose like that?"

"Well, yeah. He's bigger than me."

She smiled. After a moment, her grin faded. Chin resting on her knees, she picked at a loose thread on the hem of her jeans. "So uncool when she does that."

I shrugged. "My dad jumps on me, too, when I mouth off to him. It's like their job to—"

"No, I mean that whole adoption thing. Like anyone cares." She blew her bangs from her eyes. "And then she does that 'Perry is super awesome.' Ugh. It's pathetic. Parents shouldn't brag about their kids. I bet your dad doesn't."

Hardly. "Maybe she's just proud of you."

"Or over-compensating. She's got issues."

A part of me wondered if it was Perry who had issues.

"Enough drama." She straightened and slapped her knees. "So. I gotta know. Was it hard to learn how to ride a horse?"

"I guess not. I mean, I've been riding since I could walk. Maybe earlier." Possibly during my Underoos stage.

"He's so gorgeous." She studied El Cid as he ambled over to the adjoining yard. On the other side of the chain-link fence, a Chihuahua let out a barrage of yips, threatening death and dismemberment. Ears pinned flat, El Cid leaned over the fence and sniffed. With a shriek, the dog bounced backward, still barking. "He looks like Shadowfax. You know. From *The Lord of the Rings*?"

"That's because the main horse that played Shadowfax was an Andalusian, too." I cringed even as the words left my mouth. *Could I be any more of a nerd? Nope. Not one bit. Time for me to leave.*

"I knew it!" Beaming, Perry punched her fist into the air. A dimple danced in her right cheek. Where did *that* come from? The dimple led me to look at the rest of her face.

"Hey, Matt?"

I blinked. Had I been staring like some kind of creep? Heat flooded my face. "Yeah?"

"Do you ride around here a lot?"

"Some. Why?"

"Do you think..." She paused, grinding the soles of her sneakers along the step.

"Do I think what?"

"Do you think I could get on El Cid?" she said in a rush. "Just once. To see what it's like? I've never really been on a horse. Well, except for a pony ride at the state fair, but I was six and it was more boring than a merry-go-round."

She looked at me. There was something about her face, or the way she tilted her head—I don't know what. But, whatever it was, it made me want to say yes. Why? I had no idea. Who knew why brains did what they did. "Um…"

"Guess that was kind of pushy of me." She looked away. "Listen, it's no big deal. Let's just pretend I didn't ask."

"No."

"Right. That's why I said to just pretend I didn't—"

"I mean, no, it wasn't pushy. And yes, you can ride him." I hoped El Cid was too busy with the dog to listen in. I'd have to figure out how to get him to agree. "He'll take good care of you."

Her face lit up. "Really?"

"Sure." Ignoring the way her smile made my pulse frisk around like one of Navarre's new foals, I thought for a moment. "How about tomorrow? Around ten?" I took a stab at a time of day when Ben was usually doing his own thing and I could slip away without too much of an explanation. Because I knew how *that* would go down if he found out I was going to teach a girl how to ride.

"Ten, then. Oh, wait." Perry swiveled around toward the house and yelled through the screen. "Mom? Can I go riding with Matt tomorrow? At ten?" A long silence. "Mom? *Mom!*"

"Stop bellowing. I'm right here." Dr. Vandermer appeared in the doorway. She juggled a plate of puffy muffins and two glasses of juice. I jumped up and opened the screen for her. "Thank you, Matt. And, yes, Per, I know it's cliché to bring out a snack, but stop rolling your eyes and indulge me, would you?" She passed the plate to her daughter, the glasses clinking. "Why were you yelling for me?"

"Matt said I could ride his horse. Tomorrow around ten. He'd bring El Cid here."

"We're going to be in Denver all day tomorrow, picking up equipment and supplies. Remember?"

"Do I *have* to come with you?"

"You make it sound like a punishment." Her mother's face tightened. "Spending the day with me."

Perry opened her mouth.

"How about the day after?" I offered.

Mother and daughter both looked at me, Perry's face hopeful. Then, Dr. Vandermer spoke. "Are you sure it's not an imposition?"

"No, ma'am." It gave me time to figure out how to explain it to Dad. And even more importantly, to El Cid.

"Well, okay." She smiled at me. "Saturday works for us. Thanks, Matt. Please tell your father I said hello. Perry, bring in the dishes when you're finished."

"Got it." She waited until her mother's footsteps faded away. "At least it wasn't cookies and milk." She grabbed a muffin.

I did too. They were thick with apples and heavy on the cinnamon, and best of all, homemade. Nom. Spotting us eating, El Cid stopped teasing the dog into hysterics and headed back over. The mooch. I let him have the bottom part.

"Is your dad a scientist, too?" I asked around a mouthful. It dawned on me that I hadn't heard or seen any sign of the man.

"It's just Mom and me." Before I could say anything, she continued. "What does your dad do?"

"Pest control," I answered promptly.

She frowned. "Not ranching? Or horse training or something like that?"

"The horses are more of a family hobby."

"Your mom work, too?"

"My mom died. When I was little." I waited for the averted eyes or the uncomfortable shifting. The usual response from other kids when I told them that. Grown-ups were worse. They always said they were sorry. Why? *They* didn't cause her death.

But Perry simply nodded. "Mine, too. My biological mom."

Not sure what to say, I dug out some apple bits and gave them to El Cid. I wished she'd change the subject.

She must have read my mind. "So, who's your favorite character?" she asked after a minute. "In *The Lord of the Rings*."

I stalled for time. I didn't want to go over my nerd quota for the day. I was already pretty close to the red zone with that earlier comment about Shadowfax. "Gimli's cool." I took a drink, trying not to slurp. "What about you? Oh, wait. Let me guess. Legolas, right?" Girls and that elf. I just didn't get it.

Perry snorted. "Hardly. He's too perfect at everything. And he's got better hair than I do. No, Strider's my favorite. After Shadowfax."

By the time we finished pointing out to each other why Rohan should've lost the battle at Helm's Deep, the muffins were long gone, the sun was closing in on the mountains, and El Cid was making grumbling noises.

"I better go." I stood and dusted crumbs from my jeans.

"What should I wear to ride?" She looked down at her bright green Sketchers. "I don't have boots."

"Jeans and sneakers are fine."

"'Kay." She rose, picking up the dishes with her. "See you Saturday, then."

With El Cid beside me, I walked down her driveway. I swore my feet had doubled in size since I sat down on her porch. And why were my arms swinging all goofy-like? Was she watching me? The thought made me stumble. Face on fire, I glanced back. The porch was empty.

Why did I feel disappointed?

17

All the way home, I mentally tried out fourteen ways to mention Perry's riding lesson to El Cid. And to my father. Rejected all of them.

"Perry certainly is a charming young lady," El Cid said. "It was nice of you to befriend her, seeing that she's new here."

"I didn't *befriend* her. We just hung out. And don't say anything to Dad or Ben about it, okay? Especially Ben. You know how he is."

"I do indeed."

Reaching the yard, El Cid stopped at the bottom of the porch steps and waited until I slid off. As he wandered over to the water barrel for a drink, I caught the drone of the television through the screen door. Dad watched the Weather Channel like other men watched sports. Old school rancher blood ran deep in the guy.

"We're home," I yelled.

"You two were gone a long time," Dad called back. "I was beginning to think you went to Nebraska for the soda."

"Sorry." I hesitated, then cranked up my courage. "I was hanging out with Perry. We just sat on the porch." Preemptive move on my part.

"Perry Vandermer?"

"Yeah. She and her mom are renting a house across from the 7-Eleven. Just until the camp is ready." I held my breath, waiting to see what *that* piece of information would do.

"That is nice. Go help your brother."

Mission accomplished. I trailed after the gray. Once inside the barn, I fanned my T-shirt, relishing the cool air of the building. At the back, Turk lurked in the gloom like some sort of vampire horse, afraid of sunlight.

From the corner she had claimed, Izzie nickered a greeting. An enormous pile of straw was heaped at her feet.

I eyed the mound. "Wow."

"Tell me about it." She sighed.

"Last one." Ben carried another armload over and dropped it. He spread it around with a foot. "There. Try that."

"You don't have to do this every day, you know. It's kind of overkill." She tested the pile with a front hoof. "I might get lost in that."

Ben laughed. Spotting me, he motioned toward the storage bins. "Your turn to wait on *El Chapo*." He tugged on Izzie's mane and left.

I removed El Cid's saddle and halter and hauled them to the rack. Wiping the cinch clean of sweat and hair, I glanced over at Turk. He stood motionless, head high and staring at me. He reminded me of a black cobra waiting to strike. "The usual?"

He grunted.

I opened the metal storage bin with a clang, scooped out two helpings into a bucket, and carried it to his feed tub. "Anything else?" *Mastah*. I fought a grin, remembering Perry's imitation of Igor.

"No." He bent his neck and began crunching away.

I gritted my teeth. Another warm and heartfelt exchange. What my father saw in the black stallion was beyond me. The couple of times I had asked him, he said that Turk was exactly what our family needed. Like what—a sociopath with four hooves? Why would anyone need that?

"You're welcome," I sneered.

I walked over to El Cid. My thoughts looped back around to my earlier problem. *Maybe I could just go to Perry's and not mention it to anyone. Like it was no big deal.* I eyed the gray. *But what about El Cid?* The gleam in his eyes stopped me cold. "What?"

"Something's afoot," he said.

"What do you mean?" Stalling for time, I headed back to the bins. I felt his attention on me the whole way, an itch between my shoulder blades. After filling the bucket with mixed oats and grains sweetened with molasses, I sprinkled in the powdery vitamin supplement Kathleen had left for us and mixed it with my hand.

"You're up to something," he said as I poured his supper into the feed tub, the grain pinging merrily. "I can hear your brain whirling away."

"Well, kind of." I leaned forward and whispered, "But just between you and me, okay?"

"That depends." El Cid lowered his voice, too. "Does it involve you doing something foolish or dangerous?"

"It's about Perry."

"Ah. Hazardous on another level."

"You know she's horse crazy."

"As many girls are."

I peeked over El Cid's neck. Good. Izzie and Turk were both nostril deep in their meals. "Perry asked if she could...you know."

"I do not. Enlighten me."

"Go riding."

"Horseback riding?"

"Yeah."

"On *me*?"

"No, on Turk—she's got a death wish." I made a face. "Yes, on you."

"And what was your response?"

"I told her it'd be all right. Day after tomorrow. Around ten." I crossed my toes inside my shoes and waited.

He lowered his head and lipped up a mouthful then munched in contemplation, molars grinding away. "Well," he said, a few grains dribbling out. "Since you've committed us to this course, I would be churlish to say no. However, you should speak to your father about it. You know how he is about such things."

"Yeah, you're probably right." I blew out a long breath. "Now all I have to do is keep Ben from finding out. He'll make my life miserable."

"The prerogative of an older brother."

"Man, that's for sure." I sighed. "Why couldn't I have been born first?"

అలా

All through supper, I tried to figure out some way to get Dad alone so I could ask him about Perry. I kept eyeing him as I ate, struggling to think of an excuse.

"I know that look." Dad twirled another bite of spaghetti around his fork. Thursday night was pasta night.

I made my face go as blank as a whiteboard during summer break. "What look?"

"You want to ask me something that you already know the answer to. Or you want to confess something that is going to make me wish I had stayed single and childless." He paused, the fork halfway to his mouth. "Did something happen when you were with Perry?"

"Was *that* where you were all afternoon? At *Perry's*?" Ben's face lit up. "Well, what do you know—miracles do happen. Baby brother has a girlfriend. Dude, I'm impressed. You just met her last week."

"Shut up, Ben."

"Do not use that phrase," Dad said automatically. "It is rude. Now, what happened—"

"So, have you two kissed yet?" Ben pushed his empty plate aside and leaned forward. "Or are you still at the holding sweaty hands stage? Because if you need any pointers, I'd be happy to—"

"Wait, I take it back," our father said. "Shut up, Ben. Better yet, go away."

Smirking, Ben rose and carried his plate to the sink. "Can I take the truck into town?"

"Why?"

"I don't know. Just to go somewhere."

To me, that wasn't a reason. But it seemed to make sense to Dad. His expression softened. Leaning to one side, he dug the keys out of his pocket and a twenty out of his wallet. He held up both. As Ben started to take them, he pulled them back out of reach.

"Top off the gas tank. Be back in an hour. Do not do anything stupid."

"When have I ever?" He flashed a grin and left. A few minutes later, he drove away. The bass on the radio thumped loud enough to rattle the kitchen window.

Dad shook his head then settled in his chair. "So. Matt. *¿Qué pasa?*"

"Well, Perry asked me if she could..." The rest of the words died. A flare of embarrassment swept over me. My palms and armpits grew damp. The memory of the talk Dad and I had had earlier in the year—*that* talk—came back to me. Oh boy.

"If she could what?"

I took a deep breath. "If she could try riding El Cid."

Dad rubbed the back of his neck. "I do not think that is such a good idea. Too many things could go wrong."

El Cid's words came back to me. *Talking horses and magical weapons and creatures that go bump in the night are all just too much for the average person to believe in. You know this. And what people don't understand, they fear. And what they fear, they often grow to hate.*

"And, anyway, it is up to El Cid," he continued. "I doubt he would go for it."

"I already asked. He's cool about it."

Dad's eyebrows flew up. "He is usually more cautious." A long silence. Then a hint of a smile pulled his goatee to one side. "Well, if he approved." He nailed me with his eyes. "El Cid is in charge. Ride only around Huerfano. And..."

"And what?" A part of me already regretted saying yes to Perry. The same part wished the only thing I had to worry about in life was hunting monsters. *When did everything get so complicated?*

Silence filled the kitchen. The only sound was the slow drip of the kitchen faucet and the ticking of the cooling burner on the stove.

"Dad?" I prodded him. *Just get this over with.*

Running a thumb along his jaw, he studied the air between us. "Perry seems like a fine girl. Or a young lady, I should say."

The change in subject caught me by surprise, but okay. "Well, yeah."

"And I do not have to remind you to be respectful? Especially to young ladies?"

I caught myself from rolling my eyes just in time. "Yeah, yeah. And we had this talk already, remember?"

"It bears repeating. I want people to look at my sons and say there goes a—"

"A gentleman. *Un caballero.*" I exaggerated my accent just enough to inch up to the smart-mouth line but not cross it.

Dad was pretty good about letting Ben and I stretch that line, but once across it, we knew our father would be waiting—and willing—to smack down a disrespectful son. My brother stepped across that line so many times, I wondered why he just didn't leave his shoes on the other side.

"Perry and I are just in the friend zone. Nothing more."

"That zone has a way of shifting its boundaries. Be aware." He grinned, his teeth a flash of white in his tanned face. "Your turn with dishes." Pushing away from the table, he headed into the living room and clicked on the television.

After I went to bed, I lay awake. Hands clasped behind my head, I stared up at the ceiling and thought about that zone. And shifting boundaries. How did other kids know about this stuff? Was I the only one who didn't have a clue?

"Bet you ten bucks a skinner eats Allbury by supper." Standing beside El Cid's head at the end of the Gate, I stared down into the valley.

A lanky figure paced back and forth among the boulders, a bundle of short wooden stakes in one hand. Allbury's khaki shirt matched the sand and a wide brimmed hat shaded his face. His Land Rover was parked nearby. As I watched, he thrust one of the stakes into the ground, walked a few paces, and planted another one.

"You mean, eats him *for* supper," Ben said.

Izzie chuffed. "Good one." She nudged his shoulder with the side of her nose.

I inched closer to the gray, grateful for any shade from the afternoon sun. A few feet away, Dad leaned on a boulder, his elbows propped on the top of the rock and his hat shoved back. He peered through a pair of binoculars pressed to his face.

"What's he doing?" I asked. "Looking for fossils already?"

Dad adjusted the focus. "Probably marking the location for the camp site."

"What about the coffer? What if they find the cave?" An image of the scientists opening the chest in the middle of their camp—and the skinners bursting out into the sunlight—played in my head. Just like that scene in the first Indiana Jones movie, when the bad guys opened the Ark and got melted. Nazi popsicles on a hot day. Yeesh. I ordered myself to think of something else, but another image—that smaller coffer, the Red Casket—showed up. I shoved that one away, too.

"The cave is well hidden. A person would have to know to search behind that huge block." He lowered the glasses. "He is fortunate that the skinners seem to have backed off."

"Because of us?"

"Possibly. Our increased presence may have forced the creatures to stay hidden for now. Still, we better go and talk with him. Try again."

"It'll be a waste of time," Ben said. Eschewing the stirrups, he grabbed the horn and swung into the saddle. Big show-off. "He thinks we're just a bunch of ignorant Mexicans."

"Then let us prove to him otherwise." Dad mounted and adjusted his hat. "Turk."

The black led the way at a ground-munching lope. As we neared, Allbury turned at the rumble of hooves, hesitated for a moment, then sauntered over and met us.

"Dr. Allbury."

"Hello again, Javier."

Allbury studied us through his thick glasses, eyes lingering on our iron maces hanging from the saddle horns. Turk stomped a hoof and shook his head, sending his black mane flying. The scientist eased backward. I could almost hear his thoughts: *Move slowly. Don't make eye contact.*

"Do not frighten him, Turk." Dad patted the stallion's neck. "So. Any chance of me talking you out of this?"

The man kept one eye on Turk. "You mean setting up camp here? Or the dig itself?"

"Both."

"Look." Allbury removed his hat and took a step toward Dad. He froze when Turk showed his teeth. "I don't understand why you're so set against me and my team working here." Tucking the bundle of stakes under one arm, he began ticking off on his fingers. "We're not anywhere near your ranch. We have the permission of both the federal and state authorities. And, even more importantly, this area holds some of the richest fossil deposits in the western United States."

"That will mean nothing if you are dead." Dad rested an arm on the saddle horn. "The Maze has claimed the lives of too many innocent people over the years."

"Accidents." Allbury flapped his hat, dismissing Dad's warning. "Careless accidents. Regrettable, I agree, but people need to accept a certain amount of risk if they decide to explore in here. And with any kind of field work, risk is part of the job."

"What about that dig back in the 1940s? The one under Dr. Elmer Riggs who discovered the *Apatosaurus excelsus* fossil?"

Ben and I exchanged furtive glances, my brother reining in a grin. Throwing out arcane facts and Latin words while mounted on horseback and wearing a cowboy hat was how our father rolled.

"The camp was attacked one night," Dad continued, "and most of the workers were killed. They tried to cover it up, but the few survivors claimed it was some sort of enormous dog-like creature. More than one."

For a long moment, Allbury stared at him, mouth open. "H-how do you know about that?"

"Because my grandfather was one of the locals who rode to their aid."

Actually, I knew that Mateo Francis Del Toro was the *only* local who helped after one of the survivors stumbled out of the Maze and limped the two miles to our ranch. I always tried to imagine what my great-grandfather must have looked like riding into that destroyed camp at dawn, mounted on a snow white mare and an iron mace in one hand.

Allbury shook his head. "Not buying that story. Dogs, even in a pack, rarely go after people."

"It was wolves," I blurted out. "Big ones."

He snorted. "I happen to know, young man, that there are no wild wolves left in Colorado."

"That's what makes them so dangerous." Ben picked up the corner of the fable we were weaving. "People don't believe they're still around, but they are. Folks are usually convinced when it's too late."

"Too late?"

"Yeah, right when a body part's being chewed off."

Allbury looked at Dad, who added with a straight face, "It is a rare species native only to the Maze. *Canis lupus labyrinthum*. It is much larger than a regular wolf, and with a red instead of gray pelt. Trust me, my friend. Once you have seen one, you will never forget it."

Under me, El Cid shook with silent laughter. I knew the geek side of him was dying to be part of the conversation.

Allbury's face tightened with a mix of suspicion and determination. "This dig will proceed as planned." He clapped his hat back on his head. "And just to ease your concern, I'll make sure my people are armed and work in teams. Surely those wolves, or whatever they are, won't attack a camp full of people. Not with generators running and campfires and all that?"

Dad gathered up the reins. "That depends."

"Depends on what?"

"On how hungry they are." He clucked his tongue. Turk planted his hind feet, whirled around, and lit out for the Gate. The rest of our posse fell in behind him.

El Cid caught up with Turk. "Really, Javier? *Canis lupus labyrinthum?*"

"Clever, no?" Dad winked at Ben and me.

The gray sniffed. "I thought it was a bit pedantic."

Dad raised an eyebrow. "Thus spaketh the kettle."

El Cid flattened his ears. "*I* am not pedantic. Oh, and by the way, are you certain of your Latin? *Labyrinthum?*"

Dad thought for a moment. "The declension may be wrong."

It was conversations like these that made Ben and I dream of running away and joining something more ordinary than our family. Like a circus.

Just as we reached the edge of the valley, all three steeds slammed to a stop, ears pointed back. Yanking my mace from the horn, I swiveled around, trying to spot the skinners coming for us. Then I heard a scream. A human scream.

Dad cursed under his breath. "Exquisite timing. All right, *mis amigos*. Top speed." The steeds spun around in a synchronized move and took off

"Sure would've been nice," Izzie shouted as we pounded along, "if the skinners could've attacked the guy *before* we got all the way to the Gate."

"But if he gets eaten," Turk pointed out, "that'd solve a lot of our problems."

For once, I agreed with the stallion.

Squinting into wind, I spotted Allbury. In spite of what Turk had said, I sagged in relief at the sight of the guy perched on top of a massive boulder twice the height of a warhorse. At its base, a skinner stood on hind legs, front paws clawing and jaws snapping. How Allbury managed to scramble so far up was beyond me. Guess a guy could do amazing feats when being chased by meatloaf with fangs.

"Maybe," I yelled at El Cid, "he'll believe us now."

At the rumble of our Del Toro thunder, the skinner jerked its head around and bared its teeth. With a snarl, it slunk away, running eastward across the valley. A black cloud of flies hurried to keep up. They disappeared behind a jumble of rocks.

That's right, you piece of rump roast, I thought. *Get out of here before we go Santiago on you.*

We skidded to a halt in a cloud of dust and lots of unnecessary snorting on Turk's part. Chest heaving, Allbury crouched on his haunches, knees almost level with his ears. He squinted down at us. Something about him seemed different. I mean, beside the fact that he looked like he was about to pass out. Then it struck me. His glasses were missing. A crunch under El Cid's hoof told me where they might be. I jumped down and began searching.

"Javier. Thank heavens," Allbury gasped. "W-was that one of those *wolves*?"

"In the flesh," Ben said, "so to speak."

"It came out of nowhere." Allbury coughed, patting his chest. "And the stench was overwhelming."

"It did not bite you?" Dad studied the man.

Allbury glanced down at his arms and legs. "No. No, I don't think so."

"What exactly did you see?"

"A swarm of flies was bothering me. I knocked my glasses off waving them away. Before I could find them, I caught a blur of motion out of the corner of my eye." He laughed shakily. "I must admit, all your talk of wolves made me jumpy. I should've run for my vehicle, but I was up on this rock before I knew it."

"Your speed saved your life." Dad rose in his stirrups and looked around. "You will not be as lucky next time."

"I don't believe in luck, bad or good. I believe in preparation and strategy." Allbury took a deep breath, and another. "I was a fool not to carry a rifle with me. I should've known better after my last project in Tanzania. Hippos. Extremely territorial. And deadly. From now on, I'll be armed."

"Won't do you any good," I muttered before I could stop myself.

Allbury squinted down at me. "I beg your pardon? What did you say?"

"Nothing." I picked up his glasses. "Here. I found these." One lens was cracked. I remounted and stood in the stirrups and passed them up to Allbury.

Stretching down, he took them from me. He frowned at the broken glass, then put them on. "Thank you, Ben."

Whatever. I touched El Cid with a heel and he backed out of the way. Scooting on his bottom, Allbury inched down the rock. He slid the final five feet and landed on the ground with a grunt.

Straightening, he adjusted his glasses. "Well, that was exciting."

"Exciting enough to convince you to abandon the dig?" Dad asked.

"As I said before, risk is inherent in this line of work." Allbury began sidling over to the vehicle. Reaching it, he paused, one hand on the handle. "Thank you for running that wolf—if it was a wolf—off. I hate to be rude, but I still have a great deal to do before the first of my crew arrives next week."

"*Next week?*" My voice cracked in surprise.

"Yes, yes." Opening the door, Allbury climbed inside. "Most of them will be here by next Wednesday. Thursday at the latest. A day to settle in, then the real work begins." He started up the engine, powered down the window and leaned out. "And just so you know, as of Monday, this valley is off limits to the general public. All visitors must check in at the site's headquarters. Government safety protocol. Antiquities protection regulations. I'm sure you understand."

Without waiting for a reply, he drove off, his SUV bouncing across the uneven ground. Roaring up the slope, the vehicle disappeared through the Gate. The engine's growling echo remained.

"Are all humans that clueless?" Izzie asked El Cid.

I noticed he didn't answer.

19

Saturday morning. Operation Perry. After breakfast, I escaped to the barn, desperate not to give Ben any more big brother ammo. To kill time, I raked up the old straw and wheel barrowed it out the back door. I spread it around the field and let nature do its thing. El Cid and Izzie grazed nearby. Their teeth ripped up the grass. It sounded like giant zippers opening and closing. Some distance away, Turk stood alone. Naturally.

Finished with my chore, I stowed the tools, then stuck my head out the back door. "El Cid. Time."

"What's going on?" Izzie asked around a mouthful of grass.

"Oh, we're simply taking a little jaunt." El Cid jogged over and squeezed past me.

"Can I come?"

"Not this time, Iz." I hastily closed the door.

I groomed and saddle El Cid as fast as I could. We would've been ready sooner, but he made me comb out his mane and tail. Twice.

"You act like you're going on a date with her," I complained, detangling a couple of strands.

"And you're not? I happen to know that you're sporting a new shirt."

I made a face. He had me there. I chucked the comb toward the storage box, then swung into the saddle. "Let's move before Ben shows up."

We trotted out of the yard, both of us keeping eyes and ears peeled toward the house. I let out a sigh when we rounded the Hump. El Cid slowed to a swinging walk.

One landmine avoided. One to go.

As we traveled along, worry worms hatched in my gut, squirming. "This is worse than hunting skinners."

"She's probably just as nervous."

"Yeah, right." Was she really? That helped. A little. The whole way there, I debated turning around and going back home. But I didn't. *Courage is as much about battling our fears as it is battling our foes*, Dad's voice whispered in my head.

Perry was waiting in front of her house. She waved when she spotted us and hurried down the drive. "Hey, handsome." She patted El Cid. "Oh, and hi to you too, Matt."

"Funny." My anxiety loosened a notch. I swung out of the saddle. "You ready?"

"Beyond ready. I sliced up an apple for him." She held up a plastic sandwich bag. "Is that okay?"

El Cid opened his mouth. Just in time, I elbowed him in the ribs. "Sure. He'd like that."

He crunched on the treat, dribbling bits of fruit out of his mouth in a totally non-El Cid way, the big ham. The whole time, she studied his headstall.

"This may be a dumb question, but don't bridles have that bar thing that goes in the horse's mouth?"

"It's called a bit. And yeah, most do. But we've trained our horses to a simple halter."

"Why?"

Because it's hard to talk around a piece of stainless steel in your mouth. "Just another way of riding."

"Oh." She wiped her hands on her jeans. "Well, now that I bribed him, maybe he won't buck me off."

"He'd never do that. Like I said, he'll take care of you. He's got a reputation to hold up."

"What's that mean?"

"Nothing." I guided her around to his near side. "You always mount and dismount on the left."

"Why?"

I hesitated. Would she laugh? Then, I remembered this was the girl who pointed out the humongous plot hole in *The Lord of the Rings* that I'd totally missed. "Well, there's this old legend, and I don't know if it's really true, but most knights wore their swords on their left side, so that they could draw it with their right hand. So, when they mounted their warhorses, they had to mount from the left or they would sit on their sword."

"Even with armor on—ouch."

I grinned. The last of my nervousness faded away. "Okay, watch how I do this. Reins in your left hand. Grab the horn in front and the cantle in the back. Put your left foot in the stirrup. Give a bounce on your right leg, then pull yourself up." I did it in slow-motion, exaggerating each step. It felt awkward having to think about the separate moves. I dismounted the same way. "You try."

Halfway up, Perry faltered. She clung to the side of the saddle, her right leg flailing. A warning nicker from El Cid. Without thinking, I put my hand on her bottom and boosted her the rest of the way.

"Thanks." Legs dangling and hands gripping the horn, she stared wide-eyed at the ground. "Whoa. He's taller than I thought he'd be." She shifted in the saddle. "What do I do now?"

"Feet in the stirrups. Let me fix them for you—they're too long." I adjusted one stirrup, then the other, then guided her feet into the correct position. "Drop your heels down, like you're trying to drag them through the dirt. Keep the stirrups under the balls of your feet. That's right. Your legs and spine will act like shock absorbers, especially when he trots."

"Like when I stand up on my bike pedals going over rough terrain?"

"In a way. Now, just hold the reins in your hands, but don't pull on his halter. El Cid knows what to do. If you start to slip or get nervous, squeeze the biscuit."

She eyed me like I had grown a third nostril. "What the what?"

"Grab the saddle horn. And don't worry about falling off. There's plenty of ground and you won't miss it."

I decided making Perry laugh was a pretty cool thing. Didn't know why. It just felt good.

"There's a lot more to riding than I thought there'd be," she said, adjusting her feet.

"There's an old saying—it might help you remember the important stuff: 'Heels down and head up. Knees down and heart up. Ankles close to your horse's side, elbows close to your own.'"

Walking like he was balancing an egg on his back, El Cid made a large loop around the workday empty road. Even though Perry had good balance and a natural seat, he acted like he was afraid she would fling herself off into midair.

"She's doing great—er, I mean, *you're* doing great. Now, squeeze your legs to signal him to go faster."

Mouth pursed in concentration, Perry swayed in rhythm with El Cid's longer stride. On the next circuit, I heard her whispering to herself. "Heels down and head up..." Without being asked, he broke into a jog delicate enough to rock a baby to sleep. Perry gasped and grabbed the saddle horn, hooting with delight as she bounced along.

"Heels down." I stepped into the middle of the road and stood there like a riding instructor. "That'll keep your weight in the saddle and around your horse's barrel."

She circled me twice, beaming the whole time, before pulling back on the reins with a timid tug. El Cid slowed to a brisk walk, his head bobbing in satisfaction, then halted.

"How was that?"

"It was like..." She screwed up one side of her face in thought. "Like his legs were my legs. Oh, I can't explain it." She clapped a hand to her heart. "Words fail me. Which is a first."

"Want to try galloping?"

"Really?" Her eyes widened. "You think I'm ready?"

"Sure. People don't realize it until they ride for the first time, but a gallop is easier to sit than a trot." I pointed up the road toward our ranch. "We can go that way. Won't be any traffic."

"By myself?"

"I could ride with you." Where in the world did *that* come from?

"Would you? I mean, can he carry two people?"

El Cid snorted. I stifled a laugh.

"Like a boss. After all, this is a breed that carried knights in full armor. He could probably carry *three* people at a dead run. Slide your left foot free." Reaching around Perry, I grabbed the horn, stuck my boot in the stirrup, and swung up onto the stallion's broad haunch.

"Here." Perry held the reins out to one side. "You steer."

I took the reins, my entire being hyperaware of how close we sat. Awkward didn't begin to describe it. But, in some bizarre way, it felt *not* awkward. An abrupt move from El Cid and she fell back against me. *Really, dude?* I swore I heard him chuff with amusement.

"Sorry. Lost my balance." She straightened and gripped the horn with two hands, leaning forward more than was necessary. Guess she felt weird, too. Which was weirder because I assumed girls never felt like that.

I tapped El Cid once with a heel. He took a couple of running steps, eased into a gentle lope, and pointed his nose toward the ranch. We flew along, Perry bouncing a lot less than I would've on my first ride.

"The more you relax," I said over the creak of leather, "the easier it is. Trust El Cid. He'll never do anything that'd make you fall."

"Right." She eased up on the horn, holding it lightly with one hand. "Oh, I get it." She shifted and started moving in rhythm with his stride.

"How's that feel?"

"It's *magic!*"

Yup.

After a hundred yards, El Cid slowed to a walk. I wondered why. Then, I spotted a cloud of dust from an approaching vehicle. I sighed as I caught the bass rumble of Dad's truck.

"Is that your father?"

"Yeah. He's probably going into town for the mail." *Man, he better not be checking on me. Not cool, Dad. Not cool at all.*

"Is he okay with me riding your horse?" She sounded nervous.

"I told him the other day."

"Good. I wouldn't want him to get mad or anything. He seemed kind of...you know...when I first met him."

"You mean all serious?"

She nodded, her attention on the truck. "Mom calls him intimidating."

For a moment, I tried to see my father through Perry's eyes: a stern-faced man who acted and moved like a soldier. But all I could see was my dad. "He's fine with us riding, as long as we stay around here."

El Cid moved to one side of the road. The truck slowed with a squeal of brakes, the morning sun showing off its dirty windshield. Rolling to a stop, Dad rested an elbow on the open window frame and tugged the brim of his hat in greeting. "Perry. It is good to see you again."

"Hi, Mr. Del Toro."

"Are you enjoying your ride?"

"Beats mountain biking by a billion to one. Mom said to thank you for letting me try it." She ran her palm along El Cid's neck. "He's incredible."

"He is that." Dad's eyes twinkled. "And Matt is not too bad, either."

Parents being funny. *Gah, kill me now.* Over Perry's head, I scowled at him. Which, of course, pulled his grin wider.

"You could not have two finer teachers. But, do not ride *too* far this first time." He lobbed a silent message at me. *Do not ride to the ranch.*

"We're turning around now." I lobbed the message right back.

"I will be home in an hour. If Ben is still in bed, tell him to get his lazy self up and get his chores done. We have an appointment later."

"Got it." I could tell from his expression that the appointment involved monsters and a warhorse or two.

"Perry, please tell your mother hello from me." He touched his hat brim again and drove away.

We waited until the dust from the truck settled, then rode back, switching gaits the whole way. By the time we reached her home, Perry was holding the reins and I was trying to figure out what to do with my hands.

"Wow. That was amazing." Swinging a leg over the horn, she dropped to the ground with a grunt and looped her arms around El Cid's neck. He nuzzled her shoulder.

"You did good. Want to try again?"

"Kidding, right?"

I laughed. "Okay, we'll work another time." I clambered forward into the vacant saddle and fumbled with the reins, eyes fixed on the gray's ears. *Now what do I do? Just ride off? Dismount and walk her to the door?*

Perry rescued me. "Um, thanks again, Matt. See ya later."

Before I could signal him, El Cid trotted away. The whole time, I wondered—was I supposed to look back? Maybe wave? We rounded a bend in the road. Decision made. Oh, well. I settled into the saddle, my feet dangling past the shortened stirrups.

"Perry will make a fine equestrian," El Cid said. "She has a natural seat, a light hand, and good balance. Rather reminds me of your mother."

"She does?" Gentle warmth welled up inside of me. It dawned on me, although I must've known it, that El Cid also lost someone he loved when Mom died.

I only remembered her in tiny scenes that zipped through my memory like a television commercial, the kind with people talking in short bursts. Most of the stuff they said didn't make any sense to me. No theme music, either. Just the sound of her voice, a fall of dark hair brushing my cheek, and the aroma of soap and horses.

Of course, Ben knew her longer than I had. Her death was a lump he couldn't dissolve. Not with tears or breaking things or screaming at our father when he was younger. Or locking horns with Dad as he got older.

I think that was why my brother Greyhounded away each spring for a month or so. Just to get a break from the fighting. I had a feeling that if Ben didn't make that annual trip to the Navarres, Dad would have.

"Do you miss her?"

"I do. Celia Montoya-Del Toro was a dear friend and plucky fellow conspirator."

"Conspirator?"

El Cid nodded his head in rhythm with his stride. "In keeping a certain stubborn *hombre* safe. Even if that man complained about being coddled. I promised her, the day I arrived, that I would do whatever was necessary to keep not only Javier safe, but her and young Ben as well." He sighed.

"It wasn't anyone's fault." I repeated Dad's words. "It was just bad luck."

"Perhaps." He shook his mane. "Enough gloom. Would you like to hear something heart-warming and quite sentimental about your mother and you?"

"I don't know. Do I?"

"You've no choice in the matter unless you wish to foot it home." He settled into a swinging walk, a gait he could hold for a day and a night without tiring. "When you were just two days old, your mother carried you out to the barn. A sweet, warm, quiet spring evening, if I recall. Not anything like the wrinkly little creature she carried in a blanket."

"Hey."

He chuckled, ribs rising and falling. "Celia held you up to me and you reached out with a hand that felt no bigger than a mouse's paw and touched my nose. Then she said to me, 'El Cid, I know how much you love Jav and Ben and me, but do you have room in your heart for one more?'"

It took me a moment to make sure my voice wouldn't do something to embarrass me. "What'd you tell her?"

"Why, I told her that I had plenty and to spare." He lifted his head, letting the wind blow his forelock off to one side. Then, he spoke softly, as if to himself. "I would have never guessed that one so small would take up so much room."

"They're moving in!"

At Ben's shout, I let go of the bag of grain I was dragging along the truck's bed. He and Izzie galloped into the yard. Sweat marred her coat. The dark streaks looked like blood—the kind you get with a double nostril nose bleed.

Our father had been sending one of us to the new road several times a day since last week. He called it keeping an eye on things. We called it spying.

Leaning on the truck's open tailgate, Dad blotted his face on the shoulder of his T-shirt. "How many?"

"Two camper trailers and four other vehicles. I saw Vandermer's car, too." He jumped down from Izzie, whom he had ridden bareback and without a halter. "Thanks, Iz."

She gave a nod, then plunged her muzzle into the water barrel and began slurping. El Cid and Turk appeared, jogging around the corner of the barn, their ears pricked. All of us eyed my father. I wondered what he was going to do. Stand guard in the Maze all summer?

Without a word, Dad reached into the truck and hauled another fifty-pound bag from the bed, threw it over a shoulder, and carried it into the barn. To my astonishment, Ben grabbed another and hoisted it up as easily as our father. When had he gotten that strong? I jumped down and trailed after them, ready to be out of the sun before I melted into a puddle of Matt. The horses followed me in.

"So, what's the plan?" Ben dropped his bag on top of the others stacked along the wall next to the feed bins.

"We will drive out and talk with Liz. With any luck, Allbury told her and the others about the attack last week. We will use that as an excuse to warn them once again." Dad shifted the bags and stacked them more evenly. "Not that it will do much good at this point."

"Do you think Dr. Vandermer is going to go for the whole wolf thing? I mean, she grew up here, right?"

"All we can do is try, Matt. In the meantime, we will keep destroying as many skinners as possible."

"What about Allbury?" Ben slapped horse hair from his shirt. "He said the Maze was off limits to the public."

"He is free to try and stop us." Dad eyed Ben and me. "Can you two handle it if we step up hunting?" We both nodded. He turned toward the horses. "El Cid?"

"Need you ask, Javier?"

"Hey." An idea flared to life in my head. "Maybe we should let them get a look at a skinner or two first. Might be enough to scare them off. Problem solved."

"Or it may bring a flood of biologists and other scientists into the Maze," Dad pointed out, "making the situation even worse. No, we stay under the radar and do this our way." He looked down at his clothes. "Clean up, then we will head over there."

"Are we taking the truck?" Ben asked.

"No, you are not." El Cid stuck his nose in. Literally. "We'll be able to hear or smell if those monsters are anywhere near the camp."

"Besides," Izzie said, eyes dancing. "It's a hoot watching Allbury's reaction to us warhorses. Especially you, Turk. Make sure you snort and stomp in a threatening manner when you're around the man."

"I could stomp *on* the man," Turk offered.

Twenty minutes later, we were all spiffed up and the horses saddled. Dad made us put on clean tees, while he pulled on a crisp white Western shirt, tucking it in neatly and even dusting off his black Stetson.

"Hoping to impress a certain female paleontologist?" Ben teased.

I wondered about that too, but I wasn't going to be the one to ask. Nope, crossing the line with our father was Ben's specialty.

Dad shrugged. "A sign of respect when visiting others. Speaking of impressions—what is this?" He flicked a finger at Ben's hat, a seldom-used straw one that was battered and folded to just the right amount of cowboy vintage coolness. Stampede strings hung down the back, decorated with a hawk feather. "Tell me, my son, are you hoping the crew might include a female college volunteer or two?"

"Never crossed my mind." Ben straightened the hat with a cocky grin. "Just a little protection from the sun."

"Oh, *sí*." A corner of Dad's mouth quirked. "The sun."

Trotting toward the new turnoff, I spotted something in the distance. We rode closer. A sign with an official looking seal was stuck on a post where the two roads intersected.

"'Research Project in Session. Approved Visitors Only,'" I read aloud. "'Thank you for your cooperation. The Field Museum, Chicago.'"

"I hear that's in Illinois," Ben said.

I shook my head. "Man, I can't believe he said that to you, Dad."

"It is the way of things, my son. People will judge us by our name and our looks and my accent. They will think we are uneducated ranch hands, or migrant workers, or illegal immigrants. Or worse, drug dealers or other kinds of criminals. There are a multitude of stereotypes they will assign to us." He nailed Ben and me with eyes the color of El Dorado gold. "I expect my sons to prove them wrong every time."

I made sure I rode tall in the saddle the rest of the way. I noticed Ben did, too. As did our father, of course.

Caballeros all.

છ૦ન્જી

"Holy moly." I stared down at the camp. "They sure didn't waste any time."

Tucked in the southwest corner of the valley, the two trailers sat parked nose-to-nose on either side of a large sandy area cleared of vegetation. In the middle, a fire ring and camp chairs were ready for use. Open air tents, with folding work tables underneath, were clustered to one side of the site. As we watched, personal tents were popping up beyond the trailers, creating a cluster of Gore-Tex igloos.

"Then why are we?" Turk grumbled. "I didn't come here just to stand around and pass gas." He jogged down the slope with my father.

Ben and I followed, choking with laughter. Reaching the valley floor, we laughed even harder when Izzie fell in behind the black stallion and began strutting along, stomping her hooves in imitation. Ears pinned flat, Turk whirled around, almost unseating Dad.

"Uh-oh. Crazy Ivan." She leaped sideways, avoiding the black's snapping teeth, and slammed into El Cid, pinning my leg between them.

I winced. "Hey, watch it."

"Isabel." El Cid staggered a step. "Mind what you're about."

"*Me?*" the mare said. "Jerk's the one who can't take a little teasing."

"That is enough," Dad narrowed his eyes. "Isabel, if you cannot take this seriously, then you and Ben may return home."

"But—" Ben and Izzie said at the same time.

Dad ignored them. "Turk? Stop overreacting to everything. It just encourages them."

"But—" Turk began.

My father turned on me and El Cid. "And you two."

"*Us?*" I pointed at my chest. "*We* didn't do anything, did we, El Cid?"

"Not yet," the older stallion said darkly, glaring at the other horses.

Dad closed his eyes, aimed an index finger at his temple, and mimicked pulling the trigger.

❧❦

We rode into camp under the curious stares of a dozen or so people. Most of them wore shorts and hiking boots and wide-brimmed hats, and all of them were busy hauling crates or unpacking equipment. The area rang with voices calling and the clang of tools. A heavyset woman, brown braids almost to her waist, ducked out from under a canopy.

"Can I help you gentlemen?"

"Good afternoon." Dad tugged at his hat. "I would like to speak with Dr. Vandermer."

"Liz," the woman shouted over her shoulder to the nearest trailer. "You've got a cowboy on horseback who's asking for you."

"Matt."

At the sound of my name, I twisted in the saddle. Perry hurried toward us. She slowed and approached the horses from the front. Smart. I noticed she kept her distance from Turk. Smarter.

"Hey, Perry."

"You guys just get here?" She stroked El Cid's shoulder and beamed up at us. "Hi, Mr. Del Toro. Hi, Brad."

"It's *Ben*," my brother said.

"Oh. Right. Sorry."

"Javier." Liz Vandermer appeared in the trailer's doorway. "I thought that might be you." She walked down the aluminum steps. Her Doc Martins rang on the metal treads. Allbury appeared after her. He grimaced at the sight of us. "Glad to see you ignored Philip's rather rude suggestion that you're not welcome here."

"Liz." Dismounting, Dad removed his hat. "Did Allbury tell you what happened last Friday?"

I noticed all the other scientists had gathered around, listening. So was Perry.

"The attack?" Allbury jumped in before Dr. Vandermer answered. "Certainly. I told everyone, in fact. Although I still find it hard to believe. Wolves in Colorado? Is that possible, Dr. Lewis?"

Lewis flipped a braid over her shoulder and shrugged. "There've been reports of wolves sighted in the northern part of the state. Probably migrated down from Wyoming. So it *is* possible, but highly unlikely. My guess is that it was probably just a feral dog."

At that, the crew relaxed. A few even laughed.

"But you cannot be certain—" Dad began.

"That's right, we can't," Allbury said in a loud voice. "And that's why everyone knows to take the appropriate precautions when they're away from camp. We're not letting a stray dog or two stop us. We've all worked too hard to get chosen for this project and to secure the funding for it. We can't stop now."

Before Dad could try again, the workers nodded, then headed back to their tasks. I overheard one woman say she wouldn't mind adopting any stray dog who might need a home.

Dr. Vandermer raised an eyebrow. "Dog, eh?"

"If only that were so." Dad pulled a slip of paper from his shirt pocket and offered it to her. "Cell reception is sporadic in the Maze, but just in case, here is my number. Call me if there is a need. Any time. Day or night. We will come."

"Goodness, Javier. You keep this up, and I'm going to start thinking there really *is* something to this whole monster thing." With a bemused expression, she took the slip. "But I appreciate your concern. I really do, my old friend. Perry? Back to unpacking."

"Hey, Perry?" An idea formed in my head. "Do you still want to go riding again?"

"And there you go, joking around. You know I do."

"Would that be okay, Dr. Vandermer? We could ride around here." I saw my father stiffen. I widened my eyes and shot a glance at him. *Trust me, Dad. I know what I'm doing.*

"That'd be nice, Matt. Thank you. It'll give Perry something to look forward to. You're welcome any time. All right, let's go, young lady."

Perry scowled. "Come sooner than later. I'm begging you." She dragged after her mother. Allbury smiled coolly and walked away. Soon, we were standing by ourselves.

"Well, that was a bust," Ben said in a low tone.

"Perhaps." Dad swung up on Turk. Worry etched new lines in his face.

We trotted in silence to the Gate. Once through it, Dad asked me, "Matt, what was that all about? Riding with Perry?"

"It gives El Cid and me a reason to hang around camp. We can keep an eye out for any signs of skinners." Would he go for it?

"We don't need a reason to enter here," Turk growled. "Or permission to hunt."

"No," Dad said slowly, "but we do need to keep a low profile. And Matt visiting Perry gives us a cover."

"What good is it sending these two?" Ben jabbed a thumb at me and El Cid. "They're not exactly the A-team. No offense, El Cid."

El Cid mumbled something under his breath.

"Don't you see?" Izzie spoke up. "It gives the rest of us an excuse to tag along. Like we're worried about Matt riding this far from home alone or still worried about that so-called feral dog or something like that. He can even say that's why he carries a mace."

Dad nodded. "And we will alternate pairs. Not only will it give the horses a chance to use nose and ears to spot any skinners, but we also might be able to slip away for more hunting." He slapped me on the back. "Clever, *mijo*."

"More clever than his older brother," El Cid said. "No offense, eh, Ben?"

21

"**M**att." Someone shook me. Hard. *"Matt!"*
I jerked awake, confused as all get out. "D-Dad?"
My tongue didn't want to work. For a second, I
wondered why he was getting me up in the middle of the night.

"Get dressed. Meet us outside. Hurry." He bolted from my
room and yelled for Ben to saddle the horses. Footsteps echoed
up and down the hall.

Heart thundering in my chest, I threw back the covers and
scrambled out of bed. I dropped every article of clothing twice
and managed to pull my T-shirt on inside out. *Boots. Where are
my stupid boots?* I snatched them from under my bed, stomped
my feet into them, then raced to the living room. Dad's and
Ben's maces were missing from the hooks by the door. Grabbing my own weapon, I kicked the door shut with a heel and ran
for the barn. Already saddled, Turk waited in the yard, nose lifted high and ears aimed northward.

"What's going on?" I panted.

"Skinners. At the camp. Vandermer managed to get a call to Javier before her phone went dead."

I darted inside the barn. Ben saddled Izzie, his face pale in the glare of the single bulb above the saddle racks. Nearby, Dad tacked up El Cid for me, his hands moving at warp speed and lips pressed in a razor-thin line.

I hurried to take over. *Please let them be okay. Let Perry be okay.* My stomach twisted tighter and tighter with every second.

For the last week, I had ridden with her almost every day. And every time, Dad or Ben had trailed along behind, pretending to watch over me as they hunted for any signs of skinners. And every day, they came up with a big ol' bucket of nothing. Not even a fly. And even with the whole public-not-allowed thing, Allbury smirked and waved each time he saw my father or brother riding around the perimeter of the valley. I marveled that Dad didn't punch the guy.

But, in spite of the skinnerless-ness, I was having the best summer of my life hanging out with Perry. I could talk with her about everything. Well, *just* about. I think she felt the same way about me.

"Get me out of here," Perry said yesterday as I rode up to her trailer mounted on Izzie. Next to me, El Cid trotted along with an empty saddle, stirrups swaying. Dad was already a small figure on horseback trotting toward the valley's western wall.

"Uh-oh. What happened?"

Her face a thunderstorm, she hopped off the aluminum steps of the trailer. "Mom's driving me insane. If she could, she'd bubble wrap me and stick me in a closet for safe keeping."

"Still won't let you leave camp by yourself?" *And, thank you, Dr. Vandermer.*

"Heck, she barely lets me go with you. It's like she's trying for Helicopter Mother of the Year. Sub-category: western re-

gion, adopted children, families with less than four members."
Fuming, she mounted El Cid.

We headed east toward the far side of the valley and away
from the dig site. The dust rising from beneath the horses'
hooves tasted like June. Cinnamon-y, with a metallic whiff. For
a while, we rode in silence.

"At least you got a mom. Although Dad's okay. And Ben,
when he's not being a jack's hindquarters."

"I'll trade you."

"Your mom? Sure, you can have Turk."

"Tempting." She sighed. "It's not like I *hate* my mom. I
love her. It's just that she tries too hard, you know?"

"Yeah. But *you* don't have a brother or sister who fights
with her on a regular basis. About the stupidest things in the
world." I noticed El Cid swiveled his ears, listening. So did Izzie. I glanced over. "Is that offer to trade still open?"

We laughed. So did the horses, chuffing in low grunts. Perry must have noticed, because she had a way of pursing her
mouth to one side when she was thinking about something or
concentrating.

"You know what, Matt? Maybe our families seem messed
up more to *us* than to the rest of the world." Both horses snorted
in agreement, tossing their heads. Perry beamed. "It's like they
understand me."

"Well…"

"Wouldn't it be cool if they really *could* talk? Like in books
where the characters' dragons or wolves speak to them?"

"Cool. Yeah." Through the saddle, I felt Izzie swell from
suppressed laughter.

Now, as I fumbled with the stallion's cinch in the semi-dark
of the barn, I wished I had told her the truth.

"I'd give anything," El Cid said, "to tell you that it'll be all
right."

"I know." I finished buckling the strap, then leaned against him for a moment, soaking up his warmth, the iron mace heavy and cold in my hand. "Okay. Let's do this." I pushed away and climbed into the saddle.

My brother mounted, too, speaking to Izzie in a low voice. Then, he straightened and pointed his mace at me. "Watch yourself. Stick with El Cid no matter what. Okay?" To my astonishment, he leaned over and gave me a rough one-armed hug.

Dad was waiting for us outside. He nodded once, then said, "Turk." The black stallion whirled around. In two strides, he was gone, swallowed up by the night.

Side by side, Izzie and El Cid raced after him. We galloped around the Hump and down the road, the horses picking up speed on the straightaway. Ahead of us, the lights of Huerfano shone in the darkness.

The land rolled beneath El Cid's hooves. I rose and balanced in the stirrups, trying to ride as light as I could. The night air whistled in my ears; it seemed like hours since I had left my warm bed.

The whistling rose to a shriek. Was it wind? Was a storm coming? I looked up. Clear night, with the stars so thick, they covered the sky in blobs of light.

The shrieks turned into howls.

Skinner howls.

I almost begged El Cid to take me home again. Then I wanted to knock myself on the head with my mace for even thinking that. *Those people need you.* Perry *needs you. You want to be a hunter like Dad? Well, here's your chance.*

We reached the intersection, Dad still in the lead and Ben right on his heels. Ribs heaving, El Cid took up the rear. Ahead of us, the mesa was a giant's castle, black against the stars.

The roar of engines filled the night. Vehicles raced toward us, their headlights slicing the dark as they careened along the dirt road. The first one blasted its horn and zoomed past. Two more followed in a tight row, bumpers to fenders. I coughed, choking on the dust.

Allbury's Land Rover appeared. Dad urged Turk in front of it. The stallion planted himself in the middle of the road, legs apart and head lifted in a surreal game of chicken. The SUV kept coming.

"Dad," I yelled. "He's not stopping. Get out of the way."

"Turk, stand your ground."

At the last second, the vehicle swerved, its engine complaining as it angled off the road and into the tall grass. I spotted Allbury at the wheel. Workers and scientists packed the other seats.

A woman powered down her window—Lewis. Her face was stretched in terror. She gestured frantically. "That chest. Something…some creature," she yelled as they bounced past us. "Liz and Perry. They're trapped and—"

Allbury gunned the motor. The rest of her words were lost.

The warhorses lowered their heads and ran. We blasted through the Gate. The corridor was as dark as the inside of my closet where monsters used to live until I was old enough to learn they existed *outside* my house. El Cid took the slope so fast, I swore his hooves never touched ground until halfway down. Hitting the valley floor with a grunt, the horses gathered their legs beneath them and sped up.

Electric lanterns, scattered around the camp, were smudges of light. Slowing, we dropped to a jog and picked our way through the camp. The only sound was the heavy breathing of the horses.

Tents hung in shreds. Several tables were knocked over, their equipment scattered across the ground. A lone work boot smoldered in the dying campfire. The reek of burning leather made my eyes water.

I glanced at Ben riding next to me. "I don't see any bodies."

"Me neither." He looked as relieved as I felt. "Guess everyone made it out in time."

Except Perry and her mom. Guilt knifed me in the gut. *Why didn't I warn her about the skinners? If she's dead, it's my fault.*

El Cid slammed to a stop. Body tight as a drum, he stared into the shadow of Allbury's trailer. "Javier. Look."

"*Madre de Dios.*" Dad leaped from Turk's back and knelt down.

Please don't let it be Perry. El Cid and I inched closer. "Oh, no," I whispered.

The coffer. It squatted on the ground, the lid twisted and mangled, and wide open. Dad prodded it with his mace. Iron clinked on iron.

"H-how did they find it?" I leaned over. Skinner tracks, too many to count, led away in all directions. "The cave's practically impossible to discover."

"Not impossible enough." Turk curled his lip. "Well, those idiots got what they deserved."

"How can you say such things?" Dad whirled on him, fists clenched. For a split second, I thought he was going to punch Turk right between the nostrils. "No one deserves that kind of death. Especially not innocent—"

A scream rent the darkness. A woman's scream.

"From the north," Izzie shouted.

She and Ben wheeled around. Not bothering with stirrups, Dad grabbed the horn and vaulted into the saddle. Turk was at a dead run even as my father hit leather.

Another scream, this time a girl's.

A massive boulder, like a giant's bald head, loomed ahead in the darkness—the same rock where Allbury had climbed to safety. It seemed like a hundred years ago. Two figures crouched on top, silhouetted against the stars. Skinners danced around the base, snarling and howling and tripping over each other. The hum of flies filled the night.

Rearing up on its hind legs, one of the creatures began clawing its way up the rough surface. The taller of the two figures raised a club-like object and swung. With a yelp, the skinner fell back.

"Ben, you and I will draw the pack away," Dad shouted. "El Cid, you and Matt get them out of here. Head for the Gate."

"He can't carry three," I protested, "*and* run all the way back." *Plus, I don't want us to split up.*

"Watch me," El Cid panted.

"He only has to reach the Gate. Ben and I will fight clear and catch up." Dad raised his mace. "Get ready."

El Cid slowed. A sliver of my brain wondered why he was going along with such a stupid plan. Turk and Izzie rocketed forward, racing neck and neck. The howls grew louder.

"*Santiago!*"

Turk smashed into the pack, sending skinners flying into the air, their paws clawing. Stomping and kicking, he smashed one creature after another under his massive hooves. Dad's mace rose and fell in a blinding speed. Globs of wet meat splattered everywhere. On Izzie's back, Ben clung to the horn as he swung his weapon in a scything action.

Then, we were past.

El Cid skidded around the far side of the boulder, then slid to a halt, mane flying. "Quickly now."

I stood in the stirrups and called out. "Perry. It's me."

Perry's face appeared above my head. "Matt?"

"Hurry." I reached my hand up.

"Matt, what on earth?" Dr. Vandermer appeared, holding a baseball bat. "You need to get out of here. There's wolves or rabid dogs or—"

"I know. My dad and brother are drawing them off. You and Perry need to come with me." I could tell Dr. Vandermer was seconds away from full-out panic mode. I knew exactly how she felt.

"We're not leaving this rock!"

"El Cid and I'll take you to our ranch. It's safe there." At that moment, I heard Dad and Ben gallop away. Had the skinners follow them? I strained to hear as the snarls faded. An odd quiet filled the night. "Listen. They're gone."

Bold words. Wished I believed them. I couldn't stop myself from visualizing skinners hiding on the other side of the boulder. *Knock it off. Don't think about that. Just get them out of here.* "Dr. Vandermer, we really need to move. Like right now."

"Mom." Perry pushed at her mother. "Go with Matt. We can trust him."

"It's too dangerous." She grabbed her daughter's arm. "No, stay here."

"Until what? Help arrives? Mom, this *is* our help." She shook loose. "Follow me." She scooted down the rock on her bottom, then jumped the last few yards and landed with an *oof.*

Dr. Vandermer trailed behind, moving slowly with one hand; the other hand still held the bat. I gritted my teeth and fought the urge to snatch it from her and fling it away. *It won't do you any good*, I wanted to scream.

The whole time, El Cid's ears swiveled around. I wanted so badly to ask him if he heard anything. Or if I was doing this whole rescue thing right. Weird. Not to be able to talk with my best friend when I needed to the most.

"C'mon, Mom," Perry hissed. "Just jump."

As soon as the woman's feet touched the ground, I dismounted and helped her into the saddle. Perry climbed up behind her. Then, I backed away, knees shaking at what I was about to do.

"Change of plan, El Cid. Get them out of here. I'm staying. I'll hide up top of this rock and catch a ride with Dad or Ben. And I bet Dr. Vandermer will let me borrow her bat." Sure hoped I sounded braver than I felt.

Dr. Vandermer looked around, her hands white-knuckled on the saddle horn. "W-who are you talking to?"

El Cid snorted. "We do not have time for a mutiny, Matt. Mount up. *Now.*"

"Not going to happen." I took another step back. "You'll never make it with three."

"You do realize that since I'll not leave you behind, you're ruining any chance of getting Perry and her mother to safety. Perhaps even consigning them to death by skinner."

A gasp from Perry. Both mother and daughter wore identical expressions: wide-eyed with mouths hanging open in disbelief.

"Um…" *How do I explain?* I felt time galloping away. *Just tell them already and step on it.* "Okay, this is going to sound nuts." I paused then blurted out, "Thehorsescantalk."

A long silence.

"Thor's kin tock," Perry said. "What does *that* mean?"

Okay, maybe I said it too fast.

El Cid swung his head around and fixed them with an eye. "What Matt said, albeit a bit awkwardly, is that we warhorses have the gift of human speech. And human intelligence, although overlaid with an equine instinct and world view."

Mouth even wider than before, Perry stared down at me. I could just make out her expression in the darkness. Her lips moved. A sharp inhale. "No. Freaking. Way," she breathed. "H-how…"

"It's a long story."

"And Matt will explain everything. Once we're safe." El Cid flattened his ears. "*All* of us. Right, Mateo?"

"Fine." Ignoring El Cid's gloat of victory, I stepped up on a rock, then squeezed in behind Perry. I felt like I was about to shoot off the gray's hind end.

El Cid started around the boulder, nose held high. He snorted in disgust. "Bleh. The whole area still reeks of those creatures. Amazing how long the stench lasts and—"

A skinner burst from the shadows. It hurled itself at El Cid, jaws snapping like castanets. The stallion staggered from the impact. His back legs buckled.

I fell backward, grasping at the air. For a split second, Perry's fingers gripped mine, then tore loose. With a sickening *whump*, I hit the ground.

Body vibrating from the impact, I lay spread-eagled in the dirt clutching my mace. A voice screamed in my head and ordered me to move my worthless self.

Breathless, I rolled over and scrambled to my feet, swatting at the flies bombing me. The creature crouched a few feet away. It bared its teeth. I bared mine right back and raised my weapon. *Well, c'mon. Show me what you got, Chuckie chuck roast.*

A trumpeting neigh.

El Cid threw himself between me and the skinner. Perry yelled at her mother to hold on, hold on. The monster darted behind and dived low, trying for the stallion's tendon.

Fury erupted in my chest. "*Santiago*," I yelled. For just a moment, I swore I heard my father's voice. Planting my feet, I swung. The mace's iron weight caught the skinner on the side of its jaw. Chunks of teeth and bones and other nasty bits exploded like shrapnel. The headless creature flew through the air and slammed against the boulder. A second later, it vanished with a *pop.*

"Y-you guys okay?" I gasped, my body trembling from the adrenaline rush. Dr. Vandermer nodded. "Perry?" She gave me a thumbs-up.

El Cid flexed a hind leg a few times. "We need to go. Now."

I scrambled onto his back. Struggling to keep my seat— both from El Cid's jarring trot and from sitting practically on the base of the stallion's tail—I craned my neck. Across the valley, dark shapes ran back and forth. A faint shout from Ben. Turk screamed a challenge. *They're still fighting. They're still alive.* I allowed myself a tiny flame of hope. *But for how long?*

Passing through the camp, we slowed to a walk. Dr. Vandermer kept glancing around. Was she looking for bodies, too?

"It's okay," I said before she asked. "I think everyone made it out in time."

At a lope, we headed toward the Gate. With every other stride, I looked back. *C'mon, Dad. Ben. You said you'd catch up.*

"Not to fret, Matt," El Cid said, one ear pointed behind. "They're approaching." He halted with a sigh.

I heard them before I saw them. The kettledrum of hoof beats. Then, two mounted figures raced up. Even before Turk skidded to a halt, my father leaped out of the saddle.

"They are right behind us," Dad gasped. "Liz, you will ride with me. Perry?" He plucked her off the gray and tossed her up on Izzie. "Go with Ben."

Dr. Vandermer slid down awkwardly, legs shaking. Dad helped her onto Turk, then flung himself up behind her. I scooted into the vacant saddle.

Just in time. The pack burst out of the night, eyes popping and venom dripping from every fang.

"Flee," Dad roared.

The steeds galloped flat out, nostrils wide and necks stretched. Chariot horses in the race of their lives. *Our* lives.

"Where are we going?" Dr. Vandermer shouted to Dad.

"Our ranch. You will be safe there."

"But those things will follow us!"

"They cannot escape the Maze. Trust me, Liz."

We charged up the slope and into the corridor's inky blackness. I rode blind, trusting El Cid's better vision. Echoes rebounded from wall to wall.

A new worry perched on my shoulder and whispered in my ear. *Something's wrong with El Cid.* I had ridden the stallion almost every day of my life, and I knew every nuance of his stride.

And his stride was off. Big time.

I leaned forward. "El Cid?"

He just shook his head and kept running.

Final sprint. We broke out of the narrow opening and into the wide, open range. Blowing hard, the warhorses stumbled to a walk. I swiveled around and glanced back. *Sure hope those meat mutts learned their lesson last time.* The skinners milled around, keeping plenty clear of the Gate's outer boundary. After a final challenge of bared fangs, they slunk away. I let out a shaky breath.

"Man, I hate those things." Ben held up his mace and studied it. "It's going to take me forever to dig it out."

"Dig what out?" Perry asked.

"Skinner. Out of the sigils." He held the weapon out to her. "See?"

She leaned away. "I believe you."

We turned our noses for home. The horses walked with lowered heads and dragging hooves, all of them filthy with sweat and dust and leftover monster mash. I swung off El Cid and paced beside him. Worry poked me with every step.

I laid my hand on his wet neck. "What's wrong?"

"Why do you keep asking?"

"You're limping. And you sound like an anti-smoking commercial."

"I simply wrenched my knee kicking that last skinner. And you'd be a tad breathless if you'd just sprinted while carrying three people. Not that I couldn't do it again," he added hastily. "A little rest is all I need." He lowered his head and plodded along.

When we reached the ranch, I wanted to fall down and hug the dirt. Maybe lay there and sleep for a couple of days.

Dad escorted Dr. Vandermer and Perry up the porch steps as Ben and I trailed the horses inside the barn. While Turk took first turn at the water barrel, my brother and I saw to Izzie and El Cid.

I pulled off his saddle and halter, then carried them over to the rack. Over my shoulder, I spotted Ben dishing out grain for Izzie. "You want something to eat too?" I asked. "Oats? Maybe with extra molasses? Or an apple?"

"I'm not hungry. Water would be nice, though, as Turk seems determined to hog the barrel."

I filled a bucket from the hose attached to the outside spigot and carried it over, sloshing water on my jeans. "Here you go."

He drank deeply then raised his head with a sigh. "Oh, that's better." Water dripped from his chin. "Are Perry and her mother all right?"

I glanced through the barn doors toward our house. "Outside of being in shock, I guess so. Dad's taking care of them."

"Good. I'll rest a bit, then perhaps take you up on that offer of oats and molasses in the morning."

"Let me wipe you down before everything hardens. Your coat's a mess." Gore and muck streaked his chest and belly and legs.

"I'd rather just rest in peace, if you don't mind. You can fuss over me later." When I started to protest, he nudged me toward the house with his nose. "Ben's already inside. Go join your family."

Odd statement. "You're my family, too, you know." I smoothed his forelock.

"I always will be." He closed his eyes.

22

I dragged my sorry self across the yard, up the steps, and into the house. The smell of grilled cheese hailed me from the kitchen along with a cheerful sizzle. My stomach gurgled a greeting back.

Perry and her mom sat at the table, blankets tucked around their shoulders and mugs of hot chocolate, loaded with a mound of whipped cream, in their hands. I spotted Dad pouring a splash from a certain bottle into Dr. Vandermer's cup, then his own. Ben stood at the stove, spatula in hand. Smoke rose from the skillet.

"But if you're descendants of knights," Perry was saying as I joined them. My father pushed a hot mug across the table at me. "Why not swords?"

Dad and I exchanged glances. "You explain while I stop your brother from burning our meal." He rose and stepped over to the stove and took the spatula from Ben. "In case you have forgotten, it is called *grilled* cheese, not *scorched* cheese."

I sipped the cocoa and whipped cream concoction; it spread through me like warm toffee. I swiped my lip, just in case, then repeated the familiar lecture. "The mace was a traditional weapon of cavalry back in the day—that's what they were used to fighting with. When the knights went to war on the creatures attacking the people of Spain, it was the weapon they asked the kings and queens to bless. In fact, the mace became the symbol of the Order of the Knights of the Coffer."

"Then, afterward, your ancestor—Santiago Del Toro, right?" Dr. Vandermer pulled the blanket higher. "He *volunteered* to come to the New World?"

"He did," Dad said. "As a sworn knight, he and the others believed they had a duty to not only rid Spain of the invading menace, but also to ensure that those evil creatures would never be a threat to others, especially the indigenous nations of this region. In one of the letters home to his family, Santiago stated that he wanted to make up, to some degree, for what many of the *conquistadors* were doing to this land and its people "

"Good for him." Dr. Vandermer raised her mug. "But, it still seems like an exile. What did he do for a living? Ranching? Mining?"

Taking another sip, I peeked over the rim at my father. I wondered how much he would reveal. Looking just as curious, Ben sank down at the table.

"While I am legally and morally bound to not disclose certain details, I trust you and your daughter enough to say this." Dad flipped a sandwich with a hiss of hot butter and melting cheddar. "The knights and their descendants were granted a stipend, in perpetuity, from the royal family's personal treasury in return for guarding the coffers. It is enough to live comfortably if one is frugal."

"Wait." Dr. Vandermer frowned. "'In perpetuity?' Do you mean that even today...the current king of Spain...?"

"His Royal Highness Felipe VI. *Sí*, every month."

As the adults continued to talk, Perry leaned over to me. "I can't believe this," she waved a hand around, "is *real*. Like *really* real. It's like something out of a movie or a book. Except a bajillion times better."

"Even when the skinners almost ate you?"

"Okay, *that* part wasn't so fun." She raised her mug in salute. "But, thanks to you guys, we're alive."

Dang, she's got guts. If I was her, I'd be a screaming mess. Not sitting here drinking hot chocolate, joking around, and with my face smudged with something best not mentioned.

"It's what we do." I lifted my own drink.

"Oh, and by the way." She socked me in the shoulder. Hard.

"Ow!" My cocoa splashed on the table. "What was *that* for?"

"That's for not telling me about the horses earlier."

"You never asked." I rubbed my shoulder. Man, she packed a punch.

She glared at me in mock annoyance. Then a reluctant grin spread across her face. "I can't wait to talk with them again, especially Izzie." Her face lit up even more. "We talked a little on the way here. She's freaking cool. And El Cid, of course." She hesitated, then added. "But Turk. I mean, he's kind of..."

"Ben and I call him Turk the Jerk."

"Ah."

After we finished the sandwiches and second mugs of hot chocolate, Perry and I were both fighting yawns. Even Ben was blinking and scrubbing his face.

"We should be going." Dr. Vandermer stood up, clutching the blanket. "Except we have no car."

Dad rose as well. "You and Perry are welcome to spend the night here. Or I would be happy to drive you into town if you would feel more comfortable in your own home."

In the end, Dr. Vandermer opted for home. I didn't blame her. While Dad drove them into town, Ben and I cleaned up the kitchen. By the time I stumbled into my bedroom, my eyelids were melting like butter. Crashing face down on the mattress, I buried my nose into the pillow, musing on how to get rid of my boots without moving a muscle.

The next thing I knew, someone was tugging my boots off, first one, then the other. Strong hands rolled me to one side, pulled my bedspread free, and drew it over me. I peeled open an eye.

The light from the bedside lamp cast a glow around the room. But it wasn't anything like the warmth on my father's face.

"You did well tonight, my son," he said softly.

"Thanks. But it was really El Cid and—" A yawn interrupted me.

Dad pulled the bedspread closer to my ears. "Sleep now." He leaned over and kissed my cheek, his beard scratching. "*Te quiero, mijo.*"

"Love you, too, Dad."

☙❧

Matt.

Someone whispered my name. Half-asleep, I lifted my head free of the pillow. Listening. Nothing. Just the normal sounds of our house at night.

Still.

I threw back the covers. Grabbing my sneakers—sneakers were for sneaking—I pulled them on and stepped out. Ben's door was closed. Okay. One down. One to go. I crept to the end of the hall and peered inside Dad's room. He lay sprawled on his back, still dressed, and snoring lightly.

Something was wrong. I couldn't say what or why, but I just knew it. I tiptoed through the house, eased the front door open, and slipped out. To the east, a pale baby blue showed above the horizon. Yawning, I stumbled across the yard to the barn, then grabbed the flashlight hanging inside the door and clicked it on.

"Matt?" A rustle from the top of Izzie's mountain of straw. "What's up?"

"Just checking on you guys." Movement, black on black in the corner, told me where Turk was. Keeping the beam low, I scanned it around. "Where's El Cid?" Uneasiness crept over me.

"Left a while ago to stretch his legs." Izzie yawned. She looked like a donkey hee-hawing in silence. I decided not to tell her that. "Mentioned something about working the stiffness out of his knee. I think."

"Oh, that's right." My anxiety faded. A little. "He said it was bothering him last night. I better go see if he's okay." I clicked off the flashlight and hung it back on the nail, then headed around the barn. The air was cool and dewy and thick with morning. I breathed in the aroma as I walked along.

A pale shape in the distance. *Yup. Just what I thought.*

At the far end of the practice field, El Cid napped with his legs curled under him and his head lowered so much that his nose rested on the grass in front of him. The picture of equine contentment.

"Guess your knee wasn't hurting *that* much," I called, "if you managed to get into that goofy position. By the way, I know your old trick. You're going to let me walk all the way out there, then you're going to jump up and run away..." The words died in my mouth.

He wavered, then toppled over and slumped to one side. Motionless.

My heart stopped. So did the rest of my body. Eyes locked on the gray form, I waited for any sign of movement. A breeze skipped along, bending the tall grasses. It lifted a hank of El Cid's mane, then let it go.

I angled my head toward the house, gaze never leaving El Cid. "Dad." It came out in a whisper. A prayer. I tried again. *"Dad!"*

The scream reminded my muscles how to work. I sprinted across the field, pumping my arms and legs and cursing with every stumble. But, no matter how hard I tried, I couldn't run fast enough.

Then, I was there.

Chest aching, I skidded to a stop and dropped to my knees. The long white mane covered his head like a shroud. I swept it aside and rested my hand on his neck.

One ebony eye, dark and soft, flickered open. All I could see was my reflection.

"Dad's coming, okay?" I threw a frantic glance over my shoulder. My father was sprinting toward us. "Just hang on."

Under my palm, the pulse in his throat jumped and sputtered. Then it slowed. I scanned his body. On his back leg, half hidden by dried muck, twin puncture wounds stared at me in accusation. Guilt sliced me and left me to bleed out.

A soft exhalation. "Not...not your fault."

I knew a lie when I heard one. "Oh, El Cid."

"Matt." Another low sigh. "M-make...room..."

I leaned closer. "What?" *Make room for what?*

His eye closed. His ribs rose once. Twice. Then, not again.

Don't move, don't you dare move, I ordered myself. I held my breath and willed just one more heartbeat under my hand. *If you don't move, he'll come back. Don't even blink. Just wait. However long it takes.*

The crunch of boots on grass. Fear gripped me. What if Dad tried to take me away? Didn't he know I had to wait? Forever if necessary. Wait right here. Until El Cid came back. I hunkered closer, fingers tangled in his mane, and rested my cheek against his.

My father sank down beside me. He placed a hand on the stallion's shoulder and bowed his head. *Dad's waiting too,* I thought. *Good. Maybe if we both stay right here and hang on, we can bring him back.*

I knew El Cid wouldn't leave me if I didn't want him to. Not if I begged him to stay. Not if he knew how much his leaving would hurt me.

But, in the end, he did.

23

The rest of the day, I watched myself from a distance. I walked around. Said words. Think I ate something. But it wasn't really me. The real me was still kneeling in the morning grass, shivering, as I waited for my best friend to come back.

Guilt. So. Much. Guilt. I marveled that my spine didn't snap from its weight. Roman's words kept clanging around in my head. *Remember, Mateo Del Toro, the comfort and well-being of our war-brothers and sisters comes first. The fact that we ride upon them does not mean they are beneath us. No, they eat before us, they rest before us. Everything for them first.*

Sitting in the shade of the porch's top step, I propped my forehead on my knees and stared at the wooden tread between my sneakers. My mace lay beside me. I couldn't stop carrying it around. Maybe I was hoping for an opportunity to use it on myself.

Through the screen, I heard Dad talking with Roman on the phone. He paused and said something to Ben, who answered back. Then the screen door whined. A moment later, my brother sat down next to me.

"Hey." He bumped me with a shoulder. "Want to go into town with me?" He jingled the truck keys in his hand. "Get a soda or something?"

I shook my head. It hurt to talk. I had cried. Hard. So hard. By the time I had finished with the first round of grief, Dad's shirt was damp with snot and slobber and tears. Not all of the tears were mine.

Ben nodded. He tucked the keys into his pocket.

The screen squealed again. "Roman and Kathleen are on their way," Dad said. "Vasco is coming with them to help us hunt down the rest of the pack. They will stay as long as we need them. Matt?"

"Yeah, I know. Change the sheets on both my beds." My room was the automatic guest quarters since it had a pair of twin beds. Which meant I ended up in a sleeping bag on the floor of Ben's room. Not that it mattered. Nothing really mattered anymore.

"What about their ranch?" Ben asked.

"Josefina can manage things. Kathleen pointed out it will be good practice for her, as she will be the one who will take over *Rancho de Navarre* eventually."

I wanted to clap my hands over my ears. *Shut up*, I screamed inside of my head. *Who cares? Who gives a rip about hunting down more skinners or managing a ranch? Or clean sheets? Nothing will ever fix what I did.*

And what I did was let El Cid die. I left him alone in the barn. Didn't take one lousy minute to examine him for bite marks even though he'd been limping. I squeezed my eyelids tight as guilt and sorrow racked me again.

"Scoot over." Dad wedged himself between us. I opened my eyes.

We sat there in silence, shoulders touching. My brain revolved in a sluggish circle. For a moment, I wondered where Turk and Izzie were. Then I remembered. They were standing vigil over El Cid until the Navarres arrived.

My father and brother had spent most of the morning digging a hole. I spent most of the morning with my head buried under a pillow. Even though they worked at the far edge of the field, I couldn't stand to hear the shovels tearing up the grass. Or the thud of clods falling to the earth.

Dad cleared his throat. "Ben? Do you recall when you were five, and Matt had just learned to walk? Oh, you were so frustrated because he could not keep up with you. So, one day, you decided to take matters into your own hands. You snuck away from both your mother and me and dragged your baby brother to the barn."

"Yeah, I kind of remember that."

"There, you looped El Cid's tail through one of the straps of your brother's overalls, then ordered the stallion to teach Matt how to walk faster."

Ben chuckled. "I remember pitching a fit because the old guy just stood there."

Dad pulled something out of his shirt pocket and held it out. A photo. I couldn't help leaning forward for a closer look.

How could a heart keep breaking into pieces if it was already dust?

In the picture, El Cid stood sideways to the camera in front of the barn. His coat was a darker gray than I had ever seen. Head lowered, he peered into the face of a furious Ben, who glared up at him with his chin thrust out and fists on his hips. And there I was. A toddler in a pair of denim overalls, tied to the stallion's tail like a dog on a leash, and beaming. Total goofball.

"As soon as your mother saw you three, she ran back inside for the camera."

"You know," Ben sniffed, then wiped his nose on his sleeve, "a normal mother would've freaked."

Dad laughed softly. "Normal is not in our family's vocabulary."

I didn't say anything. But it helped—just sitting there.

By the time Roman and Kathleen arrived, I felt, well, not better. Not even close to better. Just numb. Even before Roman eased the rig to a stop, Kathleen jumped out of the cab. Without a word, she hugged Dad, then Ben.

Then she turned to me. Before I made a run for it, she pulled me close. For a long minute, she held me. I tried not to tremble. Another failure.

"It's okay to cry, Matt. It's okay to be sad." She stepped back and laid her hands on my shoulders, eyes locked on mine. "But I promise you, you won't be sad forever."

I chomped down on my lip, tasting blood. *Why should I believe you?* I wanted to yell in her face. *You said he'd live for another ten years and maybe more.* I bit harder. It wasn't her fault. And anyway, words weren't doing it for me, so I just nodded and stepped away, playing with the leather loop on the end of the mace's haft.

Roman was gripping Dad's arm while my father stared off at the mountains, jaw clenched. Guess words weren't working for him, either. After a long minute, he took a deep breath, then gave a nod. Without a word, he and Roman walked around to the trailer, unlatched the door, and swung it open.

"Thank you, Roman," a deep voice boomed. The trailer rocked from side to side. An enormous horse, a dappled iron gray with charcoal-black mane and tail, backed out. He dipped his head at Dad. "Javier."

"Vasco."

"I'm sorry for your loss and count it as mine, as well." Vasco sighed. "He was a gifted fighter and a greathearted friend."

The stallion's eyes were sad behind a black forelock that hung almost to his nostrils.

The trailer swayed again. A brown leg, with black stockings that reached to the knees, appeared. Another horse, a bay stallion, stepped out.

The afternoon sun dusted his brown coat—the color of fine mahogany—with gold. It gleamed as he shifted from foot to foot. He shook his head, sending his black mane flying. My heart clenched when I noticed he was about the same height as El Cid, but with a more wiry build.

"This is Rodrigo." Vasco pointed his nose at the younger stallion. "He's been staying with us for a few months. He offered to come along and help on the hunt."

"Call me Rigo." The bay flexed his neck. "Vasco told me about El Cid on our way here. I'm sorry I didn't get a chance to know him." He glanced around. "Any place to get a drink?"

"Barrel by the door." Ben pointed his chin at the barn. "And there's a field to the east if you want to stretch your legs."

It was so much like the day Izzie arrived, I almost laughed. Then it hit me. A fist to the gut that knocked the amusement— and the wind—right out of me. I staggered back a step. *I don't freaking believe it.*

Rigo wasn't here to help hunt. He was here to replace El Cid.

How could Dad do that? To me? To El Cid? Confusion and betrayal and fury welled up in my chest like a bubble of lava. I prayed it would spew out and set everyone on fire. *Serve them right.*

Dad must have seen my rage, for he started toward me, one hand outstretched. "No, my son. It is not like that—"

I bolted out of the yard and flew along the road, the thump of my sneakers drowning out my father's pleas to come back. I reached the base of the Hump and slowed. A stitch burned in my left side. Panting, I started up the slope, using my mace like a cane. I marveled that I still carried the weapon.

Guess old habits never died.

Unlike family members.

I clambered up the rocky slope, using my hands and feet. Pushing myself harder and harder with each step. Punishing myself. Reaching the top, I bent over my knees, gasping, until my lungs stopped burning. Face turned away from home, I started down the Hump's north side.

It helped to just walk and think about nothing but the next footfall. When I hit the bottom, the toes of my sneakers pointed eastward for Huerfano. Fine with me. I was just along for the ride.

Ride.

Riding.

El Cid's white mane flowing over my hands. I was forever getting the reins tangled in the thick, wiry hairs.

The world blurred. Blinking hard, I stopped and scrubbed my face, then looked around. In the distance, I could see the Field Museum's sign by the side of the new road. Beyond was the Gate. Another tidal wave of guilt and rage slammed into me. I looked down at the mace in my hands. *I could do it. I could march through the Gate and into the Maze and kill every single skinner.*

What if they kill you first? an annoying voice in my head asked.

So what if they do? I answered back.

The one-two-three drumbeat of galloping hooves behind me. I sighed. Probably my father on Turk. The hoof beats slowed, then stopped. I kept my back turned and eyes closed, not wanting to see the matching sorrow in his face. A long silence—only the soft breathing of a horse. I broke first.

"I know what you're going to say, Dad."

"Wrong guy. Heck, wrong species."

I spun around. Rigo stood there, head cocked, and his forelock covering one eye. He studied me with the other.

"What do *you* want?" Rude as all get out. I didn't care.

"Just checking on you."

"Mission accomplished. Now go away."

His ears twitched at my tone. "Anything I can do for you, Matt?"

"Reverse time?"

"Wish I could," he said quietly

"Then you're not much good to me."

Even as I said it, I winced. But I couldn't bring myself to take it back. For a split second, I saw why Turk was the way he was. It was kind of fun to hurt others when you yourself were hurting.

He hesitated, then spoke. "Well, I *could* be. Of use to you, I mean. I've got two years of experience under my cinch, dealing with all kinds of monsters."

I did the math. Since Andalusians start hunting as three-year-olds, that meant the young stallion was five.

"I spent one whole year down in Arizona, helping the Montoyas when their coffer broke open. One vicious infestation of sand demons. Then another eight months over in Utah doing fire drake search-and-destroy with the Reyes clan. And for the last month, I hunted *duende* on the Navarre ranch, trading off with Vasco. Those stinkers—and I do mean *stinkers*—aren't much harder to hunt than skinners, from what Roman told me."

What? He's applying for a job? A weak curiosity stirred awake inside of me. "Don't you have a home?" A family.

He shifted a shoulder. "I like to move around."

My curiosity went back to sleep. "Well, you can move around back to the barn. I want to be alone."

"Sorry. Not an option. Javier asked me to hang out with you while they...you know."

I frowned. "While they *what?*"

"Had the ceremony."

"*Without me?*" My voice broke with disbelief.

"Your dad thought it'd be easier on you if they—"

"*No!*" I sprinted past Rigo and bolted for home, my mace a weight when I needed speed. Tears of rage stung my eyes.

Rigo trotted up beside me. "I can get you back," he said, "in like three minutes."

I don't want your help. "Fine," I snapped.

I stopped and grabbed his mane with my free hand, bent my knees, and jumped. With a grunt, I landed on my stomach, then swung my leg around. He took off with a powerful thrust of his hindquarters.

We dashed through the yard, around the barn, and across the field. My throat tightened at the sight of a mound of bare earth. *Way to go, loser. You managed to let El Cid down. Again.*

Rigo slowed, then halted. I slid off. My knees buckled. Only my hand still tangled in the bay's mane kept me upright. Ordering my legs to man up, I wobbled over and joined the circle around the mound, squeezing in between Dad and Ben. The only sound was the wind in the grass whispering a requiem.

I was suddenly and fiercely and gratefully relieved I missed the part where they slid El Cid's body into the ground. Because that would have been the last memory I had of him. And I would have hated that.

He would have hated that.

24

"**M**att."

Sprawled on Ben's bed, I rolled my head. My brother slouched in the doorway. "What?"

"We've got pizza duty. Dad already called in the order. Let's roll."

"Nah, I'm good."

He stepped closer, grabbed my arm, and pulled me off the bed.

"I said *no*." I struggled to my feet and yanked free.

"And Dad said you had to." He looked away. "And I wouldn't mind the company."

In the living room, Dad and the Navarres sat with beers in their hands, speaking in low voices. The conversation died when I appeared. I felt their gazes on me all the way to the door. *Stop staring at me. Sheesh, you act like...like...*

Like I didn't know what.

I clambered into the cab and slammed the door, then powered down the window. Usually, I got a kick out of going somewhere with just Ben. It pulled us closer like shrink wrap, the years between us melting away. Two brothers. A truck. Good times.

Not so much this time.

Nearing Perry's, I couldn't help looking at it, wondering how she was doing. "That's the Vandermers' house." The words fell out of my mouth before I caught them. A small sedan sat in the driveway with a rental sticker on its bumper.

Ben noticed the car too. "Guess their station wagon's still in the Maze."

Perry walked out the front door, a trash bag in each hand. I slid down in the seat, practically folded in half. Maybe she wouldn't notice us. Yeah right. Spotting our truck, she dropped the bags and motioned for us to stop, then called something over her shoulder. Ben slowed with a wave of his own.

"No, keep going," I hissed.

"Why?" He pulled over and put the truck into park. The traitor.

Because I don't want to talk. To anyone. About anything. "Just because."

He gave me a look then turned off the engine and stepped out. Perry, with Dr. Vandermer on her heels, met him in the middle of the driveway. I slouched lower and fastened my eyes on the dashboard. The murmur of voices, then an exclamation from Dr. Vandermer. More conversation. I caught my name once.

Footsteps. Then Perry appeared by my open window.

"Oh, Matt." The tears in her voice almost broke me. "Ben just told us."

I nodded, wishing she would go away. She must have read my mind, for she reached through the window and brushed the tips of her fingers along my arm. Then she walked away. A lump swelled in my throat; I socked my thigh with a fist to stop it.

The driver's door opened. Ben swung inside.

"Dr. Vandermer said she told the others that the biologist—the one with the braids—was right." He started up the engine. "That it *was* a pack of feral dogs that attacked the camp last night. They believed her. She also said that the team refuses to go back into the Maze. They're abandoning the dig. A lot of them have left Huerfano already. Guess a bunch of dinosaur fossils and a seventeenth century chest weren't worth it."

"Guess not."

I dragged myself behind Ben into the pizzeria. Normally, the aroma of tomato sauce and melted cheese and spicy sausage would have perked me right up. Instead, I almost gagged. I poked Ben in the back as we waited in line. "I'll be outside."

Leaning against the restaurant's brick wall, I stared down at the sidewalk. The image of El Cid lumped on the ground circled through my head until I wanted to scream. I squeezed my eyes tight.

"Hey, Matt."

I jerked my head up. Ethan was walking past me with his family. I forced a causal smile. *Just go inside. Please.* To my relief, they did. Still, I couldn't help watching out of the corner of my eye as his mother gave him an affectionate push through the door, laughing at her son's protest. Ethan grinned back.

I wished again—desperately and hopelessly again—that Mom was still alive. And El Cid.

If wishes were horses...

We drove home, half blinded by the setting sun. The smell of pepperoni rose from the boxes by my feet. Bleh. I stuck my head out the open window, letting my hair beat up my forehead.

"Matt." Ben nudged my shoulder.

I pulled my head back in. "Yeah?"

"Listen." He shifted in his seat. "It wasn't your fault. Okay?"

Liar. "Sure it was."

"Why? Because you were riding him when it happened?" He snorted. "Wow. You and Dad."

I stiffened. "What about Dad?"

"He thinks all of this is *his* fault. That he didn't check El Cid over carefully enough last night. He's beating himself up royally, even though Kathleen told him there was nothing he could've done."

"How does she know?"

Ben hesitated. "You really want to hear this?"

No. "I guess."

Fingers gripping the steering wheel harder than necessary, he spoke in a flat tone. "She examined the bite marks before we…you know. And she said from the depth and the angle, she guessed he had gotten a full dose. There wasn't anything anyone could have done for the old guy."

I thought about El Cid's behavior last night, the way he kept insisting that I leave him. "I think he knew, too."

"Why do you say that?"

"Because of the way he was acting. He told me he was fine and to go inside. Then he made up that excuse to Izzie and Turk, that he wanted to stretch his legs, then he w-walked out to the p-pasture…" I gave up. I stared out the window the rest of the drive, letting the wind dry my cheeks.

Back at the ranch, I spied Rigo alone by the ruins of the old homestead. Over by the barn, Vasco stood with Izzie, their heads close as they talked. To my surprise, Turk loitered nearby, listening.

Something made me hand the boxes to Ben. Maybe it was shame over the way I had treated the bay stallion. I knew, sure as snow in winter, that El Cid would've been hopping mad at me for acting like Turk. *And we all know what Turk rhymes with.* While my brother headed inside, I wandered over to the young stallion.

One eye peered at me through a screen of black hair. "What's up?"

"I, um…" I kicked at a broken adobe brick, crumpling it further under my boot. Dust to dust. "About earlier. Sorry."

"No worries. You're dealing with a load and a half." He bent his neck and touched his lips to one of the bricks, then raised his head. "No harm, no foul. Just want to help any way I can."

I thought back to what he had said. "Why *do* you move around?"

"Oh, I get to see a lot of the country. And there's always some hunter who needs an experienced partner on a temporary basis. Like if their war-sister is going to foal, or their war-brother got hurt or something." Even as he spoke, though, he kept shooting peeks at Izzie and Turk, then peering around the ranch.

"Matt?" Kathleen appeared on the porch. "Come eat. Rigo?" She looked past me. "You doing okay, buddy?"

He bobbed his head once. I noticed he stayed by the wall.

Kathleen motioned me over to a corner of the porch. "I have something for you. I already gave one to Ben." She opened her hand and held it out to me. My heart seized.

A slender braided bracelet, crafted from white hair and the ends tied off with red thread, laid coiled in a circle on her palm. "A lock from El Cid's mane. An old tradition from *my* people. I thought it might bring you some comfort."

Skin crawling, I picked it up. I didn't find it comforting—I found it creepy. But there was no way I was hurting anyone else's feelings. Already did plenty of *that* today. I pretended to examine it, then handed it back. "Would you tie it on?" I held out my left wrist.

She did. "There."

"Thanks." I stepped back and let her go through the door first.

Roman, with Ben's help, bustled about the kitchen. Dad stood at the sink staring out the window at the setting sun. Like he wasn't sure what he was supposed to be doing. He reminded me of Rigo.

I edged over to him. I didn't know what to say. How was I supposed to make my father feel better when I felt so lousy myself? *He* was the parent. He was supposed to make *me* feel better, not the other way around.

Everything for the warhorses first. Next, your father and brother, and the innocents of this world. Lastly, yourself. That is the way of a Knight of the Coffer. And of a true man.

I gripped the edge of the counter and did my own staring out the window. A weird awkwardness settled over me. I looked down at the bracelet. What would El Cid say? "Not your fault, you know."

"Nor yours."

Man, I wanted to believe that. I wanted to believe that in the worst way. "I feel like it was," I whispered.

"As do I." He sighed, then looped an arm around my neck and pulled me close. "He would kick me for acting like this. 'Javier,' he'd say. 'Stop brooding and start planning how to win this fight. You have a job to do, my friend, and frankly, all this maudlin behavior is becoming embarrassing.'"

In spite of the blackness, I grinned weakly at Dad's imitation. A sliver of light crept into my chest. Just a sliver. But it made the darkness a little less dark.

"Are you two going to stand there all evening or are you going to eat?" Kathleen said. "Because I don't think I can hold back Roman much longer."

We crowded around the table loaded with pizza. I selected a slice of my favorite—Hawaiian—and forced myself to take a bite. Then another. Hunger saw its opportunity. To my surprise, I ate the whole piece and reached for a second.

"So, what are we going to do now?" Ben asked around a mouthful. "Keep hunting? With three teams in the field, maybe we can spread out more and—"

"Four teams." Everyone froze in mid-chew. "I'm coming, too." *Did they think I was just going to sit around? After what happened?* They glanced at each other. I knew what they were wondering. Who would I ride?

"My son, I do not think—" Dad began.

"I can partner up with Rigo." I paused the assault on a third slice. Where did *that* idea come from?

"This *is* Rigo's *especialidad*," Roman pointed out. "Adjusting quickly to a new rider as needs be. It is why I asked him to come along."

My father chewed as he studied me. Yes or no—I wasn't sure which decision I wanted him to make. I fingered my bracelet under the table.

"I want at least one day," Dad finally said, "for Matt and Rigo to train together."

"Do we have that luxury?" Kathleen passed her leftover crust to Roman. "With their growing numbers, those beasties might pull off a breakout. You guys are always saying the wards are strong, but not infallible. And worse, once out of the Maze, they'd head straight for Huerfano. The town would turn into a skinner's all-you-can-eat buffet. Hundreds would die."

"That will not happen. Not on *our* watch. No victims will die under our Del Toro moon."

A faint stirring of something warmed my heart. I didn't know what it was, but anything was better than the coldness.

"There is another strategy we might try, my friend. You know which one," Roman said after a moment. He pointed a pizza slice at me. "Matt would give us four. Enough to take care of your skinner problem in one move."

Ben looked as confused as I felt. Four? Four what?

"The ritual has not been performed for centuries." Dad's eyes narrowed. "At least, not that I am aware of. Do you think it will still work?"

Roman shrugged a massive shoulder. "All we can do is make the attempt. We will be no worse off than before."

"What are you talking about?" I asked.

"These two lunatics," Kathleen said, "are proposing a way to capture all the skinners at one time and stuff them back in the coffer." Worry wrinkled her brow. "Besides being extremely risky, doesn't the ritual require four *knights*? I think I remember reading that somewhere in your ancestor's journal, Roman."

"Well, yes, technically. But—"

"At last count, you have two. Well, maybe two and a half. No offense, Ben."

Her husband waved a pepperoni in dismissal. "What is a knight but one who has killed in battle in defense of the inno-cent. Both Ben and Matt have bloodied their maces *and* helped rescue Vandermer and her daughter. I say they are close enough to knighthood to count." Roman beamed and winked at me. "*¿Sí, chico?*"

Nope. I felt about as far from a knight as possible.

25

"Oof!" I hit the ground, bounced once, then skidded a few feet. Dust and bits of dried vegetation flew up around me. Sprawled in the dirt at Rigo's hooves, I waited for air to return to my chest. Finally, my lungs decided to get to work. I gasped, then squinted into the afternoon sun and glared up at him. "What," I wheezed, "was that?"

He lowered his head and nosed me. "Sorry. Guess I cornered too fast."

"Gee, you think?"

His turns, his stops, his change of gaits—heck, *all* his moves were greased-lightning quick. It was like riding a jackrabbit. A big, brown, over-caffeinated jackrabbit.

"Warn me next time, would you?" I grabbed his mane. He lifted his head and pulled me to my feet. Kathleen once told me that a horse's neck had more muscle than I had in my entire body. Which was good, since Rigo had been hauling me off the ground a lot. I coughed again and dusted my jeans off.

All day, with only a short lunch break, Dad had the two of us out in the practice field. He ran us through every drill he could think of. Riding at a gallop along a row of fence posts with melons stuck on the top, pulverizing them with my mace until both of us were sticky with cantaloupe juice. Then, standing in the middle of the field and trying to swing one-handed into the saddle as Rigo thundered past. The only good part was that the bay was a couple of hands shorter than Turk, which meant I had a slim chance of getting on instead of no chance.

To the east, a low mound of bare earth watched over us. I kept looking at it. To punish myself. I knew later Dad would order a flat, square stone, engraved with El Cid's name and his favorite saying, and place it there. Just like he had done for other horses. Just like our family had done for generations. Those memorials were scattered all over the ranch. Whenever we'd run across one, Dad would tell us what he knew about that particular war horse. But always, he reminded us that the markers celebrated life and sacrifice. And love.

I wrenched my eyes away. "Where's my mace?" I searched about, finally spotting it buried in a sage bush a few feet away. Groaning, I dove for it. "He's going to kill me for dropping it."

Rigo took a stance in front of me. "Not if he doesn't know. Hurry, before he looks over here. Oh. Wait." He relaxed. "Nah, we're good—Javier missed the whole thing. He's by the barn talking to Roman. Looks like he and Vasco just got back."

"Where'd they go?" I yanked my weapon free in a flurry of pungent leaves, then sneezed.

"I think they went to check out the Maze. Vasco mentioned last night that he and Roman might try to sneak inside and do a little reconnaissance today. See what the pack of ground round was up to, and if the coffer was unguarded."

"Pretty gutsy for them to go alone. Surprised Dad didn't try to talk them out of it."

"Well, Roman knows when to take risks and when not to. And Vasco is some serious heavy cavalry."

"True that." I mounted and settled into the saddle.

A sharp whistle from Dad. Rigo struck out at a fast trot for the barn. Just as fast, my palms broke out in a sweat; I dried them on my jeans.

"No scent or sound of fresh skinner near the camp," Vasco was saying as Rigo and I rode up. "They may be keeping their heads down for now."

"And the empty coffer is still by Allbury's trailer." Roman raised his eyebrows in a silent question.

Dad nodded. "Then we stand a chance."

A chance for *what*, I wondered. "Are you talking about that ritual? How are we going to get the skinners back into the coffer if they're scattered all over the Maze?"

"If we reach the coffer first without interference," Dad said, "then *they* will come to *us*. I will explain when we reach the camp. For now, we must hurry."

Ten minutes later, my father and Roman had coiled lariats tied to their saddles and the horses had drunk their fill. Kathleen passed a couple of water bottles to Roman, who stored them in Vasco's saddle bags. Laying a hand on her husband's knee, she shot a stern glance at the rest of us.

"Don't take any more risks than you have to," she ordered. "It'd ruin my day if I have to patch up any of you—man, boy, or horse."

Roman blew her a kiss as we trotted out of the yard. The whole time I trailed along behind the others, I wondered about the ritual Dad and Roman had mentioned. Was it going to be anything like what Dad had done in the cave? Or worse?

"Oh," Rigo breathed.

I laid my hand on his shoulder. "Yeah. Pretty bad."

The site looked like an abandoned refugee camp. Tattered tent remnants snapped in the dry, hot wind. Clothing and equipment were strewn everywhere. The coffer squatted by All-bury's trailer, the lid open, and the whole thing covered in a layer of dust.

Dad and Roman dismounted and spoke in low tones, then the big hunter pointed his mace toward an open patch of ground about ten yards away. Grasping the coffer's iron rings, they hauled the container to the spot.

"What are they doing, Ben?"

"Probably something gothic and mysterious. Whatever it is, I hope the skinners'll leave us alone long enough to do whatever Dad and Roman have planned."

"Me too." I noticed Rigo's ears were pivoting like crazy. "Do you hear anything?"

"No. Nothing." He raised his head and tested the air. "I smell *something*. But it might be just leftover stench from the coffer."

"Boys. Come."

We swung down and hurried over. At Roman's request, we helped him shift the iron chest back and forth under our father's directions. The whole time, he kept one eye on the western mountains.

"*Bueno*. I think it is close enough." Dad folded the lid further back on its hinges.

I peered inside. Nothing but dust and stink. "Close enough for what?"

"We need the coffer, and ourselves, aligned with the four directions," Roman said. "It strengthens our maces' power so they can do their job."

What job? Knocking us out cold? I thought back to what happened in the cave. *What if we all fall unconscious and the skinners come back?* I swallowed through a dry mouth.

"Stand there, Ben." Roman gestured with his weapon. "Matt, the south side, across from your brother." He then stepped to the west side of the coffer while Dad took the east.

"My sons." Dad slid the mace's loop around his wrist. "Once we begin, we cannot stop. I mean, physically. We will be locked together until the coffer is closed."

"So, if you need to pee, Matty," Ben nodded toward a large chamisa bush, "go now."

Dad ground his boots into the earth—a bull preparing to charge—then he took a deep breath and raised his mace. Holding it above the coffer, he pointed it toward the sky. Roman did the same thing, touching the head of his weapon to my father's with a soft clink.

I tensed. Was something supposed to happen?

"Ben." At Dad's quiet command, my brother joined his mace with the others. Still nothing. No lightning bolts or flames. Not even sound effects.

"Matt," my father said.

Holding my breath, I licked my lips and brought up my mace. *This is lame. Nothing's going to happen—*

A sharp jerk, like a giant magnet pulling at my weapon, almost yanked the haft from my fist; I tightened my grip just in time. *Clank!* The head of my mace crashed into the others.

Kaa-rack!

Sparks exploded in a shower. I yelped when one stung my cheek. They hung in the air like fireworks, then drifted downward, sputtering out as they touched the ground.

Waves of energy pulsated through me. At first I thought it was my heart thumping. Then I realized it came from the mace.

Vibrations hummed down the shaft, along my arm, and into my body. The wind picked up and slapped my hair into my eyes.

I pulled. My weapon was locked tight—as if the four iron heads had been welded together. Then, I tried to let go of the handle. Nope.

"Holy moly," Ben shouted over the wind.

"I know. It's like we're super-glued together—"

"No." He pointed up at the sky with his free hand. "Look!"

Black clouds boiled up from nowhere good and darkened the sky. The wind increased. It whipped and spurred its way across the valley, churning the clouds in a clockwise rotation. Sand bit my eyes and stung my face and arms. Dad's hat flew off and tumbled away.

First time he had ever lost it.

"Turk," Dad yelled over the growing storm. "You and the others—stand clear. No arguing." The steeds reluctantly edged away. Their manes and tails swirled around them like pennants on a flag bearer's pole.

Tremors ran through my soles and up my legs. *Sheesh, get a grip*, I ordered myself. Then I realized it wasn't me that was trembling.

It was the ground.

"Uh-oh," I whispered.

The earth shook like a truck rattling over a cattle guard. Rocks tumbled from the cliffs and bounced down, smashing on-to the valley floor. Squealing, Izzie reared, striking out at the invisible threat. Rigo and Turk danced in place, ears flat and eyes wide. All the while, Vasco stood his ground, his legs braced apart and neck arched. A granite statue. Only his mane and tail moved, war banners rippling in the storm. The wind tore at our clothes, trying to rip them from our bodies.

"Here they come," Roman bellowed.

Movement out of the corner of my eye. I squinted, the wind half blinding me. Dark shapes appeared. They rose from the ground and into the air, swooping and rising with the wind. At first, I thought it was a flock of some kind of giant, misshapen crows. They flew closer.

Madre de Dios, protect me!

Not crows.

Skinners.

Caught up in the swirling vortex, they spun around and around, limbs paddling the air helplessly. Their howls were drowned out by the storm.

Boom! The snake-like tail of the vortex struck the ground nearby. No bigger than one of Izzie's hooves, it was still freaking powerful. It pirouetted, ripping up bushes and scrubs with every rotation. The rest of the tornado disappeared upward into the storm clouds. Skinners swam in and out of the funnel, their paws clawing for purchase. Roaring louder than any train, the tip of the funnel darted between me and my father. The force almost lifted my feet from the earth. It fingered the coffer, then jumped inside of it. Corkscrewing downward, it dragged the howling creatures with it, one by one.

I moaned. *What if the vortex grabs us, too? What if we get trapped in the coffer with all those skinners?* Muscles cramping, I tried to switch hands. Stinging debris pelted my face. A rock sliced my ear. Holding my free arm in front of my face, I squeezed my eyes tight.

"Matt," Dad shouted. "Watch out!"

My eyes flew open. A large shape tumbled past and hit the ground behind me. Still trapped, I twisted around. A few yards away, a skinner staggered to its feet. Spotting me pinned in place, it bared its teeth in glee.

I wrenched myself from side to side. "Let go," I screamed at the mace. The creature slunk closer, its fangs wet with poison and its mad eyes blazing. Over the storm's roar, I heard my father shouting desperately for Turk.

The skinner sprang. It flew toward me, its gaping jaws growing wider every second. I swore I could see down its throat and into its gut. My final destination.

I was going to die. There was no way Turk could reach me in time.

And, he didn't.

Rigo did.
Leaping between me and death by skinner, he reared, front hooves scything the air. One hoof struck the skinner and knocked it to the ground. Snarling, the creature twisted and scrambled clear of the other hoof seeking to scramble some brain.

"Matt, duck!"

Still trapped by the mace, I hunkered down as far as I could. Just in time, too. The warhorse whirled around, planted his front feet, and mule-kicked the creature. Yowling, it soared backward and disappeared into the funnel.

"*¡Olé!*" Rigo shouted.

"Whoa," I breathed.

The swirling cloud sped up. With a shriek loud enough to shatter granite, it dived into the coffer—a snake slithering back into its hole—and disappeared.

Whump! The lid slammed shut. A shudder rocked the container and the sides bulged out for a moment. The cover lifted an inch. A long, low exhalation. *Snick*. It closed again. A flash of blinding blue light. I closed my eyes tight.

With a sigh of contentment, the wind sank to a breeze, then died away. I blinked and shook the hair out of my face. The chest sat motionless, its iron a dull gray. Overhead, the clouds thinned as patches of sunlight grew

Groaning, I lowered my mace and let it drop to the ground. My arm dangled like a deflated balloon and my whole right side was on fire. I opened and closed my hand a few times, then looked up at Rigo and placed my hand on his neck. "Thanks."

"For what?"

"For saving my life. For risking your own."

"No big deal, Matt. It's what I do."

But you didn't have to, I thought. *And that makes it a big deal*. I patted his neck and looked around.

Ben rubbed his shoulder, wincing. Roman picked bits of grass from his ponytail, while my father poked at the coffer with his mace. The other horses trotted over. Izzie paused to pick up Dad's hat with her teeth from where it had snagged in a creosote bush.

I nudged the chest with the toe of my boot. "Did we get them all?"

"I think so. Oh, *gracias*, Isabel." Dad dusted off his hat and clapped it back on his head. A thin line of red decorated his cheekbone. "To the cave. Turk? Vasco?" He waved the stallions over, then untied the lariat from Turk's saddle. He and Roman fastened the ropes through the iron rings.

With their ropes dallied around the saddle horns and the coffer slung between the warhorses, Dad and Roman headed for the cave. Ben and I trailed behind. It felt weird to *not* be running for our lives. Good weird.

Once there, Ben and I helped lower the chest to the ground. Dad dismounted, then pulled the headlamp out of his pocket.

"Let me check the cave before we haul that thing back in." He removed his hat and pulled on the lamp. "The tremors may have caused some damage." Edging around the massive block of stone, he disappeared.

A few minutes later, he re-emerged, scowling. He yanked off the headlamp in frustration. "I was afraid of that."

My heart lurched. Before I could ask, Roman spoke. "How bad, Javier?"

"A section of the canyon wall has fallen and partially blocks the cave entrance. I tried, but I am unable to squeeze through." His gaze flickered over me.

With another lurch, my heart began pounding against my ribs. "You've got to be kidding me."

"Would I fit?" Ben offered. I could've hugged my brother.

Dad shook his head, his eyes never leaving my face.

"Why…" My voice cracked. I tried again. "Why can't we just keep the coffer at home? Like in the barn or something?"

"Our barn is not warded. And even though the chances of it re-opening are remote, I will not risk it. No, it must be returned to the cave."

"Aww, man," I groaned. "Really?"

"I am sorry, my son. We might be able to shift the rock or dynamite it in the future, but for now, I want that accursed thing secured." He handed me the headlamp, then pulled my mace from my hand and passed it to Ben. "You will not need your weapon."

Before I knew it, I was stumbling through the slot. Dad and Roman followed in single file, carrying the coffer between them, a lariat still tied to one of the iron rings. With every unsteady step, I fought the urge to spin around and flee. Reaching the dead end, I steeled myself and played the light over the surface.

A large slab was wedged between the walls right in front of the cave's mouth. Suspended over the sandy floor, it left a gap at the bottom, barely big enough for the coffer. And me. If I skipped breathing for a while. And didn't mind losing a layer of skin off my back. Gee, how did I get so lucky?

Dad knelt by the coffer. He handed me the other end of the rope. "Drag it inside and push it to one corner for now."

"You make it sound easy." My skin crawled like wasps were building nests under it. I crouched down and eyed the black hole. "What if that slab falls all the way and traps me in there?"

"It won't."

"But what if it does?"

"Then I will break it down with my bare hands and get you out."

I believed him.

Lying flat on my stomach and the end of the rope tied to my ankle, I forced myself to ignore the stone hanging above me. Or how loud my pulse drummed in my ears. Or how dry my mouth was. Instead, I concentrated on squeezing through the tunnel, inch by inch, using my hands to push the sand away from my face. The grains worked their way under my shirt and down my pants.

When I reached the cave, I wanted to bawl. Just to be able to stand up, even in that small space, was everything. *Still have to crawl back, you know*, said an annoying voice in my head. I told it to shut up.

"Okay, I'm through," I hollered, then untied the rope from my leg.

"Start pulling." Dad's voice echoed from the other side.

It took all my strength to drag the thing through. It kept getting caught on the sides of the tunnel or hung up in the deep sand. "You know, Dad," I complained between grunts. "You could've dug the dirt away and crawled through yourself." Finally, by sitting down and bracing my boots on either side of the opening and jerking on the rope, I inched it in.

I shoved it into a corner with my feet, then blew out a deep breath. "And, *stay* there." Coiling the lariat, I suddenly remembered the other coffer. How could I have forgotten something called the Red *Casket*? Ominous, with a touch of macabre, no? I shone the light up at the high shelf.

The high, *empty* shelf.

The hairs on my arms snapped to attention. I backed up as far as I could and steadied the light on the ledge. Had I missed it? Nope. Just a dark hole near the ceiling.

Swinging my head around, I scanned the cave. *Maybe one of the tremors knocked it off its perch.* Even as I looked, I knew I would've noticed it already.

I squatted down and yelled through the tunnel. "Dad. It's gone."

"*¿Qué?*"

"The Red Casket. That smaller one that was up on that shelf? It's not here."

"Are you certain?"

"Yeah. I can see all the way back in that hole. It's not there. It's not anywhere in this cave."

Dad's string of curse words ricochet along the tunnel; a few I stored away to share with Ben. I heard Roman's low rumble as they spoke. Once, I caught Allbury's name.

"Matt? Come along. There is nothing more you can do in there."

I didn't need to be told twice. The feel of Dad's hand grabbing my arm and pulling me the final few feet was just about the best thing ever.

"Are you all right?"

"I am now." I shuddered. "Do you think Allbury took it?"

"Who else?" Dad motioned for us to leave.

I fell in behind Roman. "What happens if he opens that one, too?" I sighed with relief when we stepped out into the afternoon light. "Skinners? Or could it hold something worse?"

"Uh-oh." Seated on Izzie, Ben grimaced at my question. "That doesn't sound good. What's going on?" He handed me my mace.

"*El Cofre Rojo* is missing." Dad mounted and pulled his hat down with a savage tug. "And I suspect Allbury."

Turk bared his teeth. "I knew I should've taken him out when I had the chance."

"Any clue where he might be?" Roman swung up on Vasco. He tied the coiled lariat to his saddle.

"No, but I know who might." Dad dug his cellphone out of his pocket and tapped on the screen. "No signal this far in." He nodded toward the Gate. "Let us hurry."

Under me, Rigo ran like an antelope on Red Bull, bounding over bushes and leaping across ravines. It made me miss El Cid so much. I pretended it was just the wind pulling tears from my eyes. I could almost hear his voice telling me to focus on the task at hand.

Reaching the devastated camp, Turk slowed to a walk. Dad checked his cell again, then grunted with approval and tapped the screen. "Liz? I need to find Allbury. Now." A pause. "Because I think he has taken another coffer from the same cave where the first one was found. This one is smaller—shoebox size—and a reddish color." Another pause, longer this time. "*Gracias*. No, we will find him." He slipped the device in his back pocket.

"Well?" Roman and Vasco said at the same time.

"Liz thinks she saw him putting something in the back of his vehicle. Something wrapped in his jacket. She did not think much of it at the time as everyone was excited about the larger coffer they had hauled back to camp."

"Does Dr. Vandermer know where Allbury is now?" I asked.

"She is not sure—he has not returned any of her calls. She did tell me that he is renting a place north of town in Mesa Rim, but she does not know which house."

Ben gave a low whistle. "Pretty fancy neighborhood. Must be good money in paleontology."

Turk sniffed. "Probably makes extra cash on the side by stealing stuff from digs and reselling them on the black market."

"We should go back and get the trucks," Roman said. "Then we can drive around that subdivision and hope we spot Allbury's vehicle."

"Not going to happen," Vasco rumbled. "You're not going after that thing without *us*."

"I agree," Dad said. "If that *tonto* managed to open the chest and let loose whatever was imprisoned, we will need our war-brothers—"

"Hey!" Izzie slashed her tail.

"—and sister," he added without missing a beat, "more than ever." He gathered up the reins. "We will head to Huerfano, then skirt around it to the north instead of going through town. The horses can make better time going cross country. Turk? Quickly, my friend."

27

We trotted and loped and trotted again along the road toward town, our shadows before us and clouds of dust behind. Fatigue and worry and numbing grief weighed me down like a sweat-soaked saddle pad. Slumped on Ringo, I half listened to Roman arguing with Kathleen on his cellphone.

Slipping it into his shirt pocket, he blew out a long breath. "She wanted to drive out and meet us, but I asked her to stay put for now." He rubbed the back of his neck. "She was not happy about it."

"I can imagine," Dad said. "How much trouble are you in?"

"Vasco?" Roman said in response. "Once we are finished here, let us keep going. I hear Wyoming is nice."

We all laughed. Except for Izzie.

"Sure hope you wanted Kathleen to stay behind *only* because of her lack of experience and *not* because she's female. Hunting knows no gender, you know, and—"

"I *do* know. Isn't my daughter one of the finest hunters of her age? And the Morrigan? Does the mare not live up to her name by the number of kills she has participated in? So, lower your hackles, my fiery Isabel."

It dawned on me that there weren't a lot of female hunters, at least not Dad's age. Well, except for his sister; Dad once mentioned that our aunt, Cristina, had been one heck of a hunter. There seemed to be more female hunters our age. Like Jo. Maybe it was a generational thing? Man, I must be really pooped if this was the kind of stuff worming around inside of my skull.

I guess everyone else was tired, too, because we jogged in silence the rest of the way to Huerfano. Skirting the town, we rode behind a group of storage units, one repair shop, and a row of back yards. A pair of little kids playing in one of the yards stopped and waved as we passed by. I waved back.

"I like your horse," one of the girls called.

"Hey, thanks," Rigo yelled over his shoulder.

"Dude," I hissed. "You can't do stuff like that."

"Why? They're kids—they still believe in magic."

Riding. Riding. The calm before the storm. The land became hillier and the houses farther apart and fancier. Tucked on the sides of rolling knolls dotted with piñon and juniper trees, each house boasted a million-dollar view of the Maze and the prairie and the distant Sangre de Cristos. Pausing by the side of the groomed dirt and gravel road that wound through the subdivision, we stopped and looked around.

"We will split up," Dad said. "I will take Matt. Roman, you and Ben—" He paused.

The rumbly hum of an approaching vehicle. It grew louder. Then, a white SUV sped around the corner of a low hill. I spotted Allbury behind the wheel. His mouth a perfect O, he slammed on the brakes. The vehicle skidded and sent up a cloud of dust. With a whine of gears, he spun around in a spray of gravel and raced back the way he had come.

"After him," Dad shouted.

We were galloping before the words left Dad's mouth. I
bent low over the bay's neck, eyes watering from the dust and
the sting of his black mane on my face. We rounded a wide
curve and burst out onto a straight section. Allbury sped up,
opening the distance.

"He's getting away," I hollered over the wind.

"Not from *me*," Rigo panted. He stretched out, head low,
and chuffed in rhythm with his stride. He pulled away from Izzie, then inched past Vasco until he reached Turk's hindquarters.
To my utter astonishment, he shifted into a higher gear. Andalusian overdrive. Flying along, he rolled up alongside the black
until they raced neck and neck.

A block ahead, Allbury wrenched the car to the left. It fish-
tailed onto a narrower road and disappeared behind a stand of
piñon trees. I caught a glimpse of his vehicle between the
branches.

Dad leaned forward. "Turk, cross country. We must cut him
off!"

Rigo leaped the low embankment. Turk matched him stride
for stride. We tore through the brush. Piñon branches slapped
me as Rigo wove around them. I crouched lower in the saddle.
Flashes of white through the trees just ahead of us.

"There he is!" My excitement faded at the sight of a high
wrought-iron fence. Allbury sped through a gate that stood open
across the road. It began to close slowly behind him.

"Rigo!"

"I see him."

Another burst of speed. Behind me, Dad shouted, ordering
me to stop. I knew I should, but something inside wouldn't let
me. Instead, I leaned forward even further, my cheek close to
Rigo's neck. Foam streaked his brown coat, whipped cream on
dark chocolate. The wind screamed in my ears.

We whipped through the gate. My knee whacked against the post, shooting a white-hot pain up my leg. I winced and swallowed a cry. One of Rigo's back hooves clipped the iron railing; he staggered a step, then regained his stride. A dull clang—the automatic gate shut behind us.

Allbury's vehicle squealed to a stop in front of an enormous timber frame house. The man jumped out and pulled something covered in a puffy jacket from the back seat. Clutching the bundle in his arms, he fled around the side of the house and disappeared. Gaining on him, we rounded the corner, then skidded to a halt. Chunks of sod flew from Rigo's hooves—divots on a golf course.

In the middle of the yard, Allbury crouched down, his hands wrapped around the Red Casket. In the daylight, the container looked battered and worn and mottled with what I hoped—and prayed—wasn't dried blood.

The chest jumped and twisted in his hold, and with each lurch, the lid flapped up and down. He threw himself on top of the coffer, trying to pin it down.

Mace in hand, I leaped out of the saddle, breaking both Dad's and El Cid's number one rule. "Stand back. I can close it up."

"More of those *things*. They're in here." Allbury's voice was shrill with panic. He rode the lid as it bucked again. "If they escape—"

"I know. If you'd get out of the way, I can seal it," I yelled over the howls coming from the coffer. I inched closer until I was right in front of the man, mace held out. My war-brother kept pace behind me. *"Move!"*

Rigo let out a brassy neigh. Allbury jerked, then rolled off and staggered to his feet, hands held in front of him as if warding off the horse.

"Sorry about this." Rigo reared and struck the man's head with his hoof. I winced at the dull thud. Without a sound, All-bury slumped to the ground in a boneless heap. The stallion stood over the figure. "Hurry, Matt."

I raised the mace. Then, I froze. Holy beans, what was the phrase? I bit down on my lip, willing my stupid brain to remember. "*Stamus...Stamus contra...*"

Rigo danced in place, lashing his tail like a twitchy cat. "What are you waiting for?"

"I don't remember the words," I moaned. Holy mother of pearl, where was my father when I needed him the most?

Or El Cid.

Bang! The lid blew open. A cloud of smoke billowed out and enveloped me. Only it didn't feel like smoke. It felt wet and clammy. Like fog or rain. And smelled something awful. Moldy leaves or the muddy bottom of a puddle drying under a July sun. The stench clogged my nostrils. With a soft hiss, the cloud coiled around my head once, leaving my cheeks wet, then shot toward the mountains and vanished.

Before I could draw a clean breath, something else moved inside the chest. A hand, with twiggy fingers and bark-like flesh, curled over the coffer's lip. I watched in horror as it fingered the latch. How could a box so small hold something the size of a human? Worse, was it alone?

Rigo pawed the ground. "Now would be a good time."

"*Stamus...Stamus contra...*" My voice ratcheted up and down with terror. Out of nowhere, the Latin phrase leaped into my head. I planted my feet, grasped the mace in both fists, and pointed the iron head at the coffer. "I'm packing a loaded mace. So get your creepy self back in there." The hand retreated until only the tips of split and broken nails showed. For a second, I wondered if the thing had tried to claw its way out. Triple yeesh. "Rigo," I called over my shoulder. "Take cover."

Heart pounding, I scrunched up my face and sucked in a deep breath. *"Stamus contra malum,"* I shouted and thrust my mace against the chest.

Neon-blue brightness blasted my vision. Then, something the size of a Mack truck hit me in the chest. I swore it drove right through my body. The sensation of flying backward. Then blackness.

Then, nothing.

෨∾෯

Why was Turk kicking me in the head? At least, that's what it felt like. I blinked. Light skewered my eyeballs, which were already beat to heck.

"Matt?" Fingers squeezed my shoulder.

I blinked again, keeping my lids at half mast, then peered up at my father on one knee beside me. Anger and something else darkened his face. For a moment, I wondered what I'd done. Then I remembered.

"Sorry, Dad." My voice creaked like wooden barn doors.

"What, in the name of all that is holy, were you thinking?"

"You're forgetting, Dad." Ben appeared. He squatted by my other side. "Matt's twelve. He's not supposed to think. Here." He held out a glass of water. "Got you some Tylenol from Allbury's house. Sorry, but he didn't have any baby aspirin."

Dad eased me into a sitting position. My head throbbed with each heartbeat. After downing the tablet and a long gulp of water, I looked around.

The Red Casket sat motionless. Just as still, Allbury lay sprawled where he had fallen; a purple lump already stood out on his forehead. Nearby, Rigo was drinking from a bucket while Roman knelt by the stallion's left front leg. He was wrapping the bay's fetlock with an elastic bandage.

"There." The hunter pinned it in place, then rose with a grunt. "Tight enough?"

The warhorse shifted his weight from side to side. "Feels good. I'll have Kathleen check it when we get back home. I mean, back to Del Toro's ranch."

"What happened?" *Great. Someone else hurt because of me.* Remorse was becoming too familiar. Not really a goal.

"Took a bad step when the blast hit me. Twisted my leg is all." Rigo shook his head gingerly. "My ears are still ringing some, though."

"So, it really worked?" I nodded toward the coffer, then immediately regretted the sudden movement.

"It appears so." My father took my arm. "Come. We need to leave before the neighbors show up wanting to know what caused that explosion."

I clung to him until my knees decided they weren't going to fold under me. "Where are the others?"

"Outside the gate. The blast from your mace knocked out the electricity and short-circuited the lock. We—Roman, Ben, and myself—came over the fence."

"You should've seen him, Matt. Dad's boots never touched the top rail, he was climbing so fast."

With Dad and Ben holding my elbows, I wobbled around the house and down the driveway. Rigo limped behind. Beside him, Roman carried the coffer under one arm.

"What about Allbury?" I felt better with each step, even though something was dancing the flamenco in my skull. "Are we just going to leave him there?"

Dad shrugged. "A blow to the head, nothing more. He is lucky to be alive after all this."

"Do you think he's going to tell others about us?" Ben asked. Reaching the gate, he began searching the post by the lock. "Should be a manual release around here somewhere," he muttered.

"Who would believe him?" Roman shifted the coffer to his other arm. "No matter how he tried to explain what happened, people would think he was *loco en la cabeza*. No, your family's secrets are safe for now."

"What are we going to do with the chest?" Izzie stuck her nose through the fence, hampering Ben's efforts.

"Vasco and I will return it to the cave. For today, I will push it through the tunnel as far as I can. Tomorrow, we can figure out how to get it in the rest of the way."

Click. The gate slowly swung open. Ben stepped aside with a wave and a cocky grin. "See? I *knew* all that breaking and entering would pay off some day." He laughed at the expression on our father's face. "Just kidding, Pop."

igo insisted I ride with him. He blew off his injury with a
horsey raspberry. "Got to finish the mission."

"What are you, some kind of equine Marine?" I joked as
Dad helped me up. I guessed he noticed my legs were still wobbly.

"*Semper fi.*"

"Here." Ben handed up my weapon. I thought he was going
to say something smart-alecky. Or Ben-alecky. Instead, he held
out his fist. "You did good, little brother."

I bumped it. "Thanks."

"Or little sister, I should say."

There it was.

We headed home, the sun in our eyes and one nightmare of
a day behind us. Reaching the intersection for the Maze, Roman
and Vasco paused. To my surprise, Ben and Izzie offered to go
along.

"Oh, I think Vasco and I can handle it." The hunter patted
his mace. Roped to the cantle, the Red Casket rested behind him

on the gray stallion's broad haunch. "After all, *El Laberinto* is now free of monsters."

"But that supernatural vacuum might have missed some. I mean, we don't know for sure," Izzie said. "Better to have back-up and not need it, yadda, yadda, yadda."

After Ben and Roman rode away, the four of us continued. Dad led the way, talking to Turk in a quiet voice. The shakes kept hitting me. I scrubbed my face to distract myself.

Rigo glanced back. "Talk about one bat-crazy hunt."

I nodded. "I can't believe it's all over. And that the skinners are locked up. At least for a while." I tapped the mace hanging from the saddle for good luck.

"Even better, you guys know what to do if they get out again."

Yeah, Team Del Toro. Just missing one member.

Sorrow almost knocked me out of the saddle. I squeezed the horn until my fingers turned white. Right then, I would have given anything for El Cid to be with me. Arguing with Turk and trading obscure references with Dad.

And telling me how proud he was of me. I hoped so, anyway.

As if he read my thoughts, Rigo spoke again. "And I meant what I said earlier. About El Cid. Wish I'd known him."

A wisp of an idea flitted through my head. I studied Rigo as he walked along, his gait nimble and light with only a trace of a limp. The idea grew. It felt wrong and right at the same time. I wondered if I should talk to Dad about it first, but then, I was pretty sure I knew what he'd say.

Maybe I should talk to El Cid first.

Would he hear me? Wherever he was? Or would he think I was betraying him? I twisted the horsehair bracelet around and around on my wrist. Okay, here goes.

*El Cid? Would it hurt your feelings if I asked Rigo if he
wants to stay? He wouldn't be taking your place. No one ever
will. Not ever. Not to me. But we could use the help. You know.
Just in case.*

I held my breath and waited.

Nothing.

Right. Didn't think so. Stupid idea. I sighed and glanced up.
An enormous thunderhead floated over the mountains. Backlit
by the setting sun, it gleamed like pale gray marble. It rolled and
tumbled toward me. Molded by the wind, it took on a new
shape.

An oh-so-familiar shape.

Tears blurred my vision. I blinked furiously.

The image of a gray horse, with arched neck and flowing
white mane, appeared. It seemed to toss its head, as if nodding
to me. Then, the wind herded it onward and sent the steed racing
through the sky. I watched it until it faded away.

Make room, Matt.

Suddenly, I realized what El Cid's last words meant. I
sniffed, then swiped my nose. Okay, then.

I cleared my throat. "Rigo? I want to ask you something."

"Hit me."

"I was wondering if you'd like to…" I hesitated. Big question, after all.

"Like to what?"

I took a deep breath. "To stay."

"Stay where?" he asked, uncertainty in his voice.

"Here. In Colorado. At our ranch with us."

"Permanently?"

"As long as you want. We could, you know, be a team. Or
at least give it a try."

Rigo walked along in silence. Then, "Yeah. Yeah, I think
I'd like that."

"Me, too."

And wasn't that a straight-up wonder—that I had room.

༄৵৵

"Hey, doofus." The next afternoon, Ben stuck his head in the bedroom we were still sharing. "Your girlfriend's here. With her mom."

In the midst of pulling on a clean T-shirt, I wrestled my face free and glared at him. "I told you before. Perry's not my—"

"Whatever." He disappeared.

By the time I got to the porch, Dad was introducing Dr. Vandermer to Roman and Kathleen. Perry was already by the barn, talking to Izzie, their noses practically touching. As I walked past, I heard Dad offering to drive Dr. Vandermer to the Maze to collect her car.

"What about those...skinners?" The scientist said it like she couldn't believe she was actually saying it.

"They are imprisoned in the coffer." Dad took her elbow. "I will explain." As they went inside, I overheard Dr. Vandermer mentioning something about Allbury and a black market for rare artifacts. That's why he wanted the Red Casket, I guessed— Turk had been right.

I joined Izzie and Perry. I hoped she wouldn't want to talk about El Cid. What if she got all weepy? Worse, what if *I* did?

I decided to head off the whole scene. "Your mom's handling this pretty good." It dawned on me that Perry was handling it even better.

"For being a scientist and all—not too shabby." She looked down and dragged a toe through the dirt. "Listen, Matt, I want to say something."

I froze.

At that moment, Rigo sauntered around the corner of the barn, ears pricked. "Thought I heard voices. You must be Perry."

I slumped in relief. Talk about timing.

Izzie and Rigo took turns telling Perry about yesterday. It was insane hearing what had happened from their points of view. They actually made me sound brave. Daring. Heroic. Total opposite of how I felt.

"You know what, Matt Del Toro?" Perry said after the horses finished their tale.

"What?"

"You really *are* a knight. Fighting on horseback with a magical weapon. Vanquishing monsters to protect the innocent villagers and all that."

My ears grew warm. I never thought of myself that way. Kind of cool that she did.

"Perry?" Dr. Vandermer stepped out onto the porch. "Time to go."

"Just a second, Mom." She grabbed my hand and tugged me inside the barn and over to one side. "How're you doing?" Still holding my hand, she peered into my face.

I knew what she was asking. I started to brush off her question then stopped. Because I *did* want to talk about El Cid. Even though it hurt just thinking about him.

"Okay, I guess. I keep forgetting he's gone, and I'll walk outside to tell him something or to ask him something. Then, I remember." I sighed. "It's like getting punched in the stomach over and over."

She didn't say anything, just nodded and squeezed my hand before letting go. "Here. This is what I wanted to tell you earlier. Give you, I mean." She pulled a folded sheet of paper out of her back pocket and handed it to me. "I wrote this for you."

On the outside, she had drawn my family's coat of arms. I started to unfold the paper.

"Wait." She laid a hand over mine. "Read it *after* I leave. Okay?"

"Perry," her mother called. "Anytime before winter."

I almost missed the quick hug she gave me. Almost. Then, she was gone.

Studying the drawing, I wandered over to the ladder leading up to the loft. With the Navarres still visiting, our house was too crowded to read my first note from a girl. I climbed up and sat on the edge, feet dangling. Dust motes floated in the air around me, tiny flickers in a shaft of sunlight. I unfolded the paper and smoothed it out on my knees.

Matt, you know how Strider had a poem that Bilbo composed for him? To explain to the world who this lonely guy wandering around Middle-earth really was? You know the one. The 'all that glitters is not gold/not all those who wander are lost' poem.

Well, I thought, why not Matt? So, I wrote you one. And, yeah, I'm too chicken to watch your face in person while you read it. It's my first attempt at this sort of thing. Don't judge me.

Here's the deal: if you don't like it, burn it. We'll pretend it never happened. If you do like it, then let me know that, too. The title, by the way, is **Del Toro Moon**—*you can probably guess why. Here goes:*

> *Empty coffer*
> *Marks the rise,*
> *Of evil old*
> *That seeks the prize:*
>
> *To feast on blood,*
> *And flesh and fear,*
> *Of trembling souls*
> *Dwelling near.*
>
> *Yet one will come*
> *During dreadful need.*
> *Armed with iron mace*
> *And steed.*
>
> *One who slays*
> *The ancient foe*
> *A* vaquero *Knight:*
> *Del Toro.*

Whoa. I read it again, my lips moving silently. Is that how she really saw me? I debated showing it to Dad and Ben. Okay, just Dad. And oh man, El Cid sure would've gotten a kick out of it. But in the end, I kept the poem to myself. For now.

Who knows? Maybe, someday, I'll even live up to Perry's words.

We Asked Darby Karchut

How did you get the idea for *Del Toro Moon*?
The story was inspired by the opening stanza in the song *From Whence Came the Cowboy*, written by Jack Hannah, singer and songwriter for the group The Sons of the San Joaquin. I've included that stanza at the beginning of this book.

I first heard the song years ago and couldn't get it out of my head. The lyrics conjured up a mishmash of iconic images: cowboys, knights, horses, and a sailing ship bearing the Spanish flag. These mental pictures stuck with me for a long time—way before I ever thought about becoming a writer. Then, about three years ago, and with twelve books under my belt, I decided to saddle up and see where those images might lead.

To my surprise, the first character to appear was Santiago Del Toro, a Knight of the Coffer, who climbed off a frigate in the 1600s and waded ashore to what is now modern-day Mexico. He carried a mace, of all things. Before I could even figure out what he wanted or why he had journeyed to the New World, a talking Andalusian warhorse appeared at his side. As I recall, the stallion was arguing with Santiago about something. And the rest, as they say, is history.

Speaking of history, is there a story behind the warhorses' names?

Names are incredibly important to me as a writer. The meaning behind a name is the foundation upon which I build the character's personality and abilities. A character becomes real when I find the perfect name for him or her.

The greathearted El Cid carries the name of one of Spain's legendary heroes and nobleman: Rodrigo Diaz de Vivar (c.1040–c.1099). A formidable warrior and strategist, El Cid ("The Lord") is the national hero of the Castile region.

Fiery Isabel is named for the San Isabel National Forest in Colorado. The forest—over a million acres in size—includes the Sangre de Cristo Range, the mountains that lie to the west of the Del Toro ranch.

Turk's name is inspired by a famous stud, the Byerley Turk, an Arabian stallion who was one of the three foundation sires for the Thoroughbred breed. The other two studs were the Darley Arabian and the Godolphin Arabian. The classic horse story *King of the Wind*, by Marguerite Henry, is the story of the Godolphin Arabian. One of my all-time favorite books. Go read it.

Turk is also a slang term for a successful young man, usually in the business world. And it rhymes with Jerk. Begs to be used.

Rodrigo's name is one of those happy accidents writers enjoy from time to time. I don't know why I picked it as a name for the bay stallion—it just seemed to fit. It wasn't until later that I realized Rodrigo is the first name of the real El Cid. The symbolic connect, on several levels, made me all kinds of happy.

In the earliest version of *Del Toro Moon*, Vasco is actually named Conquistador—Con for short. I decided Conquistador has too many negative connotations, so I went with Vasco.

Vasco is a derivative of Basque, a mountainous region in northern Spain. And since the *Rancho de Navarre* is located in the eastern foothills of the Sangre de Cristos, it's a good fit.

Quite a few fantasy books nowadays feature talking dragons. Why talking horses?
The descendants of Santiago Del Toro are *caballeros*, not dragon-riders. There's no way I could get Javier on a dragon.

What's your all-time favorite book?
Kidding, right? Okay, here goes:
The Lord of the Rings (which I've re-read over a hundred times and counting), *King of the Wind*, the *My Friend Flicka* trilogy, *The Black Stallion* books, *Billy and Blaze* series, *Storm Horse*, *Some Kind of Courage*, the Ranger's Apprentice series, the Chronicles of Prydain, the Harry Potter series, the Temeraire series, the Iron Druid Chronicles, *The Graveyard Book*, The Mortal Instruments series, *Airborn*, *The Old Testament*, *The Scorpio Races*, *A Wizard of Earthsea*, *As Brave As You*, *Lonesome Dove*, the Walt Longmire Mysteries, *The New Testament*, *Under the Same Sky*, *The Last Panther*, *Surprised by Joy*, *How the Irish Saved Civilization*, *Telling Lies for Fun and Profit*, *Boy's Life*, *On Writing: A Memoir of the Craft*, *A Handful of Stars*, *Quiet*, *Shogun*, *Star in the Forest*, *Centennial*, *The Source*, *Exodus*, and the list continues . . .

Matt told Perry that the horse who played Shadowfax in *The Lord of the Rings* movies was an Andalusian. Is that really true?
You bet your boots. Andalusian horses are popular among film directors for their cinematic good looks, trainability, and intelligence. The breed's predominate colors are bay, gray, or black. Sorrel, a reddish color also known as chestnut, is less common.

There's a line in Chapter Six that Matt's father quoted. What is that from?
Thou shall fly without wings, and conquer without any sword, O, Horse! It's from the Qur'an. I can't recall where or when I first read it, but I've always liked it.

Is the Del Toro's family sigil based on a real one?
Nope. While many royal and semi-royal families in Europe have coats of arms, I made up the Del Toro moon. However, I did borrow the sigil for Roman Navarre from the real Navarre family's coat of arms.

There are a number of Spanish words and phrases in the book. Do you speak Spanish?
Sadly, my Spanish is pretty limited, even though I was born and raised in New Mexico, and my stepdad, Onesimo Domingo Maes (O.D. to the family), was Hispanic and spoke the language fluently. Many of Javier's comments, and a bit of his speech pattern, are inspired by my stepdad.

What's your favorite breed of horse? Do you know how to ride?
Hands down, my favorite breed is the Arabian. One in particular will always hold a special place in my heart: my beloved Beau Bar-Drift, a dapple gray Arab gelding. And, yes, I rode a lot as a teen and participated in horse shows in both Western and English with Beau. He could do anything, including endurance racing. Truly, a prince of a horse.

The phrase "Don't worry about falling off—there's plenty of ground and you won't miss it" was a favorite saying of my riding teacher when I was Matt's age.

She was right. I never missed. Not even once.

Discussion Questions

1. Matt's father and brother argue a lot, which upsets Matt. Why do you think the author included this kind of family dynamic?

2. What did Javier mean when he said "Turk was exactly what our family needed"?

3. Why are the skinners so dangerous if they are contained inside the Maze?

4. How did Isabel's arrival change the power struggle between Turk and El Cid?

5. What roles do Roman and Kathleen play in Matt's life? Is there another character who fills a similar role?

6. Does Perry like Matt in the same way that Matt likes Perry? How can you tell?

7. Both Perry and Matt are big fans of *The Lord of the Rings*. How does this help them become friends? Why do you think

people become so obsessed with certain books or movies such as *The Lord of the Rings*, *Harry Potter*, or *Star Wars*?

8. When Matt thanked Turk for saving his life, the stallion responded with: "I didn't do it for you." What was Turk saying?

9. Authors often use a literary device called foreshadowing—a hint about an upcoming event or plot twist. Find three different scenes that foreshadowed El Cid's death.

10. What was El Cid trying to tell Matt when he said to "make room"?

11. Why do you think Rigo decided to stay with the Del Toro family instead of moving on?

12. Matt was surprised how well Perry handled learning about the true nature of the Del Toro family and the horses. Why was she able to do this?

13. Who do you think will eventually take over the family ranch: Matt or Ben? Why?

14. If you could partner up with any of the warhorses, which one would you choose? Why?

15. What other books remind you of *Del Toro Moon* and why?

Acknowledgements

Dear Fellow Reader,

All my life, I've read the Acknowledgements at the end of books. I always wondered who all those people were, how were they involved in the book I held in my hand, and why did the author thank them.

Now I know.

And now it's my turn.

First of all, thank *you* for joining me on this ride. *Del Toro Moon* was a whoop and a hoot to write. Thank you, too, for recommending it to others. I enjoy hearing from you and I answer every email. Yup. Every single one. So, you can find me over at www.darbykarchut.com. Stop by and say hi.

It took a whole herd of two-legged folks to produce *Del Toro Moon*. This is where I get to say *muchas gracias* to

Emma Nelson of Owl Hollow Press for her enthusiasm for this story (heck, her enthusiasm for life in general), and for her eagerness to share Matt's adventures with the world. I will never forget that phone call—it was like coming home. While her official title is "Publisher," Emma is much more to us authors. I'm proud to be a part of the flock. Or parliament. It is Owl Hollow Press after all.

Hannah Smith (acquisitions) for spotting the diamond in the rough, for wanting more of Javier's story, and for sharing a love of all things equine.

Olivia Swenson (editor) for riding point on this manuscript. She is an editing genius, as well as a straight up delight to work with. I would hunt skinners with her.

Caroline Geslison (publicity manager) for all the heavy lifting she does for me, and all the authors, at Owl Hollow Press with grace and humor and creativity. And because I never promised *not* to mention it, Caroline can drive a car while wearing a mermaid costume.

Risa Rodil (cover artist) for creating a magical cover that exceeded all my hopes and expectations, and makes me goofy-grin every time I look at it.

Amanda Rutter at Red Sofa Literary, whose passion for horse stories is just one of her super powers.

Timothy Valdez, who took time from a crushing work load to read and comment on the story, offer insights on the Hispanic culture of the Southwest, and encourage me to pursue diversity within diversity. Tim also checked and corrected my Spanish. Any mistakes in the book are mine.

Fellow authors Laura Resau, and Todd Mitchell for their support and endorsements. I also want to thank author Lydia Gil for her affirming comments during a brief elevator ride at the 2017 Pikes Peak Writers Conference, and for naming me "ally" in the on-going effort for diverse stories. Best compliment ever.

Jack Hannah, singer and songwriter extraordinaire, for graciously allowing me to use his lyrics in my book. Sir, you are a true *caballero*.

Scott O'Malley, for his kind invitation to stop by his office in Colorado Springs. Yes, this is a small world.

And, as always, Wes. *Te amo mucho.*

About the Author

Darby Karchut is a multi-award winning author, dreamer, and compulsive dawn greeter. A native of New Mexico, she now lives in the foothills of the Rocky Mountains, where she runs in blizzards and bikes in lightning storms.

When not dodging death by Colorado, Darby is busy writing for tweens and teens. Best thing ever: her YA series, *Griffin Rising*, has been optioned for film.

Visit Darby at:

#DelToroMoon

Website: https://www.darbykarchut.com
Facebook: https://www.facebook.com/darby.karchut
Twitter: https://twitter.com/DarbyKarchut

Some of Darby's other books:

Middle Grade series:
Finn Finnegan (2014 IPPY Silver Award)
Gideon's Spear
The Hound at the Gate
Finn's Choice

Young Adult series:
Griffin Rising (2011 Sharp Writ Book of the Year for Teens)
Griffin's Fire
Griffin's Storm

Non-fiction co-authored with Wes Karchut:
Money and Teens: Savvy Money Skills (2013 EIFLE for best book/personal finance for teens.

CPSIA information can be obtained
at www.ICGtesting.com
Printed in the USA
FSHW012225030919
61677FS